THE DUKE OF DEBT

THE DUKE OF DEBT

MILLCASTLE
BOOK THREE

KATE PEARCE

CHAPTER ONE

MILLCASTLE, ENGLAND 1833

"Will you come with me, Francis?" Alistair Haralson, Marquess of Hellion repeated his question. "I can't deal with that side of the family on my own."

"I agree that they are difficult, but why do you need me?" Francis Grafton, Viscount Wesley—who was known locally as Captain Grafton—shifted restlessly in his chair. "Caroline is with child, and I'm unwilling to leave her at this point in time."

They were sitting in Francis's library at his country estate just outside the rapidly expanding industrial town of Millcastle. Despite being a viscount, Francis had considerable business interests in the town and derived most of his income from trade. He and Alistair, who were distantly related, had attended school together before both joining the army, where Francis had ended up being dishonorably discharged, and Alistair had ended up in India.

"Ah, I didn't realize." Alistair paused. "Of course your priority must lie with her. Congratulations, by the way."

"Thank you. Why has the old man called you up here again?" Francis offered Alistair a cigarillo. "Didn't you pay your duty visit two months ago?"

"The invitation wasn't from him. I received a frantic scribbled note from Lilly saying that everything is *not as it seems*, and that if I wish to safeguard my inheritance, I should return *immediately!*" He grimaced and lit the cigarillo. "Not that I have any hopes of actually attaining anything, seeing as my cousin Farrell is alive and kicking."

"Farrell is an obnoxious drunkard," Francis observed.

"As were his father and grandfather." Alistair blew out a perfect circle of smoke. "One might say he is simply following family tradition."

"Since his father died, he's been running wild, and your mutual grandfather does nothing to curtail his extravagances."

"I suspect the old boy is rather proud of him," Alistair replied. "Do you think I should go, or wait for a more official summons?"

"I'd go." Francis finished his cigarillo. "Your cousin Lilly does know all the best family scandal, and if she is trying to warn you, I'd pay attention."

"You're right," Alistair agreed. "Farrell is probably in debt again and expects me to help him out, which is impossible. My finances are precarious enough as it is."

"And you a marquess," Francis gently mocked him.

"Of nothing, as you well know." Alistair mock-frowned at his favorite relative. "My father tied up what money there was tighter than a duck's arse, and his new wife took the rest."

"He never really trusted you, did he?" Francis said idly.

"No." Alistair smiled sweetly at his friend. It was not a subject he ever discussed, and he wasn't about to start now. "Which means that my stepmother and my sister live very comfortably at my expense in the only habitable property I ostensibly own."

"You don't begrudge them that, do you?"

"Not at all." Alistair stubbed out his cigarillo with unnecessary force. "It means they don't bother me, and as you know, I *do* value my privacy."

In truth, he'd rather have a decent income, but, as a gentleman, he was hardly allowed to say that. He simply watched the money from his late father's estate flow toward his stepmother, leaving him with a small income from his grandmother's trust and the surplus revenue from the estate. Frederica, his stepmother, was the same age as him and had very skillfully exacerbated the distance between father and heir. She'd also prevented Alistair from seeing the old devil when he was dying and had rewritten the will very much in her favor.

Alistair had never told her how he felt about that—he wouldn't give her the satisfaction—and was exquisitely polite to her on every occasion when they were forced to breathe the same air.

"I'll talk to Caroline. She might be relieved to see the back of me for a while, as apparently I 'fuss'." Francis opened one of the windows to encourage the smoke to leave. "Whatever happens, I can't go quite yet. We're hosting a party this weekend starting with a dinner tonight."

Alistair fought a smile. His cousin's distaste for the niceties of polite society was no secret. The fact that he was concerned enough about his wife to be called fussy was actually quite amusing.

"What's the occasion?" Alistair asked.

"It's Caroline's sister's birthday."

"Which sister?"

"Ruby. The one who fervently believes that aristocrats like you and I should be guillotined." Francis smiled as he moved restlessly around the room. "She's intent on marrying a man I employ as my bookkeeper."

"You married *your* bookkeeper," Alistair noted.

"Indeed." Francis added more coal to the fire. "Perhaps it will become a family tradition. It isn't a large party, thank God, just Caroline's family and the Blackthorns."

"I remember a very fierce lady at your wedding called Blackthorn," Alistair said. "Now, what was her name?"

"I expect you're referring to Miss Margaret Blackthorn, Adam's eldest sister." Francis checked the time. "She is almost as formidable as Ruby."

"Indeed," Alistair murmured. It was rare that someone took an instant dislike to him, but Margaret Blackthorn certainly had. She'd sized him up in one contemptuous glance, and he'd been instantly relegated to simpering fop. He'd even gone out of his way to solicit a dance with her, and, despite his best efforts to be charming, had failed to impress her at all.

It was a novel sensation, because he might not be rich, but he was titled and handsome, which worked wonders with most ladies. If she was present at the party, he was tempted to stay just to see her expression when he was announced at the dinner table.

He rose to his feet and bowed to his companion. "If I am to stay for dinner, I'd better speak to my valet and make sure I look presentable."

"You are already a veritable fashion plate compared to me, but I'm glad you've decided to stay." Francis nodded at him. "I'll speak to Caroline. If she is agreeable, we can leave on Monday."

MARGARET BLACKTHORN PUT on her new evening dress and made sure the skirts were neatly arranged over her bulky petticoats. Sometimes she wondered how she allowed herself to be dictated to by a fashion that constricted her movements so greatly. When she'd lived in the millhouse at Ravenhead with Adam and her sister, Lottie, she'd barely bothered to wear more than one petticoat. But then she'd been doing all the cooking, cleaning, and washing, while still trying to keep up appearances, and too many petticoats would've gotten in the way.

Margaret found a necklace of amber in her jewelry box and clasped it around her neck. Now she never had to do anything for herself or her family except be a lady. She sighed. Sometimes she felt so *useless*...

A tap on the door had her turning around and arranging a smile on her face.

"Are you ready, Margaret?" Her sister, Lottie, who looked effortlessly beautiful in her favorite primrose yellow, came in through the door. "Oh, my goodness! You cannot leave your hair in such a severe style! Let me arrange it for you."

Margaret sat down and allowed Lottie to fuss over her a little. Her sister had settled far better than Margaret had into the life of leisurely luxury their brother now provided for them. Despite having had to work hard, Margaret was secretly proud to have supported her family on a meager budget.

There was no need for such economy now. In the last year, Adam had opened his third mill and had rapidly become the wealthiest man in Millcastle. Margaret and Lottie had generous dowries at their disposal and the opportunity to marry whoever they wanted. Because of her beauty, Lottie attracted a lot of attention, but even Margaret had received three offers of marriage in the past year. She hadn't accepted any of them.

"There." Lottie placed some flowers in Margaret's hair and beamed at her. "You look beautiful."

Margaret knew that wasn't true, but she did look her best, even if they were only going to celebrate Ruby Delisle's birthday at Captain Grafton's country estate. She found her gloves and her reticule, and followed Lottie down the stairs into the drawing room where Mrs. Marsham awaited them. The widow wore her usual black garb and the apprehensive expression of a woman who preferred the comforts of her own home to socializing.

Her expression improved when she spied Lottie.

"You look beautiful, my dear."

Lottie rushed over and pecked Mrs. Marsham on the cheek. "So do you, ma'am, and doesn't Margaret look lovely?"

"Indeed she does." Mrs. Marsham nodded, the dainty black lace of her cap taking flight in the draft. "*Most* handsome."

Lottie glanced back toward the door. "Is Adam ready to leave? Shall I go and find him and Emily?"

"They were visiting the nursery to say goodnight to my grandson and promised to be down in a moment." Mrs. Marsham's smile softened as she mentioned her daughter and only grandchild. "That child looks so like his father."

"Let's hope he has the same disposition," Margaret said briskly. "He'll be inheriting a manufacturing empire by the time he's an adult."

"Adam has done very well for himself," Mrs. Marsham agreed. She picked up her fan and reticule, and brightened as her daughter came through the door.

"There you are, Emily!"

Emily looked her usual happy self, her fair hair piled high on her head in a cascade of ringlets. Margaret hadn't taken to Emily when Adam had first married her but had come to not only respect her, but to like her, too. Despite her fragile appearance, Emily was a strong woman and was much loved by her husband.

"You look very nice, Margaret," Adam commented.

"Thank you." Margaret curtsied to her brother, who was immaculate in his black and white evening clothes.

He studied her gown. "I told Emily that weaving the lighter silks for the new fashion of dresses would be successful."

"No, I told *you* that." Emily came to slide her hand over her husband's elbow. "Remember?"

"If you say so, my dear." Adam winked at Margaret. "Whoever thought of it has made me a lot of money, I can tell you that."

Margaret made sure that everyone remembered their shawls, reticules, and cloaks and followed them out to the carriage. It was already dark, and a slight breeze rippled through the trees, making them all hurry to get settled in.

It didn't take that long to reach the Grafton estate, but they might as well have been visiting a different world. Gone were the red brick factory buildings and smoking chimneys, and in their place sat manicured gardens and high stone boundary walls to keep out unwanted visitors.

Margaret always felt slightly ill at ease at the manor house and refused to admit to herself that she was intimidated by its size and grandeur. If it was good enough for Captain Francis Grafton, it was good enough for her brother, Adam, who was now far richer than the viscount.

She entered the hall, ascended the stairs, and was relieved of her cloak and boots by a maid. She put on her soft kid slippers, made sure her hair was tidy, and went back down into the hallway. The sound of voices drifted from the open doorway of the drawing room, but the enormous fireplace, which was big enough to walk into, commanded her attention.

"It's a relic."

She spun around as a voice spoke from behind her and a blond-haired man appeared on the stairs.

"I beg your pardon?"

He continued his descent and came to stand beside her. "The fireplace was once the end wall of the great medieval hall before the rest of this house was built around it."

"I am aware that the house is very old," Margaret said stiffly.

He pointed toward the blackened interior of the structure. "You can still see the holes for the bread ovens at the back, and the metal of the spit. It must have been quite a sight."

"Indeed."

He bowed to her. "How good it is to see you again, Miss Blackthorn."

Margaret raised an eyebrow. "You remember me?"

"How could I not?" His smile made her straighten her spine. "I've rarely met anyone who has taken me in such dislike so quickly."

If he was expecting her to dissemble and blush at his direct attack, he was in for a surprise.

"*Did* I dislike you, sir? I wonder why? I wish I could remember your name, because I have *quite* forgotten it."

He had the audacity to grin at her. "Well done, Miss Blackthorn. I am suitably put in my place."

He offered her his arm. "Shall we go through and meet our fellow guests?"

Margaret placed her hand on his sleeve and allowed him to escort her into the drawing room. She had to admit that he'd taken her dismissal quite well. She'd been told that she lacked a sense of humor, but even she could see the amusement lurking in his blue eyes. Now she just had to decide whether he was laughing at her, or with her.

Ruby rushed over to greet them. She wore a red dress with brown lace and looked her usual enthusiastic self. "Margaret! I am so glad that you could come!"

"Happy birthday." Margaret smiled at her friend, aware that her companion still lingered at her side. "Have you been introduced to—"

"As the Marquess of Hellion has been staying with Francis and Caroline for the past few days, I am *well* acquainted with him," Ruby said. "We have had some very stimulating discussions over dinner."

"Stimulating in that you annihilate my every position and leave me for dead," the marquess murmured. "I thank the Lord daily that the general populace aren't allowed to vote, because if you were in power, Miss Ruby, I suspect I would be facing certain death."

"I have no time for the landed aristocracy," Ruby declared.

"Even your own brother-in-law?" Margaret asked.

"Oh, Francis isn't one of *them*." Ruby waved a dismissive hand in the direction of her brother-in-law. "He's another thing entirely."

"I'd have to agree with you there," Lord Hellion said. "He certainly is unique."

The butler came past, and Lord Hellion procured two glasses from the tray and offered one to Margaret.

"My lady?"

"Thank you." She accepted the drink. "I can't imagine anyone getting the better of you in an argument, my lord. But as I'm part of the general populace, I'll offer my support for Ruby's views."

"That's the spirit." He clinked his glass against hers and Ruby's. "Down with the aristocracy, and *vive la France*."

Ruby was still laughing as she turned away to greet Adam, leaving Margaret alone with the marquess, which was not at all where she wished to be. He might appear to be indolent, but she was rapidly beginning to realize that his gaze was remarkably sharp.

"Where did you meet Captain Grafton?" She attempted to be civil.

"At school, where we found out we were distantly related to each other, and then we went into the army together." His smile was absent now. "We ended up in India where we lost touch for several years."

"You were in the army?"

"Indeed." It was his turn to raise an eyebrow. "Why does that surprise you?"

"Because—" Belatedly, Margaret remembered her manners. "I thought heirs to a title weren't encouraged to join up."

"That is true—unless their fathers didn't care about such niceties, but that wasn't what you were going to say, was it?" He stared down at her, a question in his eyes. "Do I not look capable of defending my country?"

"I would never say that, my lord." Margaret held his stare. "It's just that you are... so *handsome*."

He frowned. "What does that have to do with my ability to fight? Do you think I am too *pretty* to wield a sword?"

"I m*eant* that you look completely unscathed." Margaret wasn't used to being put on the back foot by anyone, let alone an idle aristocrat.

"Ah. That." He drank his wine in one swallow and bowed to her. "Not all scars are visible Miss Blackthorn."

"I am quite sure that you are right." She held his gaze. "In truth, I meant no offense, my lord. I honor anyone who has fought for our nation."

He sighed. "And there you go again, Miss Blackthorn, disarming me with your honesty."

"It is my one besetting sin," Margaret admitted somewhat grudgingly. "I am rather stubborn, but I have learned to at least be willing to admit I might be wrong."

"Which is far more than most members of our society ever accomplish." His smile was warmer this time, meant to invite her confidence rather than set her at a distance. "And I do appreciate your willingness to acknowledge fault."

"Ah, there you are, Alistair." Captain Grafton came up to his friend and patted him gently on the shoulder. "Good evening, Miss Blackthorn."

"Good evening." Glad of the opportunity to stop looking at the infuriating marquess, Margaret curtsied to her host. "Thank you for inviting me, sir."

"My sister-in-law is very fond of you," Captain Grafton replied. "And, as it is her birthday today, she chose the guests."

"That makes it sound as if you don't welcome Miss Blackthorn for herself, Francis. Surely that's not what you intended to say?"

Margaret blinked as Lord Hellion expressed exactly what she'd felt about Captain Grafton's offhand comment. There was an edge to the marquess's voice she hadn't heard before.

"I apologize for my lamentable manners." Captain Grafton bowed to Margaret. "Alistair is quite right to correct me. Sometimes I open my mouth before I have considered the consequences of my words. You are, of course, most welcome here in your own right, Miss Blackthorn."

"Thank you." Margaret bobbed another curtsey as her host turned away.

"He didn't mean it," the marquess said quietly.

"Even if he did, you didn't have to leap in and defend me," Margaret retorted. "I am well aware that men such as Viscount Grafton and... *yourself* consider us beneath them."

"*Beneath* me?" A smile hovered on the marquess's lips, and Margaret felt her cheeks redden. "Well, as to that—"

"Don't you dare." She pointed her closed fan at his wickedly smiling face, spun on her heel, and marched away, his soft laughter following her.

He was infuriating! How was she supposed to deal with a man who contained not one serious bone in his body? Who thought that everything was a joke? Margaret snapped open her fan and went to stand by the French windows that opened out onto the terrace. Yet, he'd stood up for her and had taken her attempts to set him in his place with good heart.

She fanned herself and let out a slow breath. It wasn't like her to allow a man to annoy her. In truth, most gentlemen were somewhat scared of her, and quite frankly, she preferred it like that.

The butler announced that dinner was served. Margaret turned back to the other guests and proceeded toward the door where her hostess smiled and gestured to the man standing beside her.

"Lord Hellion will be your dinner partner, Margaret."

Of course. With a resigned sign, she placed her gloved hand on his sleeve. He might be her designated partner, but that didn't mean she had to speak to him more than common politeness demanded.

AFTER ENJOYING a glass of port with the gentlemen, Alistair went into the drawing room and found Miss Blackthorn walking out on the terrace alone. He paused to admire her upright carriage and the queenly curve of her neck. She was nothing like the ladies he was used to dealing with. She met him toe-to-toe, eye-to-eye, and didn't simper or sigh. It was both refreshing and disturbing.

He strolled toward her, the cigarillo he'd lit held between his fingers. "Are you going to keep this up all night?"

She turned her rather fine brown gaze on him. "What?"

"Ignoring me." He strolled over to her side.

"I am not—"

"You barely spoke a dozen words to me at dinner."

"Maybe that was because I had nothing I wished to say to you." She smiled sweetly at him. "Have you considered that?"

"Well, no," he acknowledged. "Because I have already noted that you are a woman who prides herself on speaking her mind."

She stared at him for a long while. "You are incorrigible."

"Guilty." He inclined his head a respectful inch. "Perhaps you could explain exactly what you find so objectionable about me?"

He wasn't sure why he wanted to know, but something about her obvious dislike for him rankled.

"I believe we have already discussed this." She raised her chin. "You exemplify everything I dislike in a man of privilege."

"So, in a nutshell, you dislike me for the accident of my birth? Something I had no control over? How very... unchristian of you."

"It is not that—it's your *arrogance*, your air of being better than everyone else around you—"

He cut through her words. "Are you sure this isn't more about *your* lack of confidence in such surroundings?"

"*What?*" Her eyes flashed fire.

"Perhaps your sense of inadequacy makes you see an insult where none is offered or intended?"

She closed her mouth and then shook her head. "There is no point in arguing with you."

"Why *not?*"

"Because you—" She half turned away from him and walked to the very edge of the stone flagstones that bordered the garden.

He extinguished his cigarillo and followed her into the shadows. "Because I what? Won't behave as you wish? Won't conform to those ridiculous notions you have of how the aristocracy have ruined everything?"

She spun around to face him. "*Because* you confuse me." She looked up into his eyes. "Because I don't know what to do with you."

"As to the last, I can give you a few suggestions," Alistair said encouragingly. "Perhaps you might ask me to kiss you?"

"That's not—"

"Are you sure? Because I know I would very much like to kiss you."

"*Why?*"

"Because to be honest, Miss Blackthorn," he said with a shrug, "I'll be damned if I know what to do with you, either."

CHAPTER TWO

*A*listair was still thinking about that non-kiss a week later when he woke up encased in damp sheets at his grandfather's house to a sullen, smoldering fire and a rainstorm. He sneezed as he sat up and wondered if he was about to come down with a cold. Francis was on the verge of rebelling and returning home without him, but Alistair didn't want to leave until his awful cousin Farrell arrived. He'd allowed his stepmother to prevent him from being at his own father's deathbed, and he was foolishly reluctant to leave his grandfather alone with just his womenfolk around him on his.

Cousin Lilly had been correct that the current duke's health was declining far more rapidly than he'd been told. Alistair had spoken to his physician, who had confirmed his worst fears. He'd sent messengers down to London to alert his cousin to return immediately.

"Morning my lord." Clarkson, his valet came in, bringing a welcome pot of coffee. "Have you decided when we are leaving this godforsaken place?"

"We'll go when I'm good and ready." Alistair got out of bed

and knelt to attend the sullen fire. "And don't be rude to your betters."

Clarkson sniffed as he set down the tray. "Can't see no betters 'ere, guv."

Alistair straightened up and dusted off his hands. "Have you forgotten that I pay your wages?"

"You call that pittance wages?" Clarkson went back to the door and retrieved a jug of hot water and Alistair's shaving equipment. "I could earn better if I went back to boxing."

"Then, don't let me stop you." Alistair pulled on his shirt and breeches, shivering in the cold, and sat down to put on his woolen stockings. He'd met Arthur Clarkson at a prizefight in London after he'd been knocked unconscious and had offered him a job. "In truth, I'd quite enjoy seeing you get your face smashed in again."

"Like that would happen." Clarkson poured water into the basin. "That last time was a fluke, and you know it. Not that I'm not grateful for you letting me recover at your house." He wrapped a cloth around Alistair's throat. "Now sit back, and keep your clever remarks to yourself while I shave you, or I might accidentally slit your throat."

An hour later, suitably attired and shaved to perfection, Alistair descended the drafty stairs and went through into the breakfast room where a gaggle of his impoverished female relations were having breakfast. As usual, there was no sign of Francis, who had taken one appalled look at the ladies on the morning of their arrival and decided to take his breakfast in bed.

"Cousin Alistair!"

Lilly patted the seat next to hers. After collecting his porridge and a spoon, Alistair joined her. She wasn't technically his cousin, as she was the granddaughter of one of his grandfather's nieces. She'd come to live at the house as a child after her parents' death, and was the closest in age to him.

His family hadn't visited the duke often because the old man was not only a recluse, but also a miserable old sod who made everyone around him feel inadequate. Alistair only paid a yearly visit out of familial duty, because his cousin appeared to have none.

"Have you heard anything from Farrell yet?" Lilly inquired.

"Not a thing." Alistair helped himself to the appalling coffee. "I hope he is on his way and has no time to write to us."

His cousin was probably passed out drunk in a whorehouse, but Lilly didn't need to know such details.

"I don't think the duke is going to live for much longer, so he'd better be quick."

"Amen to that." Alistair added cream to his porridge, which at least made it palatable. "As soon as he arrives, I intend to leave."

"Why?" Lilly frowned. "You are one of the very few people Farrell listens to."

"Only when he wants to borrow money from me," Alistair said. "I'd rather not be around in case I give in to my desire to knock some sense into him."

"I'd love to see that." Lilly smiled at him. "Farrell isn't a nice man at all."

"You are correct." Alistair held her gaze. "I'd recommend that you keep away from him, especially when he's drunk."

"I already know that." She shivered. "Last time he was here, he tried to grab me. I barely got away from him."

Alistair set down his cup. "If he touches you again—"

She patted his arm. "He won't. He thinks I'm an old maid long past her prayers."

"As I said. He's a fool."

A noise in the hall beyond the breakfast room attracted his attention. He looked toward the door where the butler was just entering.

"Who has arrived?"

"The Earl of Haralson, my lord." The butler bowed.

Alistair finished his coffee and stood up. Finally, his cousin Farrell had come home.

~

UNFORTUNATELY, Farrell had chosen to bring two of his closest friends with him to the house where his grandfather lay dying. Alistair and Francis watched with increasing distaste as the three young men drank their way through dinner, scared off all the ladies, and kept drinking in the duke's study.

The only reason he and Francis were still there was because Alistair needed to speak to his cousin before he left. So far, extracting him from his boisterous companions had proved impossible. Alistair was just beginning to contemplate grabbing hold of his cousin and maneuvering him out of the room when Francis spoke quietly in his ear.

"Bottomly is about to pass out. I think I can get him to leave along with Pritchard."

"Thank you," Alistair murmured. "If you can accomplish that, I will be forever in your debt."

Francis nodded and walked over to where the younger of the two men who had accompanied Farrell was attempting to open a window.

"No need to despoil the flowerbeds, lad," Francis said in his best sergeant-at-arms voice. "Let me show you a better place to throw up your accounts." He grabbed hold of the drunk's shoulder, pivoted him around, and marched him out of the room. Alistair had forgotten that Francis owned at least one Millcastle inn and was probably more accomplished at dealing with drunks than most peers of the realm.

Alistair focused on Pritchard, who was the heir to an ancient, wealthy earldom, yet seemed intent on pissing and gambling his fortune away as fast as possible.

"Perhaps you might follow Captain Grafton and make sure your friend is all right?"

Pritchard didn't like him, but he was far too drunk to do anything about it.

"What's it to you?" Pritchard slurred.

"Well, we all know that Grafton isn't exactly a gentleman and can be quite unpredictable," Alistair said gently. "You wouldn't want him losing his temper with Bottomly, would you?"

Pritchard's gaze narrowed, but he went out through the door Alistair had conveniently opened for him. Alistair shut it and turned to his cousin, who was slouched in the chair behind the desk. He hadn't seen Farrell for almost a year, and the signs of dissipation on his bloated face had worsened considerably.

"Do you intend to stay here at Hellsdown Park until grandfather dies?" Alistair asked.

"What?" Farrell belched loudly and drank from the bottle of port at his elbow.

"I said do you intend to stay here until our grandfather dies." Alistair went over to the desk and looked down at his cousin.

"What's it to you?"

"Nothing." Alistair kept his tone polite. There was very little point in enraging a drunk. "I intend to return home, myself."

"Liar. You came here to try and steal the title from under my nose."

"As the title is hereditary, that is complete nonsense. I came because Cousin Lilly couldn't contact you and was concerned that no one from the immediate family would be here if our grandfather passed away."

"She's a stupid bitch." Farrell gulped more port. "When I'm the duke, I'm going to kick out all these parasites who live here."

"And where exactly do you expect them to go?" Alistair's patience was wearing thin. "The workhouse?"

"Why not? My grandfather only put up with them because his father did."

"It's called having a sense of family duty," Alistair snapped. "Something you appear to lack."

Farrell laughed as he upended the bottle and finished the contents, the purple of the liquid staining his lips and linen. "I don't care about any of that. You only care because that's all you have."

"Quite possibly," Alistair acknowledged the hit.

"Your own father didn't like you," Farrell continued. "He thought you were tupping his new wife."

Alistair went still. "Whoever told you that *canard?*" He dropped the bottle with a crash onto the floor.

"Grandfather." Farrell shrugged. "Don't know where he heard it, but it's funny as hell."

"Not to me." Alistair glanced back at the locked door. "Our grandfather is likely to die in the next day or so. Will you remain here to officiate at his death and burial?"

"I'll stay here long enough to make sure he's dead, and the will is read, yes."

"Excellent." Alistair nodded and went to open the door. "Perhaps you would let me know when the funeral will be so that I can come and pay my respects?"

Francis came in, his wary gaze moving between Alistair and Farrell, who was attempting to rise from his seat.

"Is everything all right?"

Alistair nodded. "Farrell intends to stay with his grandfather."

"Good. That means we can leave," Francis said.

Farrell finally got up and lurched over to the fireplace. He held onto the mantel as he fought to find his balance.

"Remembered something else about you."

"Goodnight, cousin." Alistair turned toward the door.

"Your father thinks you're a bastard."

"My father is dead and you're drunk." Alistair spun around. "Perhaps you should keep such foulness to yourself?"

"Don't like it, do you?" Farrell grinned at him, one finger pointed tauntingly at Alistair's face. "Being called a bastard."

Francis grabbed hold of Alistair's arm. "Ignore him. He doesn't know what he's saying, and he won't remember a thing in the morning."

"Oh, I'll remember." Farrell slowly tapped his forehead. "I don't forget anything useful."

Alistair shook off Francis's hand and squared up to his cousin. Farrell took an unsteady step back and grabbed the poker. He pointed it waveringly in Alistair's face.

"Stay where you are!"

"You couldn't hit me even if you were sober," Alistair said dismissively. "Now put that thing down and go to bed, you bloody great fool."

"Damn you to hell and back!" Farrell lurched forward, grazing Alistair's cheek with the tip of the poker. As Alistair recoiled, Farrell overreached, collided with the coalscuttle, and went down like a felled deer.

"Good Lord. I didn't even touch him," Alistair scoffed.

Francis pushed past Alistair. "What a buffoon." He went down on one knee and took out his handkerchief to attend to the blood seeping out of Farrell's skull.

"Wake up, you fool." Francis shook Farrell's shoulder and then frowned down at him. "I think he hit his head on the corner of the fireplace." He looked up at Alistair, who had remained frozen in place. "May I suggest you fetch one of the duke's many doctors so that they can attend to this fool and earn their wages for once?"

Alistair turned and ran through the door, shoving Pritchard, who was coming toward him, out of his way. Pritchard yelled something foul at him, but Alistair didn't stop. He descended the stairs into the kitchen, where he knew one of the three ducal physicians would be napping in the butler's apartment.

"Dr. Nettles?" Alistair didn't bother to lower his voice as he entered the room. "Can you come and attend to my cousin? He's fallen down drunk and banged his head."

The elderly man shook off his sleepiness with an ease Alistair envied, put on his coat, and followed Alistair back up the stairs into the duke's study. There was no sign of Pritchard or Bottomly. Francis was still crouched over the body.

He moved out of the way as the doctor knelt down, his somber gaze rising to fix on Alistair.

Alistair didn't need to hear the doctor's opinion. The look in Francis's eyes was enough to warn him that Farrell wasn't going to be getting up any time soon.

"Devil take it," Francis murmured in his ear. "What in God's name are we going to do now?"

MARGARET PAUSED in the doorway of the Methodist church hall to ensure that everything was going smoothly with the musical evening she'd organized to support the Sunday school. She spotted Ruby talking to Jon Ford, who was in charge of the everyday running of the hall and who also worked as Viscount Grafton's bookkeeper. At one point, she had considered him an excellent choice of husband, but he'd developed an affection for Ruby, and Margaret was not inclined to interfere with the dreams of her friend.

If Captain Grafton was happy about his sister-in-law marrying a common man, then more credit to him.

Margaret made her way around the room, nodding and smiling to the people she knew, before retreating to the back of the chapel where the minister had his office. She checked to see that the food and fruit punch were ready to serve after the concert. There was no sign of any of the serving staff she'd asked Emily to lend her from the house, but as she'd encouraged them to attend the concert first, she wasn't worried about their nonappearance.

As she was about to turn back to the hall, she heard voices in the corridor beyond and paused, her hand on the half-open door.

"But you must admit that Miss Blackthorn does a lot for the chapel, Mother."

Margaret tensed as she recognized the tremulous voice of the minister's new wife.

"Only because she has nothing else to do. Miss Blackthorn should concentrate on finding herself a husband and leave the organizing of such events to you."

"I really don't mind—"

"Well, you should mind, my dear. She has no business telling everyone what to do as though she occupied your position. If you don't put a stop to it, she'll be lording it over you with her money and her connections, and then where will you be?"

"Happily married to a man I love?"

"A man who listens more to a woman who isn't his wife? You should watch out, Beth. A plain, meddlesome women like Miss Blackthorn can cause all kinds of trouble in a marriage."

Margaret's gaze flew to the backdoor. Should she attempt to leave without letting the women know she'd overheard their conversation? Stiffening her spine, she opened the door fully and stepped out into the corridor.

"Mrs. Wells?" She smiled at the minister's wife, who visibly quailed. "What a wonderful evening we have to look forward to! Thank you so much for organizing it all."

She nodded at the other woman, who was not regarding her fondly. "Ma'am."

Margaret kept walking until she reached the hall and took a seat near the back of the rapidly filling room. She was still shaking and unwilling to expose herself to the questioning glances of her sister and brother. Had she really become a managing woman who took control of everything? She stared blindly toward the stage where the minister was now standing and welcoming everyone to the musical evening.

It was true that she was bored at home and sought opportunities to exercise her talents, but she'd never thought she was overreaching her boundaries. In truth, the new Mrs. Wells had seemed to welcome her help and advice, as had her husband. But were they only humoring her because they were afraid she would persuade her wealthy brother to stop patronizing their establishments and businesses?

It was a remarkably lowering thought.

"Miss Blackthorn?" She started as Jon sat down beside her. "Are you well, lass?"

"I'm fine, thank you." She attempted a smile. "Just a little tired."

"I'm not surprised, considering how hard you worked to make this evening a success."

"Maybe too hard." Margaret paused. "Do you think I have usurped Mrs. Wells's authority?"

"Not at all." He gave her a funny look. "She's still finding her feet. From what I can tell, she's grateful for everything you do to help her."

Margaret sighed. "Perhaps it is time I allowed her to take full responsibility for the chapel activities."

"Has someone suggested you step down?" Jon studied her carefully. "If that's what you want to do, Margaret, then do it, but don't let some old busybodies stop you doing the Lord's work."

"It's very kind of you to say that," Margaret managed to reply. "I would hate to think I was being a nuisance."

"*You*, lass?" He gave her an assessing look. "Never. Now settle in, and let's enjoy the concert."

"Shouldn't you find Ruby?"

"She's more than capable of taking care of herself, and I'm more than happy to be sitting here with you."

Margaret subsided into her seat, slightly reassured by his bracing words. Jon was a plain speaking man who wouldn't lie to her. If he thought she was overreaching, he would tell her straight out. It was one of the reasons she liked him so much.

She tried to focus on the music, but the conversation she had overheard continued to play even more loudly in her head. The problem was that there was an element of truth in what Mrs. Wells's mother had said. Margaret *was* bored and, since her financial and social elevation, she was always looking for things to do. Having a husband and hopefully children of her own was her destiny—her only destiny—when running a factory, which she was perfectly capable of doing, was not allowed.

But none of the men she'd met so far in her life measured up to her exacting standards. She'd been engaged to Emily's brother, Matthew, at a young age and had looked forward to becoming his wife, but he had been murdered by an aggrieved millhand, and she'd been left adrift at twenty-seven. She was now twenty-nine and, despite her large dowry, spinsterhood awaited her.

The thought of living in her brother's house and being dependent on him and Emily for everything did not sit well with her. Her brother would never allow her to set up house by herself, even in the town they'd been born in. And, as he currently controlled all her funds, she had no option other than to obey him. She couldn't leave Lottie behind, either, and she was fairly certain her sister would be reluctant to give up the comforts of their new home.

Margaret remembered to clap as the first performance ended and the minister stood up to introduce the next item, but her mind was not on the concert she'd worked so hard to put together. The only solution to regaining at least some independence was to marry. She would have to review the men around her and try and make a decision that would benefit them both.

ALISTAIR STRIPPED off his black gloves and threw them onto the duke's desk before helping himself to a large glass of brandy. The double funeral had just ended and the bodies had been interred in the ducal mausoleum. As the closest living relation of both men, Alistair had taken on the role of mourner in chief. He'd dealt with the church matters and the local coroner who had been summoned to deal with the expected death of the duke and the unexpected death of his heir.

Francis had left straight after the funeral. Alistair had thanked him profusely for his support over the ghastly two weeks. His cousin had died, swiftly followed by the duke, who had never regained consciousness or known that his eldest grandson had predeceased him.

"Alistair?"

Alistair looked up to see Lilly peering around the door. She was wearing black and had a lace veil pinned over her hair.

"What is it?"

"Do you intend to come and speak to the guests? There are almost a hundred people who have come to pay their respects to your grandfather."

"I'll be there in a second." Alistair poured himself a second glass of brandy.

"Mr. Brody is here as well."

"The solicitor?"

"Yes. He wishes to speak to you after the reception." Lilly hesitated. "None of Farrell's friends have turned up."

"Not even those two idiots who were with him the night he died?" Alistair asked. The pair had disappeared the morning

26

after Farrell's death was reported, without a word of condolence or thanks.

"Apparently not." She sighed. "I suspect Farrell was not well-liked."

"What a surprise." Alistair was tempted to toast her with his glass and shout good riddance to his awful cousin, but he suspected that was the brandy talking, and he had no wish to appear insensitive. "I'll be there in a minute, I promise you."

She left, and he stood looking down at the desk that was piled high with letters, presumably about the duke's passing. It was interesting that even in death, and despite his reclusively, his grandfather's rank made his passing a momentous occasion.

Alistair let out his breath, straightened his black cravat, and put his gloves back on. It was time for him to represent his family. Even if he'd despised his cousin and disliked his grandfather, he still had standards, and he would maintain them to the end.

THREE HOURS later he was back in the duke's study with the remaining family and staff while the solicitor dealt with the will. Even though he had suspected he was in line for the dukedom, the confirmation of his accession to the title was still something of a shock. He barely had time to deal with the notion before Mr. Brody was ushering everyone else out and requiring his full attention.

He'd known that the estate was in a mess, but he'd had no idea how bad it had gotten. The duke had been ill for several years and, without his oversight, the rents had fallen into arrears, and his land agent appeared to have been stealing the rest. Farrell's debts were enormous and had to be paid off, leaving the dukedom close to penury.

"You do have your own private income, do you not, your grace?" Mr. Brody inquired hopefully.

"Yes, but it is remarkably small," Alistair said. "My father left almost everything to his second wife, and, as she is not much older than I am, I doubt I will live to inherit her share."

Mr. Brody sighed. "Then we will have to make some economies."

"Indeed we shall." Alistair stood up, unable to stand the claustrophobic space for another second. "Perhaps you could gather as much information as possible about the estate and other properties, and we can start from there."

"An excellent idea, your grace. Will you be staying here for a while?"

Alistair looked around the shabby room and grimaced. "It doesn't look as if I have much choice, does it?"

CHAPTER THREE

"*I* don't understand what is wrong with you, Margaret," Lottie complained. "You no longer have to work in the kitchen, do the laundry, or sew Adam's shirts, yet you seem miserable."

"I *am* miserable." Margaret set down the book she had been attempting to read before Lottie had come to find her. "I'm... bored."

"Bored with all this?" Lottie spun in a slow circle, her hands spread wide. "The finest house in Millcastle, sister to the richest man in town, and with a magnificent dowry to boot. How can you possibly be bored?"

"I don't know." Margaret hesitated. "Perhaps it's that before Adam grew wealthy, I felt my efforts to support our family were more *valued*."

Lottie came to sit beside her. "They were valued. After mother died, you kept our family together, but you don't have to do that anymore. We're safe now." The relief in Lottie's voice was unmistakable, but Margaret couldn't share it. "After father died, I was always so scared—so afraid that something else would happen and we'd lose everything."

Margaret patted her sister's hand. "There is nothing to be scared of anymore. You are truly safe here."

"Then why don't you feel the same?" Lottie asked, reminding Margaret that despite her pretty blond looks, her sister was a sensitive creature and well-attuned to her sister's feelings. "Why can't you allow yourself to enjoy it?"

"You think I deliberately make myself miserable?" Margaret asked. "I can assure you that is not the case. I just feel... useless."

"Yet you are always busy, helping out at the factory schools and at the chapel. Why, Mr. Ford said he wouldn't know what to do if you didn't help out so much."

Margaret rose to pace the room. "Actually, I've decided not to do so much at the chapel anymore. I suspect Mrs. Wells thinks I am interfering."

Lottie snorted. "That meek-as-milk little miss? She's too scared to manage things herself and relies on you and her awful mother far too much."

"Then, from now on, she'll be relying on her undoubtedly awful mother alone. I cannot be seen to be interfering, Lottie." Margaret stared out of the window into the barren garden below. "I need to find something to *do*."

"Get married, then. That is the only career open to a woman who likes to be busy."

Margaret turned to see her sister smiling at her.

"To whom exactly?"

"Any man who takes your fancy. You can afford to pick and choose these days."

"And I've yet to meet a man who appeals to me," Margaret retorted. "They are either afraid of me, or they patronize me. If I marry, my husband will own my money, my children, and me. I have to pick very carefully, indeed."

"What about that blond man who is friends with Captain Grafton?"

"That *blond* is a marquess."

"So what?" Lottie winked at her. "You can afford him if you want him, Margaret."

"He is…" Margaret paused. "Infuriating."

"And yet, you still like him."

"Why would you think that?"

"Because I saw you that last evening at the Graftons. He followed you around all evening, and you disappeared with him out on the terrace for quite a while. When you came back in, he was smiling, and your cheeks were flushed."

"We were *arguing*." Margaret became aware that her cheeks were heating up again. "He thinks he is very clever and far above such mortals as myself. I simply attempted to make him aware that I was on to his games."

"You *do* like him," Lottie announced and clapped her hands. "I *knew* it."

"I do *not*—"

Margaret was profoundly grateful when the door opened, and Emily appeared, a note in her hand.

"I'm glad you are both here. We've been invited to the Graftons to dine, if you wish to come?"

"Of course we'll come," Lottie said and nudged her sister as if they were five again. "If one wishes to meet a member of the aristocracy to marry, then the Graftons is definitely the best place for it."

OF COURSE, the first person Margaret saw after entering the drawing room at Grafton Hall was her blond marquess. He had his back to her and was staring out of the window, hands clasped behind him, his fair hair a stark contrast to the black of his coat. Despite herself, she couldn't help but move toward him, aware that something was not right.

When she reached his side, he started and looked down at

her, his smile, for once, absent.

"Miss Blackthorn. Good evening."

"Good evening, my lord." She studied his expression. "Is everything all right?"

"With me, or with the world in general?"

Trust him to make a sincere inquiry into something it was not.

"I merely wondered why you look so tired," Margaret said stiffly. "Which is, of course, none of my business, so please excuse me."

"Don't go just yet. I am tired." He took her elbow in a gentle clasp. "I rode down last night to speak to Francis, and I'll have to return tonight."

"Return where?" Margaret asked.

"My grandfather and cousin passed away two weeks ago. As the nearest relative, I have been dealing with their affairs."

"I'm sorry for your loss, my lord."

"Don't be. To be perfectly frank, I'm glad to see the back of both of them. My grandfather was a mean-spirited old man, and my cousin... Well, let's just say that his determination to drink and gamble himself to an early grave proved remarkably successful."

She looked in vain for his usual lurking smile, but it remained absent.

"One should really not speak ill of the dead, but they do sound rather awful," Margaret ventured.

"Indeed." He finally smiled down at her. "You are a remarkably practical woman, Miss Blackthorn."

"Thank you." She curtsied. "I believe most families have members who might easily be described as black sheep."

"Even yours?" His keen gaze swept over her brother and sister, who were talking to their hosts.

"My father liked to gamble and lost control of our family

mill," Margaret admitted, surprised to find herself revealing something so personal.

"Ah." He turned back to look at her. "That is a vice I have never had the funds to indulge in. Thank God. My cousin incurred many debts of 'honor'."

Margaret heartily agreed with him about that, at least. "Do you really have to leave tonight?"

He sighed. "To be honest, I'm not sure if I should make the attempt." He glanced out of the window at the gathering clouds. "I'm tired enough as it is, and it looks as if it might rain."

"Perhaps you would be better to stay the night here and leave early in the morning when you are suitably refreshed," Margaret suggested. "I doubt your late grandfather's estate will fall apart in your absence."

"You are probably right." He chuckled. "It will fall apart regardless of whether I am there overseeing its demise, and I'll still be left holding the pieces."

"Is it fixable?" Margaret asked as he helped himself to a glass of wine from the butler.

"Everything is fixable, Miss Blackthorn, if you have enough money." He drank from his glass. "Unfortunately, I do not have enough, and, as my grandfather's heir, I am liable for all his debts."

"My brother Adam faced the same challenges, my lord. It took him years to pay off my father's creditors," Margaret said. "Have you consulted with your bank?"

"Yes, but that isn't the whole of it. Unfortunately, my cousin didn't believe in banks and merely borrowed money against his expectations from various sources who are now rather keen to get it back."

"It does seem rather unfair that you are now liable for everything," Margaret said.

"Thank you." His smile twisted. "I'm sure I'll come about at some point." He took her hand and brought it to his lips. "And now, having bored you with my affairs for long enough, let's turn to you. How are you, Miss Blackthorn?"

"The same as ever." It was Margaret's turn to lose her smile. "I try and keep busy."

"Doing what exactly?"

She shrugged. "Helping out at home and with the factory schools, knitting and sewing for the poor, attending functions."

He looked down at her. "With all due respect, Miss Blackthorn, I can't see any of those tasks keeping you occupied for long."

"Unfortunately, as a woman, I'm not allowed to do much else," she admitted. "Sometimes… it annoys me."

"I can see why." He looked up at his host came toward them. "If it will not inconvenience you, Francis, I might stay the night after all."

"Good." Their host nodded. "No point in rushing off. I assume you'll be heading down to London at some point to speak to your bank?"

Lord Hellion shuddered. "Yes. I can't say I'm looking forward to it. I suspect I'll uncover even more unpaid bills and assets left to rot."

"It's a veritable scandal what that pair did to the estate." Francis slapped his friend on the back. "I'll do what I can to help, but you need an influx of capital, my friend, and quickly."

Margaret excused herself as the two men continued to chat, and walked over to sit by the fire. She had money, but it was all tied up in her brother's hands, not to be released until she decided whom she wanted to marry. She doubted her financially astute brother would permit her to lend all her capital to a man she'd only met on three occasions. Why she was even contemplating helping that particular man was not something she was willing to delve into, either.

It just seemed unfair that he should have to pay for the sins of his grandfather and cousin. She suspected that her father's debt paled into insignificance beside Lord Hellion's relatives. She stared into the fire, her hands grasped tightly together in her lap.

But what if there was a way to help him? Did she have the courage to broach the subject, and what would he think of her if she did?

~

ALISTAIR MANAGED to avoid the gentlemen after dinner by declining the port and proclaiming his tiredness and need to go straight to bed. He had no desire to sit in a room full of hard-headed businessmen and be grilled as to his lack of capital and unlikely chances of ever restoring the dukedom.

Francis would help him restructure his loans, but the burden of sorting out the estate and repaying the staggering debts was all on him. For a moment, he paused in the hall as the weight of it settled around him before shrugging it off and continuing onward. He'd managed on his reduced expectations from his own father; he'd even survived a military career. He'd be damned if he'd allow his cousin's debts to drown him.

"Lord Hellion?"

He turned at the bottom of the stairs as Miss Blackthorn emerged from the shadows, her expression grave.

"Yes?"

"May I speak to you?"

He frowned and mentally consigned her to Hades, even as he wondered what she might wish to say to him.

"I was just going up to bed."

"Oh!" She bit her lip, but still met his gaze. "Well, never mind."

"You could join me?"

"In your bed? I hardly think that would be proper."

It occurred to him that he wouldn't mind it at all. He

pictured her there, brown hair down on her shoulders, and her strong, lush body beneath him...

With a sigh, he gestured at the study. "We can talk in there, if you wish? I don't think we will be disturbed for a while."

"I can't stay long. My sister will wonder where I am." Margaret followed him across the darkened hall to Francis's study.

He shut the door and bent to light the candles on the desk from the fire partially illuminating the large room.

"How can I assist you, Miss Blackthorn?"

She regarded him warily, her hands fisted at her sides, her head tilted at an angle. He liked the simplicity of her green dress and the smoothness of her upswept hair, which suited her far better than the laces and curls her sister preferred.

"You will probably think I have gone mad."

"I won't think anything unless you start speaking."

She took a visible breath that made her bosom swell over the narrow lace-trimmed neckline of her bodice. "I know that you need money."

He shrugged. "I cannot deny it."

"Then I have a suggestion for you. I thought that maybe I could lend you some of my capital and act as your banker, but then I realized my brother would never allow me access to my funds."

Alistair sat on the corner of the desk and regarded her in fascination. "I should imagine not."

"The only way for me to access my dowry is to marry."

Silence fell, disturbed only by the ticking of a clock and his companion's harried breathing.

"Are you *proposing* to me?" Alistair finally asked.

She turned and walked away from him, presenting him with her back. "I thought that maybe we could come to some business arrangement, whereas—"

"*Business* arrangement?"

"As in a marriage of convenience that would suit us both."

"I fail to understand how such an arrangement would benefit you, Miss Blackthorn," Alistair countered. "Your fortune would become mine and so would you. What could you possibly gain from such a union?"

"My freedom?"

"In what sense?" Alistair frowned.

"That married women are allowed to do so much more than single ones. That you would be a—a complacent husband and would not stop me from expanding my interests."

"Complacent as in letting you have lovers?"

"No!" She swung back around, her expression appalled. "I wouldn't even expect you to want that for yourself."

"Why not?"

She blinked at him. "Because you would be agreeing to a business arrangement, not a marriage for love."

"And what if that was one of my conditions? That our marriage had to be consummated?" He was so tired and over-whelmed by his current circumstances that he'd forgotten how to dissemble. He also knew that the plain-speaking woman in front of him would not have tolerated anything less than the truth.

"You would really want that?"

He raised an eyebrow, aware that he was starting to enjoy himself and having no idea why, because the whole idea was laughable. "Don't you want children?"

"Yes, but—I wouldn't wish to impose my needs on you."

"Miss Blackthorn, bedding you would not be a hardship, I can assure you."

"Then you will consider my offer?" She took a step toward him, her expression hopeful.

He helped himself to some of Francis's excellent brandy as he considered his options. "You are offering me what amounts to a marriage of convenience. I gain control of your fortune, and you gain control of your life."

"Exactly." Miss Blackthorn bit her lip. "From the look on your face, you really do think I have run mad."

"Not at all, although I must confess that I did not expect such an... offer from you."

"I'm not sure why I thought of it, myself." She drew herself up. "And I quite understand if you wish to pretend that it never happened. I will certainly never refer to it again."

She went to move past him, and he took possession of her hand. "Wait. Sit down. I need to think." He led her toward the chair behind the desk.

"I cannot stay much longer, my lord. My sister will be wondering where I am."

"I'll be as brief as I can." He brought another chair up and sat next to her. "If I agree to your proposal, we will need to talk further about the details. If I go to your brother now and ask to marry you he would rightfully be suspicious of my motives."

"Agreed." She gave a decisive nod.

"Then perhaps we can meet tomorrow at breakfast, and plan this ridiculous idea through more thoroughly?"

"Tomorrow? I thought you were leaving at dawn."

Alistair smiled at her. "As you said, Miss Blackthorn, the estate is hardly going to fall down in one more day."

"I'll ask Caroline if I can stay the night so that I can see you in the morning before you leave," Miss Blackthorn said.

"An excellent plan. I'm an early riser."

"So am I. When we lived in the millhouse I used to get up at six to see Adam off on his shift." She shrugged as if embarrassed by the memory. "Even after all these years, I can't seem to stay abed any longer."

"Then I will look for you bright and early." Alistair stood up when she did and cupped her cheek. "May I kiss you goodnight?"

Her sigh was almost comical. "I suppose if we are to be intimate, we have to start somewhere."

He gently pressed his lips to hers and then kissed along her jawline to her ear. Her hand came up to curve around his neck, and he returned his attention to her mouth, seeking entrance, which she eventually offered him on a gasp of breath.

"Mmm." He explored her mouth until her tongue tangled with his, and her whole body was pressed against him. "That's nice."

"That's—"

He kissed her again, and she forgot to speak, her fingers curling into his hair as he drew her deeper into the caress. When he reluctantly released her, she pressed her hand to her mouth, her eyes wide with a mixture of emotions he was too tired to read.

"I should go."

He stepped back and bowed. "Good night, Miss Blackthorn."

HE LET HER LEAVE, and remained where he was, sipping his brandy and staring into space. Of all the solutions to his problems, marrying an heiress had not occurred to him. Members of his own class would be quite aware of the state of the dukedom and unlikely to risk allying their daughters and families with a sinking ship. Miss Blackthorn, however, was different.

Did she want a title? He had no sense that it was important to her, and he had learned to detect and depress such eagerness in other women over the years. If he married her, would he regret the chance to seek out his one true love? He had to suspect that by the time he'd dug the estate out of debt he'd be too old and exhausted to be hanging out for a bride, and he didn't particularly believe in love, anyway.

Which left the unpalatable fact that marrying Miss Blackthorn would be a good thing for him. He finished his brandy and still didn't move. She was very pleasant to look at, with a stately grace that intrigued him, a little sharp-tongued, and nobody's fool. He could do a lot worse...

Half disgusted with the mercenary nature of his thoughts, Alistair set the chair back in place and went back out into the hall. Light shone from the drawing room where the ladies were enjoying their tea before being joined by the men. He started up the stairs, his mind in a muddle as exhaustion seeped into his bones. He'd sleep and speak to Miss Blackthorn again in the morning—if she hadn't instantly regretted her impulsive offer to marry him.

MARGARET APPROACHED the breakfast room with some trepidation, and only let out a relieved breath when it became clear that Lord Hellion was the only person sitting at the table. It hadn't taken much effort to persuade Lottie to stay with her at Grafton Hall while Emily, her mother, and Adam returned home. She'd woken early and left her sister fast asleep in their shared room.

"Good morning, Miss Blackthorn." The marquess stood and bowed to her with his usual fluid grace.

"Good morning, my lord." She went over to the long side-board that sat against the wall and helped herself to some food from the silver-domed plates. "I doubt my sister will join us, but what about Captain Grafton and Caroline?"

"Francis has already left for Millcastle, and Caroline is not an early riser. We are quite safe, and if anyone does come in, we can remove ourselves to the drawing room or somewhere quieter."

He pulled out the chair beside his, and Margaret sat down. She fussed around with her food before she gained the courage to look up at him. His eyes were very blue and marked underneath with purple shadows.

"Did you sleep at all?" she asked.

"I tried." He shrugged. "But there is so much going on at the moment that as soon as I sort out one issue, another pops into my brain, and off I go again." He paused. "Have you changed your mind?"

"About our potential marriage? No, I have not." It was Margaret's turn to hesitate. "What about you?"

"I must confess that the idea appeals to me, but I'm also aware that I'm being very selfish." He met her gaze. "I have to be honest with you. Even your inheritance might not be enough to save my estates."

"I am not quite sure of the exact amount, but I can assure you that it is quite substantial. And having available capital would give you the standing to borrow more, yes?"

"Indeed."

He was looking at her as if she were a very strange beast.

"Do young ladies of your class not talk about money?" Margaret hazarded a guess.

"No, they don't, but I wish they would. It is mightily refreshing to have an honest conversation about my finances." He sighed and shoved his fingers through his thick blond hair. "I would hate to drag you down into debt with me."

"I doubt that will happen," Margaret said stoutly. "My brother would not allow it, and if the worst came to the worst, he would always offer us a home."

A faint shudder ran through her companion. "You, perhaps, but he'd be justified in kicking my arse all the way to the poorhouse if I brought you that low."

"I have faith that together we will manage to avoid that fate, my lord." Margaret took a hasty breath. "And, as to that. If we do marry, I would prefer it if you consulted me about financial decisions." She braced herself for his rejection of her bold plea.

He nodded. "Understandably, as it will be your money keeping us afloat."

"You... would allow that?"

"I would." His smile was wry. "But I could be the kind of man to say anything in order to get his hands on your money and then renege on every promise."

"One would assume that my brother could put something in the marriage contract to protect me from such behavior," Margaret countered.

"He could, but how enforceable it would be in a court of law is debatable. In my experience, the law tends to side with the husband in such matters." Lord Hellion sipped his coffee. "What else?"

"What do you mean?" Margaret asked.

"What other conditions do you have for me?"

"I can't think of anything else right now." Margaret gave her attention to her plate. "What about you?"

"Good Lord, I'm the one receiving your splendiferous dowry. What on earth would I have to complain about?" He finished his coffee and poured himself another cup after offering her one that she declined. "Before you make your final decision, you should come up and see the estate."

"Which is where, exactly?" Margaret asked.

"The main one is about twenty miles from here."

Margaret dabbed at her mouth with her napkin. "That would mean we'd have to stay overnight."

"Indeed. I might admit Francis into my confidence, and ask him to arrange an outing for you, your sister, and hopefully a chaperone. What do you think?"

"My brother will be suspicious."

He shrugged. "Then he can come, too."

There was a hint of autocratic impatience in his reply that reminded Margaret of the very different worlds they inhabited.

"Adam is rarely able to take time away from his businesses."

"Then he'll have to trust you or send his wife." Lord Hellion set down his cup. "I'll speak to Francis when he returns—if you are agreeable."

"Yes, I am." Margaret offered him an encouraging smile.

In truth, the prospect of some excitement in her life was remarkably invigorating. She had no idea of the extent of Lord Hellion's estates or his new responsibilities, but, to her astonishment, she was more than willing to find out.

CHAPTER FOUR

To Margaret's complete surprise, in less than two days she found herself in a carriage accompanied by Caroline's mother, Mrs. Delisle, and Lottie, heading up toward Lord Hellion's family estate. She wasn't quite sure how everything had been arranged so quickly after the Graftons became involved, but she wasn't about to grumble.

It was the longest journey Margaret had ever been on without her brother, and thus a delight in its own way. They passed through many villages and a few towns that reminded her rather too much of Millcastle. Mrs. Delisle was determined not to sit in the carriage for hours and had arranged for their accommodation at a reputable inn along the way.

"Not far now, Lottie, my dear," Mrs. Delisle called out, waking Margaret from her slight doze. "It was very kind of Lord Hellion to ensure that our journey was made in such comfort."

"Lord Hellion?" Margaret asked as she yawned and rubbed her eyes. "I assumed that Adam had arranged everything."

"We decided not to bother Mr. Blackthorn," Mrs. Delisle said firmly. "Caroline and I agreed that the less he knew about your plans the better. But without Lord Hellion's detailed instructions, I doubt I would've had the courage to venture forth at all."

"What will Adam think when half the women in his household are missing?" Lottie chuckled. "I know our brother is a busy man, but even he might notice *that*."

"Emily will explain to him that we are staying with Caroline for a few days to keep her spirits up," Mrs. Delisle said. "And, if nothing comes of your visit, Margaret, then we will have nothing to tell Adam."

"A clever plan," Lottie said approvingly. "What Adam doesn't know, won't hurt him, and Margaret hasn't decided what she is going to do yet, anyway."

"What makes you think I have anything to decide?" Margaret parried. "We were all invited to visit Lord Hellion, not just me."

"Oh for goodness sake, Margaret, I'm not Adam. I am *quite* aware of what is going on." Lottie grinned at her. "You are visiting Lord Hellion's estate to see if he will suit you."

"I am not—" Margaret might as well not have bothered as Lottie continued speaking.

"And very wise of you, too. He is quite a catch by anyone's standards."

"Lottie, he might have a title, but he has no money."

"But you will be a marchioness!" Lottie clasped her hands to her bosom. "*Lady* Hellion."

Margaret sniffed. "I have never aspired to be a member of the aristocracy, Lottie."

"Which is why this whole thing is so amusing to watch. You like him *despite* him representing everything you despise."

"I don't despise the aristocracy, I just happen to think that they are rather… *useless*."

Lottie's peal of laughter brought a reluctant smile to Margaret's face. Each mile they traveled brought her closer to making a decision that would affect the rest of her life, and her bright confidence in her ability to *make* such a decision was waning. She hardly knew him. He'd pointed out to her that he could abscond with all her money, and there was very little she could do about it once they were married. At least he'd tried to be truthful about that…

Yet there was something in his eyes that drew her to him—a sense that, despite his levity, he was an honest man, a *strong* man. She'd never met a man she could speak her mind to before, and it was quite exhilarating. And when he touched her, kissed her, she wanted so much more…

"Ah, here we are." Mrs. Delisle sat up straight and looked out of the window. "The village of Hellsdown, which belongs to the estate."

After they passed along the main street, the carriage took a sharp turn to the left under a sturdy stone arch, past an octagonal gatehouse, and onto a badly rutted drive lined with elm trees.

As they bumped about, Lottie caught Margaret's eye. "One can already see why Lord Hellion might be needing your money."

"I'll make certain that it is the first thing that is fixed," Margaret promised, her gaze on the overgrown trees and what passed as a park beyond them. The grounds were sadly overgrown, and didn't improve as they came closer to the house.

"Goodness gracious!" Lottie squeaked as they finally drew up at the front of the house. "This place is enormous!"

No one emerged from the house, so Margaret opened the carriage door and got out to look up at the imposing stone and crenellated façade of the building. She'd imagined Grafton Hall was large, but this place was easily ten times the size of it. The enormity of her suggestion to marry into such a family hit her anew. What did she know of such a place and such people?

The front door opened a crack, and an elderly man in a faded livery tottered down the steps to greet them.

"Mrs. Delisle?"

"Yes, indeed." Caroline's mother inclined her head a friendly inch. "I assume Lord Hellion is expecting us."

"Yes, ma'am. Please come in."

Margaret stepped into the large black-and-white tiled hall that rose to the towering height of a cathedral and fought to keep a pleasant smile on her face and not gawp like a country bumpkin.

"I'll take you through to Miss Lilly and Mrs. Grantham in the small morning room, ma'am. Your bags will be taken up to your rooms."

"Thank you," Mrs. Delisle said.

Margaret, Mrs. Delisle, and Lottie followed the butler down what appeared to be a mile of corridor lined with faded wainscoting and unidentifiable artwork. There was a pervading scent of damp and lack of use in the air, which made Margaret even more nervous.

The morning room, however, was full of sunlight and furnished in a comfortable, if shabby, way. The young woman who rose to greet them wore black and appeared to be of a similar age to Margaret and Lottie.

"You must be Alistair's guests. How kind of you to come and visit us." She smiled uncertainly at Margaret and Lottie, as if wondering why on earth they had decided to visit at all. "I'm Miss Archer, and this is my aunt Maud, Mrs. Grantham. We are both related to the last duke, but on somewhat distant branches of the family tree."

Miss Archer gestured for them all to join her around the meager fire, which did little to warm even such a moderately small room. Margaret guessed the chimney hadn't been swept for quite a long while, which would explain the lack of vigor of the flames. She settled on the couch where she could still see the door.

"Williams will bring us some tea, which will sustain us while we wait for Alistair." Miss Archer smiled. "He has been somewhat busy in the last few weeks as he attempts to deal with the estate."

"I can imagine." Mrs. Delisle glanced over at Margaret and Lottie. "We were very sorry to hear of the loss of his grandfather and cousin."

"Indeed, we expected Great Uncle Norris to die because he had reached a great age and had been unwell for several years, but not his oldest grandson." Miss Archer sighed. "Poor Alistair has been left with a houseful of dependents, an estate that has been allowed to slide into disrepair, and a title that he never wanted."

As if summoned by his cousin's words, the door opened, and the butler came in with the tea tray, followed by the unmistakable figure of Margaret's potential husband.

"His Grace, the Duke of Thorsway," the butler intoned.

Margaret slowly came to her feet as he approached, her gaze taking in his brown coat, buff colored breeches, and gleaming top boots. His blond hair needed cutting and his cravat was a crumpled, knotted mess. Her fingers itched to remove it from his neck and offer him a freshly ironed one.

"Mrs. Delisle, Miss Blackthorn, Miss Lottie." He executed a perfect bow. "How kind of you to visit me."

He kissed Mrs. Delisle's gloved hand, winked at Lottie, and came over to Margaret, his blue eyes dancing with that subtle amusement she was never sure was aimed at her.

"Miss Blackthorn, a pleasure indeed."

"You are a *duke* now?" Margaret blurted out.

"For my sins, yes. I inherited the title from my grandfather after my cousin's demise." His mouth twisted. "A duke of debt and ruin as you can probably already tell." Keeping hold of her hand, he turned to Miss Archer. "I'll take the ladies on a tour after they've had some tea, Lilly."

"If you really wish to, Alistair, although there is not much to see." Miss Archer sat down and started pouring the tea, her smile disappearing. "The state rooms are all shut up, and the rest of the house is in much need of repair."

"I still wish Miss Blackthorn to see everything," Lord Hellion replied. "She is very interested in such things."

"Indeed she is," Lottie agreed. "There is nothing my sister likes more than a stimulating project."

"Then perhaps she can advise you, Alistair." Miss Archer's smile had completely disappeared. "Lord knows, we need all the assistance we can get."

"Then I will stay here with Miss Archer and Mrs. Delisle while you go and explore with the duke, Margaret," Lottie said with a wicked smile. "I'm sure you will have plenty of advice for his grace."

And just like that, Margaret found herself walking alone with the new duke of Thorsway along the dank corridors of his newly acquired mansion. He opened random doors as they progressed, commenting on what he thought the room's purpose was. It was difficult to see much with the shutters up and the majority of the furniture in holland covers.

"I didn't grow up here, so I'm not that familiar with the place," he confessed as they reached yet another stairway. "My father didn't get along with his brother or his father, so we rarely visited."

"Has it always been like this?" Margaret asked as she turned a slow circle.

"No, when I was a child it was perfectly kept. After my grandmother died, and grandfather became ill, things changed for the worse." He hesitated. "Recently, my cousin brought a rather unscrupulous land agent in to wring as much money out of the estate and farms as possible. Those desperate endeavors have weakened the entire estate, left the tenants unhappy, and half the farms empty."

Margaret walked over to the window and rubbed a small hole in the grime on the glass. In truth, the whole place gave her the horrors. She tried to imagine how it once might have looked and found it impossible. The new duke was watching her intently now, one shoulder propped up against the window frame and a hand thrust into the pocket of his breeches.

"It's appalling, isn't it? This is exactly why I suggested you visit before committing yourself to any foolishness."

His tone was light, but she could sense the bleakness beneath it. The house was so quiet she could hear mice scratching behind the skirting boards and paneling. To set this place to rights... to make it into a showplace would take a lifetime.

She let out a long, slow breath that seemed to take forever.

"It would certainly be an interesting challenge." She walked toward him.

He regarded her warily. "How interesting?"

"Interesting enough to marry you for," Margaret said.

He reached out and caught her chin in his hard fingers. "Perhaps you should reserve judgment until you have spent a whole day here."

"I doubt it will get any better, and it will probably get worse." She paused. "Are you sure that you don't want to accept my offer now?"

He leaned in very slowly and kissed her on the lips. "No, I believe you should be given every opportunity to run away as fast as your legs will carry you."

"I'm not a coward," Margaret insisted.

"But you are a reckless fool to want this." He kissed her again, his tongue seeking admittance to clash with hers until she was leaning fully against him, one hand anchored on his shoulder as he ravaged her mouth.

He was the first to draw back and scowl at her. "Stop being so damned enticing."

"I am hardly that." Margaret sounded breathless even to herself. She wanted to press against the hard planes of his body, to slide her fingers beneath the badly starched collar of his shirt, and rip it off...

She took an unsteady step back. "Mrs. Delisle will be wondering where we are."

"I doubt it." He offered her his arm. "But I sense that you have had enough of me and wish to return to your family."

"I am merely tired after the carriage ride and would welcome a moment to set myself to rights," Margaret countered. In truth, she needed to gather her resources against him, but she had no intention of telling him that.

"You look perfectly beautiful to me."

"Beautiful?" Margaret sniffed. "I suspect you are referring to my sister. She is the acknowledged beauty in the family."

"Says who?"

"*Everyone.*"

He stopped walking and turned to face her, his gaze traveling up her body until he finally met her eyes. "Perhaps you are not beautiful in the current way society demands, Miss Blackthorn, but you are a strong, handsome woman. The kind of woman who doesn't break easily—the kind who would dare to marry a man desperately trying to survive."

For some reason, his words made her want to cry. Before she could embarrass herself further, he dropped a kiss on her nose, and offered her his hand again.

"Shall we go? Your tea will be cold, but I'll order up another pot. We can, at least, afford that."

ALISTAIR SPENT an inordinate amount of time simply watching Margaret Blackthorn navigate her way around his family and his estate. She answered all the questions about her brother and Millcastle with a refreshing honesty that still surprised him. She wasn't ashamed of her family tree and obviously didn't care about the supposed nobility of his. But why would she, when her brother had succeeded from nothing, and Alistair had inherited a rotten branch of an aristocratic family who had singlehandedly destroyed their worth and wealth in less than two generations?

After a dinner, which had barely been edible, he slipped away to his grandfather's study to smoke a cigarillo and plan what to do with Miss Blackthorn for the remainder of her stay. He intended to show her the worst of the place, so that she could never say he'd tried to bamboozle her into marriage.

He blew out a ring of smoke. But why was he so determined to put her off when he already liked her and definitely lusted after her? Just for once, couldn't he forget his damned stupid scruples and take advantage of the situation?

"Alistair?"

He spun around to find that Lilly had come into the room and was hovering nervously by the door.

"What is it?"

"May I ask why you invited the Miss Blackthorns and Mrs. Delisle to visit us?"

He raised an eyebrow. "Isn't it obvious?"

"That Miss Margaret has aspirations to your title, yes, but—"

"She isn't like that," Alistair said abruptly. "The only one aspiring to anything here is me."

"You... care for her?" Lilly whispered.

"I think it's too soon to be talking in such terms, but I certainly admire and respect her."

Lilly gripped her hands together and came farther into the room. "But what about me?"

"I don't understand," Alistair said slowly, although he had a horrible idea where the conversation was heading.

"Everyone is expecting you to marry *me*."

Alistair stubbed out his cigarillo and prepared to hurt yet

another person in his life who didn't deserve it. "I've always liked you, Lilly, but I think of you as a sister."

"And yet you feel it is better to marry someone you hardly know and 'respect' than a woman who has always been your friend?"

"It's not that simple, and you know it." Alistair held her gaze. "If I am to keep this place going, I need money. The estate on the verge of bankruptcy."

"And Miss Blackthorn is wealthy."

"She is."

"And she is from a family who a generation ago worked in a *mill*."

"Yes."

"She is not *like* us, Alistair. She will not know how things are *done* here. She will—"

He held up his hand. "If she decides to marry me, her wealth will save the estate."

Lilly gathered herself up and, for the first time in his life, glared at him. "I never thought of you as mercenary before, Alistair."

He shrugged. "Perhaps I learned a lesson or two about being too nice last time I inherited nothing."

She shook her head. "If you go through with this foolish scheme, neither of you will be happy. Miss Blackthorn will be out of her natural position in society, you will be dragged down to her level, and—"

"And what, Lilly? I'll save the estate? Do you even begrudge me that opportunity?"

She spun around and walked out, shutting the door quietly behind her. Alistair slowly exhaled, more shaken by the encounter than he had expected. If Lilly, who had always been his only ally in the family, refused to accept his union with Margaret, then he was in for a great deal of trouble.

But if he didn't marry soon and well, the rest of his family would be losing their home anyway, because he wouldn't be able to support the estate, and it would have to be sold off. He doubted they would believe that his choice was so stark. He suspected that many of them would rather endure penury than lower themselves to marry for money.

He wasn't like that. He'd barely survived the gradual stripping away of his inheritance and responsibilities by his father at the behest of his stepmother. He wasn't prepared to have a title and empty coffers again. Part of him relished the thought of his stepmother finding out what he'd done. She hadn't bothered to write to him about his accession to the dukedom, presumably because she knew the state of his inheritance and was reveling in the thought of his further discomfort.

If he married Margaret, he'd make damn sure not to invite his stepmother to the wedding... He'd even be in a position to offer his sister a home if she was willing, and his stepmother hadn't turned her completely against him.

Alistair rose to his feet and made sure that the fire was out before he left the room. He wanted to marry Margaret. He'd show her the worst of the estate over the next day, and, if she was still willing, he would ignore the inevitable outcry and make her his wife.

"Do you think you'll marry your duke?" Lottie asked as she tucked herself in beside Margaret in their draughty bedroom.

"I'm still not sure." Margaret grimaced as she pulled the damp covers up to her chin. "He seems to be doing everything in his power to persuade me otherwise."

"Which, knowing you, is very clever of him, indeed," Lottie agreed. "I quite like him."

"He certainly is attempting to be honest with me, and this place..." Margaret's gaze drifted around the faded curtains, smoking chimney, and the frayed silk wall hangings. "It is far worse than I envisaged."

"Well, you weren't expecting to become a duchess, either," Lottie reminded her. "Adam will be beside himself."

"He won't care in the slightest, as long as I am happy," Margaret defended her brother. "The only thing he will object to is the idea of his money pouring into what he would consider a lost cause."

"This place could be beautiful," Lottie said wistfully. "Lilly was telling me how it was when she was a little girl. It was quite hard to imagine."

"Lilly doesn't like me."

"Of course she doesn't." Lottie nudged her. "She believes she's in line to be the next duchess."

Margaret sat bolt upright. "She told you that?"

"Not in so many words, you know how these aristocratic ladies can be, but the general tone of her conversation was all about what 'she and Alistair' hoped to accomplish with the estate."

"Do you think he is betrothed to her?" Margaret asked.

"Surely not." Lottie frowned. "Isn't that a legal contract that cannot be broken? You should ask your intended." She chuckled. "Perhaps it is a family tradition. Adam broke off his relationship with the schoolteacher to marry Emily, didn't he?" She hastened to add, "Although that was never formalized."

"I received the impression from Lord Hellion—I mean, his grace—that Lilly was like a sister to him."

Lottie snorted. "Men can be rather blind sometimes, can't they?"

"It would certainly explain her dislike of me," Margaret agreed. "Not that she is openly hostile, of course. She is merely cold and distant."

To be fair, most of Lord Hellion's family had treated her with that same indifference—as if her presence was not only unwanted, but to be ignored. It made quite a change to the constant adulation she and her family received in Millcastle. She remembered her first reaction when Adam had told her he was going to marry Emily Marsham. She'd wanted him to recover their father's lost wealth and position, but hadn't held a high opinion of Emily, who had seemed far too meek to interest her formidable brother.

She'd been proved wrong about that and had come to like Emily very much, indeed. Perhaps if she married Lord Hellion, his grace, the Duke of Thorsway, his family would come to appreciate her finer qualities as well.

Even as she lay back on the pillow and closed her eyes, Margaret smiled at the absurdity of that fanciful notion. They would never approve of her, but they'd be too well-bred to openly oppose her, which might work in her favor. Despite everything—in fact, because of all the negatives—her resolve to thumb her nose at everyone and marry the new duke was strengthening.

CHAPTER FIVE

"Mr. Blackthorn will see you now."

Alistair nodded his thanks to the clerk and went through into Adam Blackthorn's office. It was the first time Alistair had ever been inside a mill, and he devoutly hoped it would be his last. The bleakness of the surroundings, the dull thud of powerful machinery that reverberated through the whole building, the *people*...

Adam Blackthorn stood as Alistair approached his desk, his sharp gaze running over Alistair as if he were an impudent parlor maid. He wore a plain black coat with a blue waistcoat and very white linen, which Alistair wondered how he kept clean in such a gritty environment.

"To what do I owe this honor?"

"I wish to marry your sister, Margaret," Alistair said simply.

"Do you, now." Adam gestured at the chair in front of his desk. "Sit down."

Alistair complied and crossed one leg over the other in an attempt to display a nonchalance he was far from feeling.

"I understand that you have recently inherited a dukedom."

"That is correct." Alistair nodded.

"I suppose you think that means you're better than me."

"Not at all." Alistair raised an eyebrow. "I wish to marry your sister, not engage in a pissing contest with you."

Adam's lips twitched slightly. "I can see why my sister approves of you."

"She *is* a great believer in plain speaking," Alistair agreed.

"She told me that she wants this marriage."

"Then surely all you have to do is give me your approval, and we're done?" Alistair suggested.

"I've done some investigating into your current financial state." Adam picked up a pile of papers from his desk and studied them. "You are in debt, your estates are crumbling, and your own father left all his money to his second wife rather than trust you with a penny." He looked up. "Why in God's name would you think I'd be willing to allow my sister to marry *you?*"

"Because she is aware of all this and still wishes to become my wife?" Adam went to interrupt him, but Alistair was quicker. "And please don't tell me that she doesn't know her own mind or her own worth because she is a mere female. She knows exactly who and what I am."

"Perhaps you have beguiled her with false promises and kisses."

Alistair almost laughed. "Beguiled *Margaret?* Good Lord, man. Do you not know your own *sister?* If I'd been anything less than honest with her, she would've walked away in a second!" Alistair sat forward. "We like and respect each other and believe we would be compatible, which gives us more in common than most couples who entertain the notion of marriage."

Adam allowed the papers to slide through his fingers. "You are aware that she has a good dowry?"

"Of course I am."

"And you need that money to rebuild your estates?"

"Yes."

"At least you aren't trying to pretend otherwise." Adam reached for another stack of paper on his desk, his clipped Northern vowels emerging more strongly with every word. "If she marries you, and I said *if*, there are several financial conditions I will insist are put in place to safeguard her interests."

"I would expect nothing less from you."

Adam pushed the papers toward him. "I suggest you read through the marriage settlement and then come back and speak to me and my solicitors again."

"Can you summarize the parts that you believe will be contentious?" Alistair asked.

"To be honest, I don't think you'll like any of it." Adam's smile was both triumphant and predatory. "I'll have you by the ballocks, and if you put one foot wrong with my sister, I'll have no problem cutting you off."

Alistair winced. "That sounds painful." He leaned forward to gather the papers in his hand. "I'll be staying at the Graftons for the next few days. I will send you a message when I've had time to read through the document."

"As you wish." Adam stood, and Alistair followed suit. "I'll give you credit for turning up here and asking straight out for what you want."

"The credit for that belongs to your sister," Alistair confessed. "She told me not to come down here with any fancy airs, but to look you right in the eye and speak to you like a businessman."

"She was right." Adam came around the desk and briefly shook Alistair's hand. "I have to visit my other mill now. Can I drop you anywhere?"

"In the nearest river, perhaps?" Alistair murmured. "Thank you for your attention, but I have my own horse." He bowed and turned toward the door. "A pleasure to meet you again, Mr. Blackthorn."

"Likewise."

Alistair strode out of the office and kept going until he reached his horse, threw a coin to the boy who'd been watching it for him, and left the premises. The taste of smoke and what he could only assume was cotton or wool lingered on his tongue, making him thirsty.

He rode into Millcastle, left his horse in the stable yard, and went into the inn Francis still owned in the market square.

"Is Captain Grafton here, Nancy?" Alistair asked the landlady.

"Yes, he's upstairs in his old rooms, your lordship." She waved him onward. "I'll send up a fresh bottle of brandy."

Alistair knocked loudly on the door and went in without waiting for an answer. Francis was sitting at his desk poring over his account books.

"You survived, then?"

"Barely." Alistair whistled. "My God, he is quite formidable isn't he?"

"*Quite?* Adam Blackthorn is terrifying. He makes me look like a lamb," Francis said.

"Hardly that." Alistair accepted the bottle of brandy the maid offered him and opened it. "Thank you."

He didn't bother with a glass, but took a long swig directly from the bottle.

"That's better." He drew the package of papers out of his pocket. "He gave me his list of demands and suggested he'd own me."

"It's interesting that he drew up a marriage settlement at all," Francis remarked. "You should be encouraged."

"I haven't read it yet." Alistair drank more brandy. "Do you have a solicitor in town?"

"Don't you have your very own ducal retainer?" Francis looked pained.

"I do, but I don't want him to see anything until I've hammered out the details."

Francis laughed and held out his hand for the brandy bottle. "If I know Blackthorn, he's hoping you'll walk away with your tail between your legs."

"If that's what he's hoping, he doesn't know me and, what's worse, he doesn't know his sister, Margaret. If she wants this marriage, she'll not let him stand in her way."

~

"WHAT DO you mean you saw the Duke of Thorsway in your office this morning?" Margaret demanded.

Adam raised his eyebrows and put down his wine glass. "You heard me quite plainly, lass, why are you asking me to repeat myself?"

"Why didn't you tell me until now?"

"Because he came to see me, not you." Adam refilled his plate from the serving dishes at the center of the table. "This is very good lamb, Emily."

"Thank you, my love, but perhaps you might address Margaret's concerns?" Emily glanced nervously at her sister-in-law.

"Which reminds me," Adam started talking again. "How exactly did my sister get to know a duke well enough to extort a marriage proposal from him?"

"*Extort?*" Margaret glared at her brother.

"For goodness sake, Adam, Margaret hardly had to do that when the man was literally following her around like a besotted lamb at the Graftons' last dinner party," Lottie entered the fray on her sister's behalf. "And, to be frank, it is Lord Hellion who needs Margaret, not the other way around."

"We decided that we would suit," Margaret said. "It was a mutual decision. What did you say to him?"

Adam's smile was wicked. "Don't you want to know what he said to me first?"

"I know what he said!"

Her brother sat back in his chair and regarded her. "I'll give you one thing, Margaret. I never expected him to turn up at the mill and ask me right out for permission to marry you. He's a lot braver than he looks."

Lottie rolled her eyes. "He was in the army with Captain Grafton, Adam. He's hardly a coward."

"He's still a damned aristocrat, a species Margaret insisted were worthless until quite recently." Adam winked at her. "But he stood up for himself. I like that in a man."

"Did you agree?" Margaret asked, her hands locked together under the table, her heart beating far too wildly.

"I gave him a copy of my proposed marriage settlement." He grinned at her. "We'll find out what he's made of when he reads through that!"

"Do you have a copy, yourself?" Margaret asked.

"Yes, do you want to read it?" Adam reached inside his coat and produced a folded document. "He'll hate every sentence."

Margaret took the papers. "You are enjoying this, aren't you?"

"Aye." He shrugged, his smile dying. "Remember, I am doing everything in my power to protect you. When I married Emily, her father made no effort to safeguard anything for her in the way of a settlement. I got everything." He glanced down the table at his wife. "I've remedied that now, but mark my words, sister, I will not allow any man to drag you into penury, duke or no duke."

"I understand." Even though it was hard not to instinctively protest his hardline stance, Margaret had to appreciate his genuine concerns for her.

Despite their differences, the bond between them was unbreakable. After their father's death by suicide, they'd held the family together, both of them working to provide for their mother and younger sister until Adam had climbed back up the ranks to regain his position and substantially increase his wealth.

"If I did allow him to beggar you, you'd never forgive me, either," Adam reminded her and reached for her hand. "We'll see what he's made of now, won't we? And whether he deserves you."

Unfortunately, sometimes Adam knew her far too well. Margaret scowled at her brother even as he grinned triumphantly back at her.

~

"THESE TERMS ARE RIDICULOUS, YOUR GRACE," Mr. Simpkins repeated stubbornly as Alistair set his jaw. He was sitting in the solicitor's office with Francis, attempting to find a way through the impasse of Adam Blackthorn's draconian marriage settlement.

"If you sign this agreement, Mr. Blackthorn will have the ability to foreclose on the estate and strip it of everything of value if you do not comply with his terms."

"He *is* offering to buy up all my debts and mortgages, Mr. Simpkins. Surely such a large outlay of capital on his part at the outset of my marriage deserves some security?" Alistair asked.

"Yes, but not the whole damned estate, Alistair," Francis intervened. "Perhaps it might be better to suggest a compromise? You could offer to set aside a portion of the estate in his name in trust for your children."

"I'd rather he wasn't involved long term at all," Alistair said stubbornly. "I thought to use the clean slate he's offered me, along with Margaret's dowry, to make the estate profitable again."

"Which you won't be able to do if you are too busy servicing the extortionate interest rates of his proposed loans," Francis reminded him.

Alistair read through the complex document again.

"What if I agree to use half the dowry to fund settlements on Margaret and our future children, and allow Mr. Blackthorn to take on a smaller percentage of the outstanding debt at a more reasonable repayment rate?"

"It would take longer for you to make the estate profitable, but at least you would have some capital, and won't be owned like a dog," Francis remarked.

"I would suggest settling a quarter of Miss Blackthorn's dowry on her and your issue, sir," Mr. Simpkins advised. "The rest should be sufficient to start improving the estate and pay Mr. Blackthorn back for the percentage of debt you allow him to take on."

"Then perhaps you will draw up the counter offer and deliver it to Mr. Blackthorn, Mr. Simpkins?" Alistair stood up. "Thank you for your advice, and let us know when Mr. Blackthorn or his solicitor responds to you.

As they exited the house, Alistair looked over at Francis. "Do you think Blackthorn will accept such a compromise?"

"I doubt it, but you can only ask." Francis shuddered. "God bless your soul if he chooses to take exception to your proposals."

"Ah, but I have one thing in my favor," Alistair reminded his distant cousin. "If Mr. Blackthorn isn't willing to strike a deal, his dear sister will never let him hear the end of it."

~

"MARGARET!"

At Adam's shout, Margaret came across the hall and into her brother's study, her bonnet still dangling in her hand. She'd been out shopping with her sister, not that there was anything worth buying in Millcastle, but she'd needed something to occupy her time while Adam and her potential husband wrangled over terms. It was somewhat frustrating to feel like a bone caught between two dogs.

"Whatever is the matter?"

He held up a sheaf of papers. "Your intended's counter offer."

"May I see it?" She took the document and read through it as quickly as she could before raising her gaze to her irate brother's.

"I don't know why you are so annoyed. You could hardly have expected him to turn the whole estate over to you."

"I was intent on safeguarding your interests."

"By making him totally beholden to you for every financial decision about the estate? By offering him interest rates that even the most gullible of businessmen wouldn't accept?" Margaret handed back the pages. "This all seems quite reasonable to me."

"*Reasonable?*" Adam frowned. "He seems to think he is better able to judge his own financial needs than I am."

"And maybe he is. How many dukedoms have you run, Adam?" Margaret asked sweetly. "Perhaps, for once in your life, you might settle down and learn something."

"And what would you say if I refuse to concede a single inch?"

She held his gaze. "That you would never do that because it would make me unhappy."

He frowned. "Would you marry him if I refused my help and my money?"

"Of course not! He needs my dowry, and that comes from you."

"That's my girl." Adam's smile slowly returned. "At least you admit it."

Margaret exhaled. "I love you very much, Adam, but I really do wish to marry my duke."

"Other aristocrats in dire straits would be more than willing to accept my terms. With your dowry, you could probably attract a royal duke."

"But they wouldn't be Alistair," Margaret said. "I want the *man*, not the title. You know that."

She held her breath as her brother sat down and drew the two sets of documents in front of him again, one under each palm as if he were weighing them against each other.

"Whatever terms I agree to, if he doesn't succeed, I'll make certain that he pays for it, and you don't."

"I understand that."

"And if he comes running to me wanting to change the agreement later, I won't listen to him."

"I doubt he will do that."

He looked up at her. "I'd agree with you. He's less of a coward than I anticipated."

"You were hoping he'd walk away."

"I wouldn't have minded that, lass—if he wasn't the right man for you." He shrugged. "But I appreciate a man who offers me a bold counterproposal these days when so many are afraid to even try."

"So you will agree terms with him?" Margaret asked.

"With a few amendments." He winked at her and drew the new agreement in front of him. "I can't let him think he's bettered the great Adam Blackthorn, now, can I?"

CHAPTER SIX

For about the fifteenth time, Margaret went over to the window and peered out into the gloom of the rapidly darkening sky. There was no sign of the Grafton carriage. She was wearing her best blue gown, and Lottie had arranged her hair in a swathe of curls and jeweled pins.

"Margaret, he's not due here for another quarter of an hour at least," Lottie reminded her as she tidied up the brushes and ribbons.

"If he comes." Margaret turned to her sister. "I have no way of knowing exactly what terms Adam settled on and whether his grace will appear here merely to throw them back in my brother's face."

"Adam did seem quite confident that he would get his way," Lottie said doubtfully. "But I think your duke has rather more backbone than Adam imagines."

"I wish he'd bothered to speak to me about everything." Margaret gathered her shawl. "He's been staying with the Graftons for a week and hasn't deigned to visit me here at all."

"Probably because he's been busy negotiating with our brother and his solicitors and didn't want to be distracted."

"I could've helped him," Margaret insisted.

Lottie chuckled. "I doubt he considered that, and he is a *duke*, Margaret. He probably has a whole retinue of solicitors and lawyers to advise him about what is best for the estate." She turned to the door. "Are you ready to come down? Adam and Emily will probably be in the drawing room by now."

"I'll come." Margaret touched Lottie's shoulder. "Thank you for doing my hair."

"You are most welcome." Lottie kissed her cheek. "Your duke will be beside himself at your great beauty and instantly agree to even the most ridiculous of Adam's terms."

"I do hope not," Margaret retorted, which set her sister off chuckling again. By the time she reached the drawing room, she was smiling herself and quite unprepared for the sight of the duke, resplendent in a dove-grey coat and silver waistcoat talking to her sister-in-law.

He looked up as she entered and held her gaze, a slow smile warming his expression until it reached his dancing blue eyes.

"Miss Blackthorn. How delightful."

She went to him, drawn by that invisible thread that had tied them together since the first day they'd met, and he'd taken her hand in his.

"Your grace. I didn't realize you were coming alone."

"Francis took the carriage and went back to pick up Caroline and her mother while I made my way here on horseback." He paused. "You look rather worried. Is everything all right?"

"You tell me." She met his amused gaze.

He shrugged. "I'm here, am I not?"

Her smile faltered, and she attempted to ease out of his grasp. "You don't have to be here if you don't want to be."

"Good Lord, not this again." His grip tightened, and he drew her away from the rest of her family and into the hallway beyond. "Please excuse us, everyone."

"Where are you taking me—?" Margaret protested as he

opened the nearest door and brought her into the darkened room. "What are you doing—?"

"This." He drew her into his arms and kissed her thoroughly. "It seems that I have to regularly remind you just how desperately I want to kiss you before you immediately assume the worst."

"I do *not*—"

He kissed her again, and this time she returned his efforts until she was pressed against him from knee to shoulder. He eventually drew back and cupped her chin.

"Now, where were we?"

"I merely asked how you were," Margaret said stiffly.

"And made assumptions about my willingness to be here." He smoothed his thumb along her lower lip. "When I have spent the last week battling your overbearing brother and his obsequious solicitors for the right to marry you."

"Does that mean you have won?" Margaret asked suspiciously.

He grimaced. "Perhaps it would be fairer to say that both sides have suffered grievous wounds, but that we have declared a truce in order to placate our fair lady." He leaned in and kissed her gently. "Will you marry me, Margaret Blackthorn?"

She pressed her palm against his chest and held him at bay. "Will marrying me help or hinder your current financial situation?"

"As your brother might say, you're a canny lass." He grinned at her. "I should've asked you to negotiate the marriage settlement alongside me."

"I would've done so if you'd asked."

"And set you against your brother?" He shook his head. "I wouldn't do that to either of you. All is well. You are more than welcome to read through the settlement before you accept my proposal."

"I will do so," Margaret stated.

"I knew you'd say that." He slid a hand inside his coat and brought out some rolled up paperwork. "Be my guest."

He set about lighting the lamp and rekindling the fire while Margaret sat down to read through the documents. As she'd already seen the originals and her intended's response, she was quick to note where things had changed once more. Eventually, she sat back to find him regarding her from his perch on the edge of the desk. He'd somehow found Adam's brandy and helped himself to a glass.

"My brother has been..." She hesitated.

"Remarkably fair, has he not?"

"Yes." She swallowed hard. "He loves me very much."

"So he told me when he threatened to rip my ballocks off if I ever caused you the slightest pain." He glanced down at his torso. "I *did* tell him that procuring an heir for the dukedom would be remarkably difficult if he followed through with his threat, and that you might not wish to be married to a eunuch."

"I'm beginning to understand why you did not want me involved in these negotiations." Margaret rolled the papers up and tied the ribbon around them again, her fingers trembling. "Then we can marry?"

"Yes, my little doubting Thomas, if we both wish to do so."

She bit her lip. "There is one more thing."

He sighed. "Of course there is—out with it, then."

"Your cousin Lilly seems to think you are going to marry her."

He stowed the papers away and came around the desk to draw her to her feet.

"I can assure you that the thought never crossed my mind," he said firmly. "I have always liked her, but I've never seen her as a potential bride."

"Poor Lilly," Margaret murmured as her duke took her in his arms again. "I was worried that you might have been formally betrothed at some point."

"No." He kissed her. "Never. Now can we go and have dinner with your family and the Graftons? Much as it pains me to have to look at your brother's face, I cannot deny the fact that I wish to get on with our engagement." He paused. "I almost forgot."

He rummaged in his coat pocket and produced a faded velvet box. "The Thorsway betrothal ring." He opened the box to reveal a diamond and ruby ring that in Margaret's eyes was rather ugly, and in desperate need of cleaning. "Luckily for us, my cousin hated rubies and old-fashioned settings and neglected to sell this off to pay his gambling debts. It's been in the family for about two hundred years."

He slid it onto her third finger, his expression for once, quite serious. "I know that it is hideous, but it will have to do until I can afford something better, or we can have the jewels reset."

"It's lovely." Margaret gazed at the enormous ruby, which was surrounded by diamonds and seed pearls. She'd never seen or worn anything of such antiquity before. "Thank you."

"There is a tiara and a necklace in the set as well. I couldn't fit them into my pocket."

"A *tiara?*"

He kissed her hand and urged her toward the door. "Indeed, which will look very well on you when you are presented at court."

"Wait…" She dug her heels in as he opened the door. "You are jesting, yes?"

"No. We'll both have to be presented at some point. It's a damn nuisance." He raised a taunting eyebrow. "Don't tell me that the bravest woman of my acquaintance is *afraid?*"

"Of course not!" Margaret rallied and moved toward him. "Perhaps we should start with dinner and announcing our engagement, and worry about everything else on another occasion."

As soon as they stepped into the drawing room, all eyes fell on their joined hands. Adam Blackthorn didn't look very happy, but Alistair wasn't in the mood to tease the man. He had, after all, accepted most of Alistair's revised terms, which had been a complete surprise. With the money he received from Margaret's dowry, which was far more extensive than he could possibly have imagined, and the new structure to his debts, he would at least have a chance of restoring the dukedom to solvency.

He went straight over to Adam and bowed elaborately. "Thank you for inviting me to your house this evening."

"You're most welcome." Adam's gaze fell to Margaret's left hand. "I assume you have something to share with us?"

"Yes, indeed." Alistair turned to face the other guests. "Miss Blackthorn has agreed to marry me."

Lottie clapped her hands and ran over to hug her sister. "Good lord, my sister is going to be a duchess!"

Margaret, who was still slightly flushed from their kisses, glanced uncertainly up at Alistair. "I keep forgetting about that."

"Trust me, you will do fine. If there is anyone less qualified to be a duke than I am, I have yet to meet him, but we'll muddle through."

Lottie went on tiptoe to kiss his cheek. "Welcome to the family, your grace."

"Thank you." Alistair turned to Adam, who was regarding him with rather less enthusiasm. "I owe it all to your brother."

"Wait until Mrs. Wells hears about this, Margaret. She'll probably swoon away on a fit of jealous rage!" Lottie chuckled. "Just think, you will never have to put up with her or her saintly daughter again."

Francis, who had just arrived, came over with Caroline at his side, and held out his hand. "Congratulations my friend."

"Thank you." Alistair shook Francis's hand, and then turned to kiss Caroline's gloved fingers. "And thank you for lending me your mother to act as a chaperone when Miss Blackthorn came for a visit."

"My mother is a romantic and she enjoyed every minute of it," Caroline said. "Apart from the smoking chimneys, the moth-eaten bed linen, and the food, of course."

"I intend to put all those things to rights," Alistair assured her. "Tell her that next time she visits us, things should have improved greatly."

Caroline linked her arm with his and drew him farther down the room, away from the gathering around the fireplace. "You do realize that this will be difficult for Miss Blackthorn, don't you?"

"In what way?"

"That, as your wife, she will be entering the aristocracy after growing up in a millhouse?"

"Don't tell me you share my cousin Lilly's views that Margaret can never be considered good enough?" He met her gaze. "I'm surprised at you."

Caroline frowned. "That's not what I meant, and you know it. I'm merely concerned that there will be a lot of... opposition from your family, and that you should be on your guard for it."

"I am already aware of it. I was hoping that a gentle reminder that if I do not bring some money into the family, they will all be out on their ears might work."

Caroline didn't seem convinced. "Their disapproval will be more subtle than that—I've been on both sides of that divide, and I don't envy her." She touched his sleeve. "I hope you don't mind me speaking frankly to you about this matter?"

"Not at all. I value your opinion."

Alistair looked over to where Margaret was conversing with her sister-in-law, her smile bright and her eyes full of amusement. He wanted to take her hand and run away from the lot of them.

"She's stronger than she looks," Alistair remarked. "I suspect that if there are battles to come, there will only be one victor." He paused to consider his words and continued with a wry smile. "And it probably won't be anyone from my side of the family who wins, and that includes me."

After an excellent dinner at which Adam toasted the engaged couple with champagne, Alistair decided to forgo the port and went to find Margaret in the drawing room. He accepted a cup of tea from his hostess and persuaded his betrothed to move away from the other women and speak to him privately.

She looked even more exhausted than he felt. For a second he doubted his confident assertion to Caroline that she would deal with her elevated status and responsibilities in her stride. He took her hand and stared down at the betrothal ring. It truly was hideous.

"Are you happy with your choice, Miss Blackthorn?"

Her chuckle surprised him. "Now who is the doubting Thomas? I am very content."

"Good. Do you wish for a long engagement to gather your trousseau together and organize a grand and opulent wedding?"

She raised her eyebrows. "I would rather we just got on with it."

"Which part of marriage in particular are you keen to... embrace?"

"All of you?"

He considered her for a long moment. "You have the most damnable way of answering me with your truth and making me want you." He reached forward to touch one of her brown curls. "I'd like to see your hair down around your magnificent shoulders." His finger traced a line down from her chin to her shoulder blades, making her shiver. "And the rest of you, of course."

"I think I would like that." She met his gaze without fear.

"Oh, you will," he assured her. "I'll make damned sure of it."

CHAPTER SEVEN

*F*ive weeks later, as she awaited her new husband in bed, Margaret wasn't quite so certain of anything anymore. Since their engagement had been announced, she'd hardly seen Alistair Frederick James St. John Haralson. He'd been dealing with financial matters concerned with the estate, and she had been busy organizing her wedding. She'd had a lot of help from her sister and Emily, but she was still exhausted.

They'd married in the Church of England because Methodists were not authorized to solemnize marriages or issue certificates. Apparently, if you were marrying a duke, such things mattered to your potential heirs. With Lottie's help and immaculate style, Margaret had chosen a simple cream-colored gown and veil made from fabric produced in her brother's mill and sewn by a local seamstress. Her new husband had appeared to approve of her choice as he'd kissed her more than once and complimented her extravagantly.

He hadn't invited anyone to the ceremony.

Margaret bit her lip as she remembered the uneven nature of the congregation. Most of her guests had looked uncomfortable in the unfamiliar pews of the church, but at least they'd been present. On one of the rare occasions she'd seen Alistair before the wedding, she'd asked him for a list of his guests. He'd airily promised to send her one and never done so.

Had he even informed his own family that he was getting married? Her brother had put a notice in the local papers but not the London *Times*. He'd told her that was her new husband's decision. Did Lilly even know she'd been ousted?

"Ah, there you are."

Margaret jumped as he came in from the dressing room. They were spending their first night in the guest suite at Grafton Park, which had recently been renovated and was now very grand. He wore a threadbare silk dressing gown and nothing else. He paused to study her and then came to sit on the side of the bed.

"You look worried."

She tried to find a smile. "It's been a very long day."

He grimaced as he took her hand. "I'm sorry that I haven't been here very much to support your efforts, but I must say that it all went off very well."

"I suppose it did."

"What's wrong?" He smoothed his thumb over hers in a regular pattern. "Are you regretting your decision?"

As usual his tone was light, as if everything was an amusing joke that she was the object of, making her response rather sharp.

"Even if I was, there is very little I can do about it now, is there?"

"Good Lord, I expected to get a few good years out of you before you realized I was quite worthless."

She tried to pull her hand free, but he wouldn't let her.

"Margaret..." He leaned in closer. "Will you please look me in the eye and tell me exactly what is bothering you?"

She reluctantly raised her gaze to meet his. "I am just... tired."

He cupped her cheek, his gaze searching. "You do look exhausted, but it's more than that." He paused. "Can we please start this marriage off as we mean to go on by being honest with each other?"

"I don't know where to start," Margaret blurted out.

"If that's the case, I should probably make myself comfortable." He walked around to the other side of the huge four-poster bed and got in. She stiffened as he sat beside her and dropped a casual arm around her shoulders. "Now, start at the beginning."

She looked desperately down at her joined hands. She wasn't used to feeling unsure of herself, and she didn't like it at all.

"I've hardly seen you."

"I know, and I can only apologize for that. The finances of the dukedom were in such a precarious state that I had to personally visit all my main creditors in London, and reassure them that they would eventually be paid." He sighed. "Your brother and Francis offered themselves up as my guarantors, which helped tremendously, but I still felt like a beggar."

Margaret recognized the thread of tiredness in his voice and the lines on his face and reminded herself that her brother was often absent from home because of his work commitments, and that she should not hold dedication to fixing his problems against the new duke.

"What else?" His fingers gently rubbed her shoulder.

"You didn't invite anyone to the wedding."

"Ah." This time it was he who paused before finally answering her. "I decided not to do that."

"Why?" She turned toward him and found herself nose to nose with him. "Are you ashamed of me?"

He blinked at her. "Of course not! I'm merely reluctant to introduce you to my awful family en masse. I did write to my father's wife to inform her of my recent elevation to the dukedom and my upcoming marriage. I asked her if my sister

Phoebe could come to the wedding. She didn't bother to reply to me."

"I didn't even know that you had a sister."

"I haven't seen her for a while. Frederica doesn't allow it."

"Your stepmother?"

"As she is the same age as me, I prefer not to think of her like that. Now can we change the subject to something more pleasant?"

For the first time in their acquaintance she'd discovered something that obviously irked him. If she were not careful and persisted in her inquiries, they would soon be having the first argument of their married life.

"It's a shame that your sister didn't come. I am looking forward to meeting her." Margaret let out a breath. "I'm not sure which worried me most—that you had invited everyone, and they had refused to come, or that you had decided not to invite *anyone* because you were embarrassed to be marrying a mill owner's sister."

"If anyone should be embarrassed, it's me."

"Why?"

"Because everyone knows that I need your money."

"You do need it," Margaret agreed.

A tremor of laughter shook through him. "True, but it is attached to you, and I do believe I need you more."

"You would never have married me unless I'd had money," Margaret said stoutly. "And I was the one who suggested it."

"I'm not sure about that." He held her gaze, his fingers curling into the back of her hair. "I was attracted to you from the moment you looked down your rather haughty nose at me and pretended that you'd completely forgotten my existence."

She found herself smiling into his glinting blue eyes. "That's because you are far too used to being adored."

"*Adored?*" He leaned in and kissed her mouth. "If there is any adoring to be done, I'll be in charge of that." He kissed her again.

"Do you know what happens between a man and a woman in their marriage bed?"

"Of course I do. I wasn't brought up like a sheltered lady."

"Good." He rolled over and pinned her beneath him. "Then you won't be shocked when I strip off your nightgown and feast my gaze on your nakedness."

She gasped as he expertly wrestled with the buttons on her nightgown and drew it swiftly over her head, leaving her exposed to his gaze. It took all her courage not to curl up and cover herself.

"Mmm…" He kissed his way down her throat. "You are even more beautiful than my feverish imaginings." He cupped her full breast and brought it to his mouth, making her catch her breath. "Let me taste you."

After a few moments when she thought she might die of need, he slowly raised his head to look at her.

"You have my full permission to touch anything you want."

"Anything?"

His smile was wicked. "Oh, yes." He bent his head and gently bit her nipple, making her writhe against the sheets, her legs instinctively parting to allow him to kneel inside her thighs. "God, you are beautiful."

He stroked her breasts, alternating his kisses and nips between each side until she was breathing hard, her fingers tangled in his hair, holding him exactly where she wanted him. He moved lower, caressing her hipbones, making her arch toward him with an unspoken plea that her body understood far better than she did.

She stiffened as his fingers brushed against her mound, parting her fold with ease to discover the slick secrets within.

"You're wet for me." He raised himself more fully over her, his mouth plundering hers.

"Is that permitted?" Margaret whispered.

"Not only permitted, but greatly encouraged because it

means that you want me, and that when I finally ease inside you, you're going to come."

"Come where?"

"Around my cock, against my mouth, my fingers..." He flicked his fingers, pinching her most tender pulsing flesh, making her surge up against him. "Wherever you desire and for as many times as I can make you."

"You are... quite indecent."

His smile was laced with lasciviousness. "When I want something, yes I am." He kissed her mound. "And I want you, my duchess, very much indeed."

She moaned his name as he bent his head and licked her most private secrets. He used his tongue to push inside her, making her even wetter.

"Please." She pulled his hair. "I want..."

"Me?" He raised his head to stare at her, running his tongue over his lips, tasting her with a thorough enjoyment that made her stare avidly at him. "I want to make you come first."

"I don't know if I can—"

He raised an eyebrow, settled one elbow on the bed, and rested his chin in his hand. "You've never given yourself pleasure?"

"I've tried, but—" She forced the rest of the words out. "It's always frightened me—the letting go—the losing myself."

He nodded as if her words made perfect sense. "The man you were intending to marry, did he not help you?"

"Help me?" She gaped at him. "Matthew barely liked being in the same room with me, let alone touching me."

"He sounds like a fool." Her husband eased himself up the bed until he was lying alongside her.

"He made me feel as if it were my fault," she confided. "That I lacked something."

He kissed her gently on the mouth. "You lack nothing. One

hates to speak ill of the dead, but he sounds bloody awful. Why on earth did you agree to marry him?"

"To restore my family's position in Millcastle?" Margaret shrugged. "That makes me sound very mercenary, indeed."

"Because you wished to save your family? I can understand why you would want to help them." He searched her face. "Especially as I am doing exactly the same thing. The difference being that I am so bloody grateful that I intend to spend the rest of my life proving it to you." He kissed her very thoroughly. "Now where were we?"

Margaret surrendered herself to him completely, because it was much easier than arguing, and it was such a revelation to be wanted for herself. She hadn't realized how deeply Matthew's contempt had hurt her until she'd encountered the exact opposite.

And her new husband seemed remarkably competent...

She eased her mouth free of his. "Have you had many lovers?"

"Yes." He met her gaze squarely. "And they've all taught me something useful to bring to my marriage bed."

"That is an... interesting way of putting it."

He kissed her very slowly, his knee pushing hers apart as he settled himself over her, one hand caressing her bud in time to each thrust of his tongue. Soon she forgot about speaking as the need for *something* consumed her. His finger slid inside her in the same rhythm while his thumb pressed and circled her throbbing center.

"I... can't," Margaret gasped.

"You can, if you just stop fighting and let me show you the way of it."

She glared at him. "It's too much."

"Yes, it is, isn't it?" He held still over her. "I can feel your need under my thumb, coiling up like wire, wanting release." He slid down between her thighs again and set his mouth over her. She groaned as the friction of his stubbled chin rubbed over her, and his teeth...

"*God...*" She screamed then, turning her face into the pillow as her whole world shrank to the sensations of need and pleasure he had aroused in her. The slow clench of her muscles around his questing fingers set off another rippling wave of excitement.

"That's better." He returned to face her. "Now do that again while I'm inside you."

He eased his member inside her and everything went still again. His smile wasn't quite so cocky anymore.

"Hold onto my shoulders. Bite me if you must. I don't care what you do as long as you let me have you."

She nodded and settled her hands on his shoulders. She wasn't sure when he'd shed his dressing gown, but it was gone now, and he was as naked as she was. She couldn't see where he was now joined to her, but she could feel the thick, hot head of him pulsing at her entrance.

"It might hurt this first time," he cautioned her.

"I am aware of that, but just do it, *please*."

His laugh was harried. "As you wish, duchess." He drew his hips back and then plunged forward, taking her from pleasure into jarring discomfort, and then that too was gone, and he was rocking himself deep inside her.

"Are you all right?"

She slowly opened her eyes and considered him. "Yes."

"That's all you have to say?"

"Yes." She experimentally moved her hips, catching her breath at the sensation of him inside her. "Are we done now?"

His slow smile held all the elements of wickedness she had come to associate with him. He pressed forward and then retreated, leaving her wide-eyed and completely focused on his face.

"Not *quite* yet."

～

SHE WOKE UP LATER, draped across his body, to the sound of his faint snores. It was almost dawn, and the bed was striped with light because they had forgotten to close the curtains. She was a little sore and was looking forward to a bath to ease the stiffness of her limbs. With one tentative hand, she touched the fair hair on his chest and traced the line of his ribs down to his waist where there was a particularly vicious scar.

"Keep going."

His softly murmured words buzzed against her ear, but she didn't move away. Her fingers curved around his hip and followed the trail of hair lower to his groin.

"Mmm..."

She paused there, aware that he was rather more awake than she'd anticipated.

"Lost your nerve?" he inquired.

"Never." She closed her eyes and wrapped her hand around the base of his shaft, slightly alarmed when it leapt to her touch.

"Ah... Be gentle with me, duchess."

"As you were with me, last night?"

His hand closed over hers. "Did I—"

She gripped him harder, making him catch his breath. "I was being honest. You were... very patient with me."

He chuckled and pushed against her restraining fingers. "It was my pleasure, I assure you. Now do you want to learn how to drive a man to his knees?"

She rolled onto her side so that she could see his face, and found him leaning back against the pillows, eyes closed, with one hand behind his head.

"Yes, please."

He glanced down at her working hand. "Then simply continue what you are doing." His smile invited her to join him in mischief. "And if you want to make me your slave forever, there *is* a way to do that, too."

"How so?"

"Did you enjoy my mouth on you?"

"Yes." It would be pointless to deny it when she had screamed his name into her pillow, lost in pleasure. Her fingers slipped through the wetness now covering his shaft as she considered the implications of his words. "Oh."

"Exactly." He sighed and slowly circled his hips. "Please, be my guest."

ALISTAIR HAD LEFT his valet Clarkson sulking at Hellsdown Park and borrowed one of Francis's footmen to assist him with his morning ablutions. He left Margaret in bed and went down to breakfast, feeling more at peace with the world than he had in years. There was still an enormous amount of work to do to salvage the ducal estate, but at least he had his finances in some kind of order and a wife who wasn't afraid of hard work.

"Good morning, Alistair." Caroline greeted him as he came into the sunny morning room. "Is Margaret still sleeping?"

"Yes. Weddings are remarkably tiring things, aren't they? Especially when you have the likes of Adam Blackthorn breathing down your neck, and you know full well that the rest of the guests think you are a useless, idle aristocrat stealing a decent God-fearing woman's money."

Caroline raised her eyebrows. "My, you are quite opinionated today."

He grinned at her. "That's because married life obviously agrees with me. Is Francis here?"

"Yes, but he is working on his accounts, and does not want to be disturbed until midday." Caroline patted her slightly rounded stomach. "Unless I am dying, in which case, he will make an exception.

"I assume those were his exact words?" Alistair helped himself to bacon, eggs, sausages, and baked ham from the serving dishes. He'd hardly eaten anything on the previous day, which had passed by far too quickly. "I thought you were supposed to be a civilizing influence on him?"

"My influence can only go so far." Caroline buttered another piece of toast. "How long are you intending to stay here before you need to return to Hellsdown Park?"

"That rather depends on your continuing desire to be hospitable and my new wife's organizational skills. I suspect she will wish to take quite a lot of things up to her new home, including half her brother's staff, if he'll let her."

"From what she's told me, you have nothing to worry about. She is already as well-organized as a military campaign."

"She probably is." Alistair set about eating his breakfast. "You will come and visit us, won't you?"

"It depends how the roads are and whether I could bear all that bumping around," Caroline said. "But you are both very welcome to visit us here whenever you like."

"Thank you for that." He met her gaze. "You and Francis have been very kind to me."

"From what Francis has told me, you deserve some kindness in your life." Caroline poured herself more tea. "Your step-mother sounds appalling."

"I won't argue with that." Alistair kept eating. "I'm fairly certain that Margaret intends to visit her family in Millcastle regularly, so I expect I'll be accompanying her."

"Good." Caroline offered him an approving smile. "You'll be going down to London, too?"

"I have no choice." He groaned. "I have a townhouse there that needs looking at, and then there's the House of Lords. I suppose I should really make sure that Margaret is properly introduced into society."

"She will certainly make an unusual duchess," Caroline commented drily. "I doubt any other wife of a duke grew up in a millhouse."

Alistair chuckled and reached for the coffee pot.

A slight disturbance made him turn his head to see his wife framed in the door, one hand gripping the frame and a militant look in her eye that made him instantly leap to his feet. She'd probably overheard Caroline's comment and had rushed to a thousand conclusions. Despite appearances, he'd already learned she wasn't quite as impervious to insult as she looked.

"Are you hungry, my dear?"

She took a deep breath and raised her gaze to his. "Yes."

"Then come and sit down and allow me to set a plate before you."

She advanced somewhat reluctantly into the room and sat in the chair he held out, her back rigid and her chin high in the air. Even as Alistair went to speak, she turned to Caroline.

"I did grow up in a millhouse. I am not ashamed of that."

"Why would you be?" Caroline blinked at her.

"You implied that it was a laughable matter."

Caroline wasn't the sort of woman to back down, and she fixed Margaret with her own indomitable stare. "I suggested it was unusual because it is. That was all. I intended no insult."

For a moment, Alistair held his breath and wondered if he would have to throw himself between the two women and what Francis would say to him if he inadvertently upset Caroline.

"One would hope not, seeing as you once considered working in the mills yourself," Margaret responded.

Caroline smiled. "And I am probably the only viscount's wife who has worked as her husband's bookkeeper *and* mistress."

Margaret's own smile was slow to come but eventually appeared. "Then we both know our own worth, don't we?"

"I agree, and we will not allow ourselves to be cowed by the aristocracy." Caroline held up her cup and Margaret picked up hers to gently chime them against each other. "Are you not getting Margaret some breakfast, Alistair?"

"Indeed I am." He hurriedly filled a plate for his new wife and placed it in front of her. "I just didn't want to get in the way in case you two decided to duel or something."

They both looked at him with identical pitying expressions and then ignored his foolishness, which was perfectly fine with him.

Caroline excused herself on a household matter, which left him alone with Margaret, who was happily eating her way through the plate of food.

"She didn't mean anything." Alistair said.

"So she said."

He watched her for a while. "Are you truly not offended?"

"Why should I be? She is right, and I expect I will hear the same words said with far less friendliness in the future." She looked up at him. "But I refuse to hide who I am, and where I come from."

"I would never ask you to do so," he reassured her.

"Only because you are the sort of person who enjoys making others squirm, and having a wife who is from the lower classes will amuse you greatly."

"That's a little harsh," he protested. "I might enjoy their discomfiture if they are expecting you to turn up with a shuttle stuck in your hair, bare feet, and an incomprehensible accent, but I would never allow anyone to insult you."

She studied him carefully while she finished her tea.

"You are quite appalling, you know."

"It is my besetting sin," Alistair admitted. "But I've always been of the opinion that if one doesn't laugh, then one might cry, and that would not do at all."

"Why ever not?"

"Because crying is beaten out of most men before they reach adulthood." He frowned at her. "You know that. I can't imagine your estimable brother goes around weeping every time he doesn't get his own way?"

"He always gets his own way."

"You're deliberately missing my point." He held her gaze. "I choose not to take life seriously."

She raised her eyebrows. "Then it is lucky for you that I am often accused of taking everything *too* seriously."

"Which is why we are a perfect match. How long do you think it will be before we can leave for Hellsdown Park?"

"Do you not intend to visit your sister and stepmother first?"

"God, no." He shuddered. "Let's start with the remnants of my grandfather's family. I suspect they will be far easier to deal with."

Margaret set down her fork. "We can leave tomorrow if you wish?"

"You are ready to go?"

"I've been packing for a month, so yes." She shrugged. "I hate being disorganized. We can say our goodbyes in Millcastle today and be ready to travel onward tomorrow morning."

He gazed at her in admiration and bent to kiss her hand. "Yes, duchess. We will indeed."

She balled up her napkin and threw it at his head.

CHAPTER EIGHT

*H*ellsdown Park was even worse than Margaret remembered. When they pulled up at the front door with all the baggage, no one even appeared to assist them. After shoving open the protesting door, Alistair went inside and bellowed for help so loudly that Margaret could hear him in the carriage.

Eventually, two young men appeared and Margaret's maid Eileen began directing them where to take her mistress's belongings. Alistair came around to hand her down from the carriage.

"I need to go around to the stables and make sure the horses are properly seen to—although that is one area of the estate my cousin and grandfather lavished money on, so I suspect it is still well-staffed. Do you think you can deal with our baggage?"

"Of course." Displaying far more confidence than she felt, Margaret nodded.

"Good. I'll meet you upstairs in our bedchamber as soon as I am able."

He went off and she was soon busy making sure that every-thing was unloaded carefully from the second carriage. When the majority of the items were inside, and it began to drizzle with rain, she stepped into the cold stone hall.

Lilly appeared, and Margaret offered her a warm smile, which was not returned.

"How lovely to see you again, Lilly. Can you direct me to Alistair's suite?"

"It's straight up the main staircase and to the right."

"Thank you." Margaret paused to take off her bonnet. "Would you order some tea to be sent up to me?"

Lilly looked her up and down. "Surely that is your job now?"

Suppressing a sigh only because she knew all too well how it felt to be supplanted by another woman in your own house, Margaret continued up the stairs. She would ask Eileen to brave the no-doubt-frosty reception in the kitchens and bring up the tea herself.

It was easy to guess which door belonged to her husband, because it was open and there was the sound of loud voices coming through it.

"You can't put all that there!"

"The new duchess says different, Mr. Clarkson."

"I don't give a fig what the new duchess says, I want you all out of here."

Margaret paused at the open door to remove her gloves and survey the chaotic scene in front of her. The bedchamber was very large, but her belongings were now taking up more than half of it. The man who was protesting both her arrival and her possessions currently had his back to her as he continued complaining. His hair was black, and he wore what she could only consider a very casual attempt at a valet's uniform.

He turned suddenly, as if aware of her presence, and she simply stared at him as the two footmen disappeared behind her.

"What's wrong?" he asked. "Never seen a black man before?"

"No, I have not." She continued to study him. "Are you the duke's valet?"

"Yes, I am. What of it?"

"Then you are lamentably bad at your duties. Do you have any idea how to starch a neckcloth?"

His mouth opened and shut at least twice before he managed a reply. "Probably better than you do, your grace. How many times have you been down to a kitchen and washed and ironed a ten-foot piece of linen?"

Margaret smiled serenely at him. "Probably more times than you have, from the look of the duke's attire."

"You—" He shook his head. "You aren't supposed to speak to me like that."

"In truth, the boot is surely on the other foot?" Margaret raised her eyebrows. "You are in my employ, I pay your wages, and I expect *you* to do your job."

Behind her, someone delicately cleared his throat.

"I see that you two have met, then." Alistair came to stand between them. "Clarkson, this is my new duchess."

"I'd worked that out for myself, your grace, seeing as she arrived with enough luggage for a queen and has already told me I don't starch your neckties properly."

"She's right." Alistair smiled at Margaret. "Do you want to rest, or would you prefer to leave Eileen to get on with the unpacking and come down for tea?"

"I think I'll let Eileen make a start on this." Margaret gave Clarkson another gracious smile. "After sitting in the carriage for hours I would prefer to stretch my legs."

Alistair took her hand as they went back down the corridor. "I'm sorry I wasn't there to introduce you properly to Clarkson."

"Oh, I think we understand each other," Margaret said lightly.

"He isn't what you might call a conventional valet. I met him during a prize fight when he was down on his luck, and offered him employment."

"As your valet?"

He shrugged. "He's well-qualified. He grew up in a merchant's house and tried his hand at every task before the old man died, and he was put out on the streets with nothing but his fists to defend himself with."

"I'm sure we will get along perfectly once he realizes who is in charge."

Alistair laughed. "Ah, you see, that's where I went wrong. He runs roughshod over me."

Margaret didn't respond, her attention on the drawing room where she could already hear the murmured conversations of her husband's family. Desperate not to show that she was nervous, she gripped Alistair's hand a little more tightly.

He drew her through the door and nodded to the assembled company. "Good afternoon, everyone. I'm sure you are all eager to welcome my new duchess?"

His gaze went to Lilly, who was sitting by the fire. "You have ordered some tea. How nice."

"I thought you might appreciate it after your journey, Alistair." Lilly smiled fondly at the duke.

Just as Lilly went to pick up the teapot, Margaret leaned in and took possession of it. She might as well establish that she was the mistress of Hellsdown Park from the beginning. "May I pour you a cup of tea, Alistair?"

For a few tense seconds, it looked as if Lilly might get into an unsightly wrangle with her over mastery of the teapot, but, after one martyred glance, Lilly relinquished her spot behind the tea tray and moved over to sit by her aunt.

Keeping her smile fixed firmly in place, Margaret began to pour the tea and Alistair distributed it around the room. There was a second pot of boiling water, which she added to the pot.

"Do we have lemon?" she asked, as she finally poured herself a cup and someone sniggered.

"Not at the moment," Alistair was quick to reply to her. "There used to be a conservatory and hot house on the side of the house where such exotic fruits flourished, but it has since fallen into disrepair."

"Perhaps we should renovate it?" Margaret asked as if they were alone and she was not being stared at and judged by a dozen dependent relatives. "I will make sure to visit it on my tour."

The same person snorted, and Margaret raised her gaze to meet the hooded eyes of a man who obviously didn't care for her presence. With a murmured excuse to Alistair, she picked up her cup, and walked over to where he sat to the side of the large room.

"Good afternoon. May I have the pleasure of knowing your name?" Margaret asked pleasantly.

"I'm nobody of importance," the man growled. He wasn't as old as she had first imagined. His face was lined and his hair was greying only at the temples.

"As a relative of my husband who lives in his house, that cannot be true."

"I'm Brandon Hill."

Margaret shook his hand. "I am very pleased to meet you. My name is Margaret."

He regarded her with suspicion before easing his hand free of hers. "You sound more like a parlor maid than a duchess." His own accent was as crisp and autocratic as Alistair's.

"That is probably because I was born not far from here in Millcastle. Have you heard of it?"

"I remember a village of that name, but as I haven't left the estate and village for the last ten years, I can't say I am familiar with it."

"Why haven't you left?"

He glanced down at his blanket-covered lap. "Damned legs don't work. That's why I ended up here in the first place. When I came home from India, the last duke took pity on me and let me live here."

"What regiment were you in?" Margaret asked as she set her tea down beside his.

"Life Guards." He looked down his nose at her. "What other regiment is there?"

"Is that the same one as my husband?"

"Good lord, no." He raised his voice. "Alistair can you come here and talk to your wife? She is displaying a distinct lack of knowledge about the British military."

If Brandon Hill expected her to be embarrassed, he was sorely mistaken. She greeted Alistair with a smile as he approached.

"Mr. Hill has reminded me that I don't know which regiment you served in, Alistair?"

"The Prince of Wales Hussars." Alistair glanced from her to Brandon and lowered his voice. "Is he annoying you?"

"No more than any of your relatives are," Margaret said. "At least Mr. Hill is honest about his lack of approval for me, and my apparent ignorance about all things military."

"It's Captain Hill." Brandon sighed and looked over at Alistair. "She's a feisty one, I'll give you that."

"She certainly is, and I'm fairly certain that she would prefer to be spoken to directly rather than talked over." Alistair nodded, and left them to it.

"Do you have a proper wheeled chair?" Margaret asked.

A look of revulsion spread over her companion's face. "Of course not."

"Then no wonder you are so cross." Margaret reclaimed her cup and sipped her cold, weak tea. "Being stuck in this place without any way of escaping would sour the sweetest of natures."

He cracked a reluctant laugh. "I can assure you, duchess. I was never sweet."

Margaret rose and smiled down at him. "It was a pleasure to meet you, Captain Hill."

"Likewise, your grace." He inclined his head an inch. "I suspect we are in for some changes, eh?"

"I certainly intend to improve the house and grounds," Margaret said diplomatically.

"And turf out all these hangers-on? I know Farrell intended to clear the decks, so to speak."

"I have no intention of doing that, I can assure you." Margaret met his skeptical gaze. "As far as I am concerned, you are all part of Alistair's family."

"You are far too nice, your grace, when you must know that most of these people hold you in contempt."

She swallowed the insult and concentrated on remaining outwardly composed.

"I must go and find Alistair."

His hand shot out and caught her wrist. "I'm sorry. That was unconscionably rude." He sighed. "Perhaps you should start the evictions with me."

"Perhaps I will. Please excuse me."

Margaret picked up her cup and walked back to the fire. She couldn't entirely blame Captain Hill for his comments. She was the one who had gone looking for him.

"Are you all right, Margaret?" Alistair murmured in her ear as he removed the cup from her hand. "If you wish to retire, you have certainly done your duty for the day."

"By upsetting Lilly and annoying Captain Hill?"

He smiled at her. "Absolutely."

"You—"

His fingers curled around her elbow, and he leaned in close. "You may say whatever you damn well like, my dear. I mean it. Some of these people deserve to be rattled after blithely accepting my grandfather's largesse for their entire lives and then having the nerve to complain about you."

It suddenly occurred to Margaret that she wasn't the only one who had been circulating amongst the relatives, and that Alistair was even angrier than she was.

"Perhaps we should both go and see what progress has been made on our rooms?" Margaret suggested.

He held her gaze. "What an excellent idea. And if they have managed to find the bed, maybe we should take a much-needed nap?"

Still holding her hand, he swung around to face the room.

"Such a pleasure to see you all gathered here today." He bowed. "I'm sure we'll be welcoming you all later for dinner as well, but for now, my wife and I really must get on."

No one moved from their spot, and after a nod to an unsmiling Lilly, Alistair drew her arm through his and marched them both up the grand staircase. They could already hear the shouting before they reached their suite.

Alistair paused on the landing and looked toward the still-open door of the suite where Eileen and Clarkson were still arguing. "I wish the whole bunch of them would go to the devil!"

"Your relatives or our staff?" Margaret inquired.

"The whole bloody lot of them." He tugged on her hand. "Come on."

"Where are we going now?" she protested as he towed her along with him.

"To my old room. At least I know it's clean, and there's a lock on the door."

They reached another door set into a circular wall and he opened it. "Hold my hand."

The steps were narrow and at an angle, and she had to concentrate not to bang her shoulder against the wall.

"Here we are." He unlatched the door. "I chose this room

because my cousin and grandfather were usually too drunk to manage the stairs."

Margaret stepped into the bedchamber, which contained a simple bed, a rug by the fireplace, and a spectacular view of the surrounding countryside.

"It is beautiful."

"It will be even better once I've lit the fire and set a few candles about the place." Alistair locked the door, went over to the fireplace, and busied himself there while she walked over to the narrow window and the seat beneath it.

"I feel like a princess in a fairytale," Margaret murmured.

"Which is amusing because the only person being rescued here is me." He straightened up and brushed off his hands. "The bed linen is fresh. Do you want to lie down with me?"

She glanced longingly at the bed. "There is so much to do..."

"And it will all still be there tomorrow." He sat on the side of the bed and took off his boots. "Come here, duchess."

"I do wish you wouldn't call me that."

"Why?" He raised an eyebrow. "Perhaps I keep saying it to remind myself that I am apparently a duke?"

His annoyance with his family had disappeared beneath his familiar laughing tone. It reminded her that he wasn't as easy to manipulate as one might first think.

"Won't everyone wonder where we have gone?" Margaret asked.

"They'll all be too busy gossiping about us to care." He reached her side and took her hand. "Come on, it's a very comfortable bed."

ALISTAIR SMILED as she slid off her perch on the window seat and moved with him to the bed. She'd behaved impeccably in front of his appalling bunch of relatives, some of whom who deserved to be shot for the disparaging comments they'd made about his choice of wife. He suspected that he might need to have a few intimate conversations with the more vocal of her opponents and offer them the opportunity to leave his house entirely. They'd soon fall into line if their comfort was threatened.

He drew back the covers and patted the mattress. "See? It really is quite safe."

"I doubt a bed with you in it is safe," Margaret murmured and then went red as he laughed.

"I swear I will be the perfect gentleman. If you simply wish to sleep, I will do nothing to stop you."

"I am rather tired," she acknowledged, her gaze drawn to the crisply starched sheets. "It has been a very long day."

He took off his coat and waistcoat. "Can I help you undress?" Alistair looked up at her, as she made no move to get in.

"I'm quite capable of doing that for myself," Margaret answered him. "I didn't always have a maid, you know." She paused. "I'm just not sure how much to take off."

"Everything?" Alistair asked and received a roll of her eyes in return as she struggled out of her dress. "Do you need me to unlace your stays?"

She regarded him suspiciously, and he tried to look innocent as she presented him with her back.

He took his time, deliberately touching the skin he revealed until her breathing was harried, and she was unconsciously arching her back, pressing her rather fine arse firmly against the rising swell of his cock.

"Mmm…" He buried his face in her neck. "You always smell so sweet."

She made a choked sound, and he gently released her, patting her rounded derriere as she climbed into his bed. He liked seeing her there more than he had anticipated.

He stripped off his buckskin breeches and, leaving his long-tailed shirt on, got in beside her. He lay on his back and gathered her against his side.

"If you do change your mind and wish to do something other than sleep, please feel free to tell me."

A tiny snore greeted his softly worded suggestion. He fought a smile and allowed his own eyes to close. He was the duke now, no one had authority over him in his own home, and *he* would decide when to get up and have his dinner. Sometimes privilege did have its advantages...

CHAPTER NINE

"*G*ive it to me." Margaret held out her hand.

"It's perfectly fine, your grace!" Clarkson glared at her.

"It is not. It is wrinkled, and needs to be properly ironed," Margaret said. "Give me the shirt."

With a martyred sigh, Clarkson handed it over. "What you gonna do with it, now? Throw it on the fire? It'll make an awful stink, and his lordship won't be pleased."

Margaret met his gaze. "Come with me." She marched toward the door. She had no idea where her husband was currently and half hoped he was far enough away from the main house to have no sense of what was occurring within it.

"Where the hell are you going with that shirt?" Clarkson asked.

"Firstly, mind your language, and secondly, I told you to accompany me. Are you deaf?"

Still muttering, Clarkson followed her down the flight of stairs and toward the kitchen wing. Margaret pushed open the door into the kitchen, causing consternation among the staff.

"Your grace!" The old butler, who was sitting at the table drinking tea and reading Alistair's newspaper, rose to his feet. "May I assist you with something?"

Margaret ignored him and settled her gaze on the so-called housekeeper who was keeping the butler company at the table.

"Where is the flat iron kept?"

"Doesn't your maid know where things are yet, your grace?" The housekeeper shook her head and winked at the butler. "You haven't trained her very well, have you?"

"That is hardly your concern, Mrs. Walton. I thought you were supposed to be in charge of the household and should know such simple things?"

The housekeeper gave a long-suffering sigh and stood up. "I suppose you expect me to go and find it for you, don't you?"

"No, just tell me where it is located." Margaret attempted to keep her voice steady but it was becoming harder and harder by the second.

"I don't want you ferreting around in my kitchen, ma'am, and making things all awry, and what you want with a flat iron is beyond me."

Margaret heard the ripple of amusement from the assembled servants around her and raised her chin. If the iron had been currently in her possession, she might not be responsible for where it ended up.

"You will address me as your grace, and it is none of your business what I need the flat iron for. It is merely your duty to provide it for me."

"There's no need to lose your temper, lass, now is there?" Mrs. Walton responded.

After almost a month of such insubordination, Margaret was in no mood to be pleasant. "You may pack your bags and leave, Mrs. Walton." She turned her gaze toward the openmouthed kitchen maid. "The flat iron is for his grace's shirts. Where is it stored?"

The kitchen maid pointed to a room off to the side. "In there, your grace. We iron in there."

She nodded at the girl. "What is your name?"

"Beryl."

"Thank you, Beryl. Perhaps you could assist Mrs. Walton with her packing?'

"You can't—" Mrs. Walton tried to block her path.

"Yes, I can, and if you insist on arguing the matter with me, I will have one of the footmen throw you out, and you will be deprived of your belongings, too. You have been nothing but insolent and unhelpful toward me since the day I arrived and asked for your help."

Mrs. Walton stepped out of the way and stuttered a reply. "I'll tell his grace! You can't just come in here and get rid of loyal family retainers!"

Margaret held her gaze. "I expect loyalty to *me*, Mrs. Walton, and you have offered me nothing but contempt and condescension."

"Because you aren't fit for this job!" Mrs. Walton shrieked. "He should have married our Miss Lilly."

"But he chose not to, and I am the current duchess, and you are now without an occupation." Margaret turned away. "Please be gone before nightfall. Will you arrange for a gig to take Mrs. Walton wherever she wishes to go, please Sams?"

"Yes, your grace." The butler looked warily from her to the seething housekeeper.

"Then, come along, Mr. Clarkson. We have work to do." Margaret walked through the crowd of now-silent servants toward the room Beryl had mentioned.

"Bloody hell, you're a ballsy one, aren't you?" Clarkson whistled as Margaret added more coal to the fire and studied the three flat irons on the metal plate that sat over the fire. "You've set the cat among the pigeons now."

"Good." Margaret dusted off her hands. "I am tired of being

treated as if I don't exist in my own house." She glared at Clarkson. "And, please, watch your language!"

She spread Alistair's shirt out on the wooden table and forced herself to take several deep breaths. She was still shaking, but she didn't regret what she had said in the slightest. Weeks of appalling meals, sneering indifference, and a refusal to even accomplish the most basic of her requests had brought her to a point of no return.

"Get some water and a sponge," Margaret directed Clarkson, who was grinning at her unrepentantly. "I will show you how to iron a shirt *properly!*"

"Like you would know how to do that." Clarkson chuckled. "I'll wager you've never been in a kitchen before in your life!"

"Then, please place your bet, because you would lose that wager," Margaret invited him. She stalked over to the flat iron and selected the middle-sized one, holding it up against her cheek to gauge the heat. "Now, observe, and mayhap you will *learn* something!"

Alistair had barely sat down at his desk before his study door burst open and his butler came in followed by his housekeeper. He eyed them warily.

"What is it *now?*"

"The duchess just told Mrs. Walton to pack her bags and leave, your grace."

"Ah."

Mrs. Walton stepped forward. There were two spots of color on her cheeks, and her hands were clenched into fists. "She came into my kitchen and *insulted* me, right to my face!"

Alistair had a fleeting moment to wonder why his wife was picking fights with his staff, before his housekeeper continued speaking.

"She said I had to leave by nightfall, and that if I didn't do as she ordered, she would set one of the footmen on me and throw me out without a penny to my name!" She sniffed. "Begging your pardon, your grace, we all know why you had to marry her, but I knew she had no class when she turned up here, and this just proves my point."

"Does it." Alistair regarded her until she dropped her gaze.

He glanced over at Sams. "Will you find my wife and ask her to join me here when it is convenient?"

"Yes, your grace." Sams bowed, and considering his age, withdrew with some speed.

Mrs. Walton sniffed. "I'll go back to my kitchen, then, your grace. I'm sure you'll explain how things are to your wife, and she'll come around to our way of doing things."

Somehow, Alistair doubted that, but he told Mrs. Walton to leave, and sat down to await the arrival of his wife. He had just begun to wonder whether she had left him when the door opened and she came in, her cheeks flushed, and her hair in some disarray.

"I'm sorry to have kept you waiting. I had to teach your valet to iron a shirt properly, and I didn't want to leave it half done."

Alistair, who had risen to his feet at her entrance, blinked at her.

"I beg your pardon?"

"Mr. Clarkson doubted my ability to wield a flat iron and I showed him the error of his ways." She gave a satisfied smirk. "He now owes me sixpence, and don't think I won't make sure he pays up."

He gazed at her for a long moment before she frowned.

"What?"

"Is there anything else you'd like to tell me about your excursion into the kitchen?"

"Such as?" Her smile disappeared.

"That you ordered my housekeeper to leave forthwith?"

"*Your* housekeeper?"

"You know what I mean." He paused. "You are probably unaware that the Walton family have provided housekeepers for the dukedom for three generations."

"I don't understand your point." Margaret said slowly.

"You can't just..." He snapped his fingers. "Tell a Walton to leave. Her uncle is the head groom here, and he helped teach me to ride. Her cousin is one of the gamekeepers."

"Why not?" To her credit, she looked genuinely interested and not as angry as he had expected. "If she was a worker in my brother's mill, and she spoke to him with such disrespect, he would dismiss her instantly."

"But things are different here." He tried to explain. "Families like ours have a responsibility to those who have served us for generations."

She went still. "Are you are suggesting that Mrs. Walton may say whatever she likes, treat me like an interloper, and I can do nothing about it?"

"No, of course not. She should certainly treat you with respect." He tried again. "I will speak to her and make sure of it."

"She disregards my orders, she sneers at me, and refers everything to your cousin Lilly." Margaret drew herself up to her full height. "If you let her stay, you will undermine my authority with the whole staff."

"I hardly think—"

"You will." She raised her chin, and he caught the glimmer of tears in her eyes. "If you expect me to apologize to her you will wait a long time."

"I don't—"

She nodded abruptly. "Then do whatever you wish. If you will excuse me, I have letters to write."

"Margaret." He spoke to himself, as she had turned on her heel and walked out.

He let out a harried breath and went upstairs to change his coat before dinner. His steps slowed as he mounted the stairs, and he remembered her stricken expression. Was she right? Would such a ridiculous domestic dispute really undermine her authority, or was she merely exaggerating?

The smell of a hot iron and heated linen reached him as he pushed open the door to his bedchamber and found Clarkson ironing his cravats. His valet looked up as he entered and held up the iron.

"Your missus is an unusual woman, my lord." He chuckled. "She reminds me a bit of my mum. Look at how well she ironed your favorite shirt!"

Alistair walked over to where his shirt was draped over the back of a chair. "My wife did this?"

"She bloody well did, sir. Not sure where she learned the trick, but she certainly surprised me."

Alistair imagined her lovingly and efficiently ironing her brother's shirts in the millhouse kitchen where she'd grown up and felt like a fool.

"Is Mrs. Walton rude to her?" he asked abruptly.

"The whole lot of them are." Clarkson finished one cravat and started on the next. "Bloody rude and condescending. I'm not surprised she finally lost her temper with that housekeeper today. She deserved it."

"I haven't noticed any issues."

Clarkson gave him a pitying stare. "That's because they are all too busy licking your arse and groveling to you, sir. Two-faced bastards, the lot of them." He chuckled. "You should've seen that woman's face when your lady told her to pack her bags. She got a shock, she did, thought she'd never be held responsible for anything she said."

Alistair took off his heavy coat. "Her family has been house-keepers here for generations."

"So what?" His valet frowned. "You don't owe them any loyalty. If they can't accept your wife, then they should all leave."

It was Alistair's turn to glare at Clarkson. "I thought you didn't like my duchess?"

"I don't, but I already know that she's loyal to you, and that's what counts for me."

"So you think I should tell all the staff to depart and leave us with no servants?" Alistair inquired sarcastically.

"If they act like that toward the duchess, then yes." Clarkson paused. "She might seem a bit starchy, but she's not really, and she needs someone to stand up for her."

Alistair let off a string of curses as Clarkson continued to iron and whistle like a man without a care in the world.

How DARED HE? Margaret walked out into the badly neglected gardens and away from the house at some speed. If Alistair let Mrs. Walton stay, Margaret would be relegated to a nonentity in her own house with no power or influence. Lilly would remain mistress, and she would end up having to humiliate herself by asking Alistair's cousin to get anything done.

Margaret wasn't one to cry, but she couldn't stop the tears from falling as she stomped over the uneven lawn. Her husband had looked at her with no understanding at all when she'd attempted to explain the harm he was doing to her reputation and standing in the house. How could she improve the place if no one was willing to listen to her?

For a stricken moment, Margaret stared out over the still unfamiliar green fields and wished she was back in Millcastle with people who understood her and would agree with her. She'd wanted a challenge and had been given one, but was she doomed to fall at the first fence? She'd never been the sort of woman who gave up easily, yet the thought of fighting the entire household, plus the duke, was exhausting.

Had she been too hasty offering Mrs. Walton an ultimatum without any negotiation? She couldn't decide whether Adam would approve of her actions or not. Margaret sighed. She had a temper, and, after a disastrous first month when she had felt oppressed on all sides, it had perhaps gotten the better of her.

"Your grace!" She turned at the shout to see Clarkson waving at her. "His lordship wants to speak to you in his study!"

Margaret briefly considered pretending she couldn't hear him, but she had never been a coward and had faced far worse than this. She reluctantly turned around and walked back to where Clarkson awaited her.

He held the door open. "You look like you're ready to murder him."

"Perhaps I am." She frowned at him and went past, wiping her shoes on the mat and undoing the buttons of her coat.

"Good luck to you, then." His laughter followed her down the corridor.

Margaret didn't bother to knock on the door of the study and went right in, only to stop immediately when she saw Mrs. Walton standing in front of her husband's desk.

"Ah, there you are, my dear." Alistair gestured to the two chairs set in front of his desk. "I thought it might be a good idea for you and Mrs. Walton to clear the air, so to speak."

Margaret offered him a murderous glare. "I'm not sure it will make much difference, your grace."

Mrs. Walton tossed her head, refusing to even look at Margaret.

"Both of you will sit down and at least attempt to behave like the reasonable people I know you both are," Alistair snapped, reminding Margaret that he had once commanded men in the military.

She sat, her hands folded together on her lap, and looked over at the housekeeper who had followed suit. Her husband came around to sit on the front of his desk between them.

"Mrs. Walton, my wife is the new duchess, not Miss Lilly. I expect you to take your orders from her and act on them."

"She said I was to leave by tonight, and where exactly am I supposed to go when this has been my home since I was born?" Mrs. Walton said tremulously.

Margaret leaned slightly forward. "Perhaps you should have thought of that before you made the last month one of the most miserable of my life. I *asked* you to help me."

"Yes, well—" Mrs. Walton sniffed. "I thought—"

"—that Lilly should've been the new duchess." Margaret finished her sentence. "But if his grace had married Lilly, you would all be in trouble because this place needs an investment of capital, and, whether you like it or not, I provide that." She hesitated. "I want to make this place a home for the duke and a comfortable place for us all to live. If you don't wish to be part of that, then perhaps you *should* leave."

She glanced over at her husband. "I'm sure that his grace would offer you somewhere to live, and a pension to compensate you for your years of service if you wish to go." She forced herself to continue speaking. "It was wrong of me to suggest that you should leave with nothing. I apologize."

Mrs. Walton slowly looked up at her. "Perhaps I've been too hasty as well. His grace is the only decent man in the family, and Miss Lilly was so upset. I was anxious about him marrying for money and not inclined to like you on sight." She finally met Margaret's gaze. "I should've given you a chance."

Margaret nodded. She'd had similar feelings when her brother Adam had married Emily to gain control of her fortune and the mills. "I need someone to stand beside me and help me bring this place back to its former glory, not someone who fights me all the way."

"I'd like to be part of that, your grace," Mrs. Walton offered hesitantly. "This is my home, too."

"Then shall we try again?" Margaret looked at her husband, who was listening intently. "We both want what is best for his grace, after all."

"And his grace would be very happy if two of his favorite women managed to get along sufficiently to make his life even more comfortable than it already is. I believe I would like to be spoiled," Alistair said as he set his booted feet on the floor and reached for both of their hands.

Mrs. Walton offered him and Margaret a hopeful smile. "Perhaps I should return to the kitchens to oversee dinner?"

"That would be most helpful," Margaret replied. "And maybe tomorrow we could make a tour of the house together, starting in the kitchens, to decide what needs to be done?"

Mrs. Walton curtsied. "Yes, your grace, that would be most satisfactory."

She left the study, her head held high, and Margaret gathered herself to follow.

"Thank you," Alistair said.

Margaret made the mistake of looking back at him over her shoulder. "For what?"

"Bending." He shrugged. "You... surprised me."

She turned to face him. "Did you expect me to display the coarseness of my upbringing and demand that she left, or else?"

He stiffened. "Please don't put words into my mouth."

"Then what did you expect?" She advanced toward him, hands on her hips.

"You apologized to her very sweetly and offered her the opportunity to work with you on something she loves."

"What else was I supposed to do when you had made it clear that you cared about her staying and refused to back me?"

He angled his head to one side and studied her. "You know I hate to argue, but I don't think you did it entirely for me."

"I did it because it was unfair of me to throw a woman out of the only home she has ever known," Margaret said. "I should have thought about that before I lost my temper and demanded she leave."

His smile was slow in coming and made her want to slap his face or kiss him, she wasn't sure which.

"You are a good woman, Margaret Blackthorn."

"Too good for the likes of you." She wasn't yet ready to be charmed.

"I can't argue with that." He came toward her and she stiffened. "You look rather tired. Can I interest you in a nap?"

"You expect me to sleep beside you after what you have just done?"

"*Sleep?* Not really." He shrugged. "I was rather hoping you might find a way to redirect all that righteous anger into making love with me?"

"I want to hit you," Margaret blurted out.

"Exactly." His smile was a wicked invitation. "Hit me, bite me, fight me? You may do whatever you desire, as long as you are naked and in my bed."

Margaret's breath shuddered out as he reached forward to cup her chin. "You are incorrigible."

"You knew that before you married me." His thumb brushed her lip and his voice went low, reminding her of their nights together and what they did under the sheets when no one could interrupt them. "Come to bed."

"I—"

He gathered her into his arms and kissed her until she forgot why she was angry. She only remembered when he pulled back and smiled at her.

"See how easy it is?"

She leaned in and bit his lip.

He laughed and drew her so tightly against him that even

through her skirts she was aware that he was fully aroused. He kissed her again, one hand firmly planted on her bottom, until she kissed him back.

"Come on." He eased away and grabbed her hand. "Unless you wish to be ravished on the ducal desk, let's go to bed."

CHAPTER TEN

*M*argaret rolled onto her back and considered the much-faded draperies above her head. The embroidered bed curtains were gathered together in an extravagant knot in the center of the canopy. She suspected they had never been taken down and cleaned since they had been hung, probably fifty years ago.

She also knew she was contemplating the drapery because it helped her avoid thinking about her inability to resist her husband. The worst thing was that he knew it and used it to his advantage when he wished to redirect her attention elsewhere. It wasn't as if he was trying to hide it.

She wasn't even sure that there was anything she could do about it, because making love with him was extraordinary. She shifted her limbs, aware of the heaviness of her muscles and the slight soreness between her legs. He teased her, tempted her, *enraged* her, and never, ever made her feel that she was not being ladylike or that she was too demanding. In fact, he encouraged her excesses.

There was a knock on the door and Eileen, her maid, came in with a jug of hot water.

"Good morning, your grace."

Margaret sat up, realized she was naked, and attempted to find her nightgown while Eileen bustled around the room picking up items of clothing that Margaret had dropped to the floor in her haste to get her husband into bed. Five years ago when she'd lived in the millhouse, such laziness would have appalled her, and having someone else picking up after her? A mortal sin.

"His grace said he would be out for most of the day on estate business." Eileen set a cake of soap next to the bowl and water. "He's certainly working hard to make the place better. His tenants are all singing his praises in the village."

Margaret was quite aware of how hard Alistair was working. For the last three months, he had risen at six, taken a horse from the depleted stables—he'd already sold off most of his cousin's stud—and set out across the fields, talking to his farmers and tenants about the state of their holdings. While he dealt with that matter, Margaret was intent on restoring the house. With Mrs. Walton now committed to the project, she was hopeful that much could be done.

Margaret sat down at her dressing table and studied her reflection in the mirror. With her hair around her shoulders she looked like a happy, well-satisfied woman, but where was her backbone? Where was the woman who had singlehandedly ruled the Methodist community in Millcastle? Who had preached the values of austerity and self-restraint, and declared her dislike of the aristocracy?

She feared that Ruby Delisle would be most disappointed in her. Sometimes she couldn't believe she was the same person.

"Mrs. Walton said she would meet you in the state apartments when you are ready, your grace," Eileen said as she brushed Margaret's hair and started to put it up.

"Please let her know that I will join her there as soon as I have finished my breakfast," Margaret replied. "Has the linen in the servants' quarters improved this week?"

"Oh, yes, your grace! New sheets and everything, and once all those holes are fixed in the roof, it will be grand up there."

The cost of fixing the enormous roof was not only exorbitant, but also time-consuming. Both she and Alistair had deemed it a priority to stop the house falling down on top of them. Even though locals were doing most of the work, the bills still made Margaret wince.

"Which dress would you like today, your grace?" Eileen finished styling her hair and went over to the door leading to the dressing room where most of their clothes were stored.

"Something old, seeing as I am bound to end up getting it dirty or ripping it," Margaret called out.

She often forgot she was a duchess and happily climbed up on a ledge to better clean an intricate carving or pull down a piece of curtain covered in dust. As a result, several of her new gowns had been relegated to the ragbag, and she'd reverted back to her original hardwearing gowns from the millhouse.

Only last week, Alistair had come to collect her in the gig after she'd been visiting some farm cottages out on the estate. At first, he'd failed to recognize her because she'd been in the kitchen feeding the baby while the mother bathed her older two children in front of the fire. Sometimes Margaret felt more at home and at ease in the cottages than she did in the ducal manor house.

Mrs. Walton had helped her identify where new staff members were needed, and they'd set about finding them. There were many people in the surrounding villages who would still rather work in a house than seek employment in the rapidly expanding mill towns. Having occasionally worked in the mill when her brother was shorthanded, Margaret could quite understand why.

She'd save her best dresses for when she went visiting and the hall was in an acceptable state to be visited back.

~

"Yes, indeed, Mr. Brewerton, I do understand. Please, go on."

Alistair nodded as the farmer in front of him listed off all the problems with his house, outbuildings, and land. It was an all-too-familiar tale of woe, which made Alistair long to get hold of his cousin and grandfather and smash their heads together for their pathetic neglect of their lands and tenants.

Behind him, his newly acquired secretary, the Honorable Joseph Lang, wrote copious notes and nodded in sympathy along with the farmer. Francis had sent the young man to Alistair a month ago, explaining that someone in his family was attempting to force the boy into the army, and that he didn't want to go. As Joseph was more than willing to work hard for his bed and board, Alistair had quickly ascertained that he was intelligent and close-mouthed and put him to use.

At the end of the tour, Alistair paused to look back at the moldering thatch on the roof of the farm. He'd met Mrs. Brewerton and her three children and they'd all been unwell, probably because of the damp conditions they were forced to live in. He wasn't naturally a violent man, although he had been trained to kill without mercy, but his anger with his family was coming close to boiling point.

He shook Mr. Brewerton's hand. "I have a list of all your needs now, sir, and I can only promise you that I will attend to them with all speed."

"That would be very good of you, your grace." Mr. Brewerton's skepticism was clear as day on his lined face. "I'll wait to hear from you."

Alistair gestured to Joseph, who handed over the ducal

purse. He pressed several coins into the farmer's palm. "Use this where you need it most urgently."

"Thank you, your grace," Mr. Brewerton stammered. "Thank you, very much."

Alistair nodded and turned back to where his horse was tied up by the gate.

"Come along now, Joseph. Who is next?"

He mounted his horse and waited as his new secretary consulted the extensive list from his pocket.

"The Wheldons." He pointed to the right. "It's about a quarter of a mile that way."

Alistair let out a breath. He hadn't seen a single dwelling that was fit to be lived in. The stories about the previous land agent had made him so angry he wished he'd known where the bastard had gone so he could prosecute him to the full extent of the law. But, in truth, the agent had only been doing his cousin's bidding, so the blame sat squarely on his own family, and it was up to him to make reparation.

"Your grace?" Joseph asked.

"What is it?"

"Would it be acceptable to suggest that the men who ran this estate before you were somewhat neglectful of their duties?"

"They were a bunch of lying, stealing blaggards, yes," Alistair said. "I almost wish my grandfather was still alive so I could kill him myself."

"If you did that, your grace, you would probably be standing trial for murder and not enjoying your new title," Joseph murmured.

Alistair glanced over at his new hire, who appeared to have a somewhat dry sense of humor that appealed to his employer.

"It would be worth it." He flung out a hand. "How they could bring such prime farmland so low is beyond my comprehension."

"It is not an uncommon phenomenon for a landlord to

extort funds from his holdings. My own father is quite proficient at it."

"I am aware of that," Alistair said grimly. "Sometimes I think my wife has the right idea, and the entire aristocracy should be kicked out to starve in the streets."

Joseph rode on in silence for a few moments before venturing a reply. "Is the current duchess of French origin, your grace?"

"Not at all, but she grew up in the Methodist faith and among people who value their worth in a very different manner."

"Ah, that explains it, then."

Joseph consulted his estate map and directed them down yet another overgrown narrow trail. Alistair braced himself as a dog started to bark and a figure emerged from the house with a billy club in his hands.

"After we've met the Wheldons, let's go back to the house. I need to read your notes and add my recommendations. Then I'm sure I will have some errands for you."

"Right you are, your grace," Joseph replied. "Now, watch out for that dog. He doesn't look very pleased to see us."

"No one is pleased to see us," Alistair groaned. "Why should a dog be any different?"

BY THE TIME he got back to the house, it had started to rain, and his dark mood had not improved. He went straight to his study and settled in to update his accounts books and farm ledgers as to what he had seen and what needed to be done. Despite the size of Margaret's dowry, the needs of the estate were so vast that he seriously wondered how on earth he was going to set everything to rights.

His study door opened, but he didn't look up.

"Joseph, we need to find some more thatchers. Have you any ideas as to—"

He stopped speaking as a plate of ham, pickle, cheese, and bread was pushed under his nose on top of his papers. He looked up.

"Good afternoon, duchess."

Margaret put a tankard of ale beside the plate of food. "Joseph said you hadn't eaten anything since breakfast."

His stomach growled, betraying his hunger, and he moved his papers to one side so that he could access his plate.

"Thank you."

She turned as if to leave, and he spoke through a mouthful of bread. "Stay a moment, will you?"

"As you wish." She sat down in front of his desk, her hands folded in her lap, her expression prim, which always made him want to tease her. Her brown hair was braided closely to her head in a very plain style and she wore an old patched blue dress, yet she still managed to look like a queen.

"I do wish, very much." He swallowed down some ale. "I've hardly seen you all week."

"Some might think that a blessing."

"Not me." He slathered butter on the bread and added a thick slab of cheese. His liaison with her was proving to be far more successful than he had imagined. "I enjoy being told off far too much."

"Only because you view it as a challenge to see how quickly you can make me forget my disapproval and lure me into bed."

He smiled at her. "Guilty as charged, duchess." He cut more of the sharp yellow cheese. "We visited four farms this morning. Every single one of them had the same story of rising rents, threats, lack of repairs to property, and downright extortion."

Margaret frowned. "Perhaps I should stop work on the house and do more for your tenants instead."

"With all due respect, my dear, I'm not sure you would be

welcome in some of the cottages. Feelings are running high, and the lady of the manor arriving and dispensing advice might not go down very well."

"Dispensing advice?" Margaret asked.

"You know how it is, the lady arrives in her carriage, and waits until the poor tenant comes out to her, bowing and scraping. She'll offer them a basket of goods and maybe a hand-sewn garment for a new baby. She'll inquire closely as to the state of their health, make unhelpful suggestions based on her lack of understanding of living in a cottage, and depart for another year."

"Are you jesting?"

"Not at all. That's exactly what my mother did when she was alive, and it was the same for my grandmother up here. Sometimes I even accompanied them."

She sniffed. "You already know my visits would not be like that at all. You've seen me with our home-farm family."

"I'd still prefer it if you didn't go any further until Joseph and I have at least had a chance to talk to every single tenant and tell them our plans for the future. It might not be safe."

He finished his ale and turned his attention to his plate, devouring everything except the blue pattern.

"Are you planning to go out again this afternoon?" Margaret took the plate and tankard and placed them back on the tray. "The rain looks as if it is settling in."

"I should." He sighed. "I have at least ten more farms and tenants to visit before I will have a full list of the damages and deprivations done to this estate. And I haven't even visited the other two smaller estates or the London townhouse where my cousin used to live."

Margaret came over to his chair and put her hand on his shoulder. "You are doing your best, and your efforts are already appreciated."

"Thank you for the encouragement." He covered her hand

with his own and looked up at her. "You have cobwebs in your hair."

"That doesn't surprise me." She shivered. "I have never dislodged so many spiders from nooks and crannies in my life!"

"Mayhap we should set fire to the place and build something just for the two of us."

"If we don't get the roof fixed and the chimneys cleaned, that might happen anyway. Do you know that there are almost forty chimneys in this house?"

"That sounds like a lot," Alistair agreed.

"It is a lot. We could employ a chimney sweep for a year, and he would barely manage to keep up with them."

He drew her down onto his lap and wrapped an arm around her waist. "Are we both fools? Why didn't we just elope and leave everything the way it was?"

"Because you are an honorable man, and I..." She paused. "Like to manage things."

A knock at the door had her scrambling out of his lap as the butler came in.

"A letter has been delivered, your grace. The boy who brought it says he has been asked to wait for a reply."

Alistair frowned and held out his hand for the missive, which had a wax seal on the exterior he immediately recognized.

"Thank you." He waited until the butler left before he broke the seal and read the tightly written script. "Devil take it!" He screwed the paper up into a ball and threw it at the fire.

"Is it bad news?"

Alistair looked up. He'd completely forgotten that Margaret had remained in the room. "It's from my late father's wife. My sister is apparently unwell and she wants me to come and see her."

"Then we should go," Margaret said immediately. "Do you

wish to write a note to your stepmother and tell her we are on our way?"

"Yes. I mean, no." Alistair paused. "I'm not sure whether we should go."

"Why not?" Margaret looked puzzled. "I understand that relations between you and your stepmother are strained, but this is your sister whom you love, and she is asking for you."

"I know that's what the note says, but you don't know Frederica." Alistair looked up at Margaret. "She's been trying to lure me back to Healdstone Hall for the past two years, mostly under false pretenses."

"I don't understand." Margaret was now looking at him as if he were the deranged one. "Why would she lie about something so important?"

"Because that's what she's like." Alistair wasn't prepared to explain any further. "She would use anything to hurt me."

"Perhaps if we go together, I can help with that?"

"How?"

Margaret shrugged. "By observing her as an impartial witness."

"Are you suggesting that I am biased against her?" He glared at his wife.

"It's possible, but as you never choose to discuss her with me, how would I know?" Her sweet smile held an edge of a challenge.

Alistair glared at her, picked up his quill pen, and found a sheet of paper. It seemed that the peace and harmony they had achieved together over the past few months was about to be tested.

"I'll write and say we will be there as soon as possible."

CHAPTER ELEVEN

*T*he closer they came to his ancestral home, the more distant Alistair became. Margaret attempted to discuss what might await her at the hall, but his reluctance to share more than the most basic of information was somewhat frustrating. He always responded to her questions with great politeness, but she knew that things were far from settled between him and his stepmother.

Such a deliberate rift surprised her, as he had shown a dislike for conflict, always preferring to make light of something, or let it go entirely. She glanced over and found him staring into space, all the mobile humor and lightness in his usual expression absent.

"Your father left most of his estate in Frederica's care, yes?"

"You are correct."

"Why do you think he did that?"

He turned toward her. "Would you like the real reason or the more palatable one?"

"As your wife, I would prefer it if you told me the truth."

"But which is the truth?" he replied. "Many would say I got

what I deserved, and that my father, God bless his soul, made the correct decision."

Margaret scowled at him. "Will you stop being so unhelpful?"

"I am merely—"

She held up one finger. "Alistair. Tell me both and let me decide which I believe."

He sighed. "As you wish. In his infinite wisdom, my father decided because I was stationed in India and might never return, that my stepmother was a far more suitable person to learn how to run the estate and take control of his finances."

"And what is the other story?"

"My father was dying. I was unaware of this, because, on my last leave, my stepmother had carefully engineered a series of arguments between us, which resulted in an estrangement. If I had known how ill he was, I would've immediately resigned my commission and come home to take over the estate."

Margaret studied him for a long moment until he raised an arrogant eyebrow.

"Well?"

"You would've come home. I do not doubt that for a second."

He slowly smiled at her. "Thank you."

"You are an honorable man." She sat forward, her hands clasped together on her lap. "Why would your father think otherwise and not trust you to run the estate properly?"

"That's a very good question. It's not as if I was running around London gambling and whoring my way through his fortune. I was in the bloody army."

"I thought that peers of the realm who only had one son didn't like their heirs going into the army," Margaret said.

"I had an older brother, Malcolm. He died in a hunting accident." Margaret brought her hand to her mouth, and he glared at her. "I didn't mention him because he was as awful as my cousin Farrell. He made my life hell when I was small. Part of the reason I went into the army was to escape him."

"So you weren't expected to inherit the title?"

"No. Just as I wasn't ever supposed to be a duke." He turned back to the window and peered out. "We're almost there."

Margaret pressed her lips together and suppressed the many questions that his answers had raised. She would see what awaited them at Healdstone Hall and form her own opinions of Lady Hellion and Alistair's sister.

The carriage turned into a beech-tree-lined drive and progressed toward a house settled low against the surrounding hills.

"It's lovely," Margaret said involuntarily. "All that honey-colored stone."

"It's a common building material around here, but yes, it is a beautiful house." His words were delivered in his usual light-hearted manner, but his expression gave away his quiet yearning.

They came to a stop in front of wide front door with roses growing around it. Alistair got out and came around to open the door for Margaret. After two days of traveling, she was aware that her clothing was crumpled and that she probably did not look her best.

The front door opened, and a man dressed in blue livery came out.

"Welcome home, your lordship!"

Alistair smiled at the man. "It is a pleasure to see you, Mr. Mortimer. Are you the butler now? Should I be terrified?"

Mr. Mortimer chuckled. "Not of me, your lordship. I knew you when you were a little skinny lad stealing cake out of the kitchen."

"And happily clipped me on the ear when you caught me up to mischief." Alistair's smile was warm. He took Margaret's hand. "My dear, may I make you known to Mr. Albert Mortimer? An old friend of mine."

"It's a pleasure to meet you, your grace." Mr. Mortimer bowed low. "Please come in. The ladies are awaiting you in the back parlor."

The second carriage carrying Clarkson, Eileen, and the rest of their luggage appeared on the drive, and was directed around the side of the building to the stables.

Margaret placed her hand on Alistair's sleeve and entered the house, breathing in the pleasing smells of beeswax polish and dried flower petals. It wasn't as grand as the ducal mansion, but it was charming and beautifully maintained. Whatever else Frederica Hellion was doing, she certainly didn't stint on her household or her housework.

Alistair let out a slow breath, his gaze slowly encompassing the entire hall as if he expected to see his father coming down the stairs to berate him. Had he been back since his father's funeral, or had he missed even that?

She pinched his sleeve, and he looked down at her as if he'd forgotten she existed.

"Come along, then, duchess," he murmured. "We mustn't keep the dragon waiting."

Mr. Mortimer paused, loudly cleared his throat, and announced them at the door.

"His grace, the Duke of Thorsway, and the Duchess of Thorsway."

Margaret kept a smile on her face as they entered the room, her gaze fixing on the petite woman who rose to greet them in something of a flutter.

"Oh, my goodness!" Lady Hellion said. She had brown curling hair, a petite form, and the face of an angel. "Alistair! You have finally come home!"

She rushed over and placed a hand on Alistair's chest, she

was so short that she barely came up to his shoulder. "Oh, don't look at me like that! Have you still not forgiven me?"

Alistair stepped back so that her hand fell away and bowed. "Good afternoon, ma'am. Margaret, may I introduce you to my father's second wife, Lady Hellion?" He paused. "Although now that you exist, my dear, and the titles all belong to you, I believe that should be the *dowager* Marchioness of Hellion, do I have that correctly?"

Lady Hellion laughed and turned to Margaret. "I certainly feel like a dowager these days, what with Phoebe ready to make her come out in society."

"Where is Phoebe?" Alistair looked over at the couch where an older woman sat staring apprehensively at him. He inclined his head. "Good afternoon, Miss Whipple."

He received an agitated squeak in return.

"Phoebe is upstairs in bed." Lady Hellion sighed. "She felt too weak to attempt to come down."

"Then I will go and see her," Alistair stated. "Who is caring for her?"

"Dr. McNeil is due to arrive in an hour." Lady Hellion hesitated. "Would you object to waiting until he has seen Phoebe and can make his report directly to you?"

"Not at all." Alistair bowed. "It will give me time to show my wife around the house."

"And have something to eat." Lady Hellion looked inquiringly at Margaret. "You must be exhausted after traveling all this way."

"Something to eat and a chance to refresh my clothing would be most welcome," Margaret allowed.

"Then we can easily manage all three. I'll take you up to your bedchamber, and when you are ready, come down and partake of some victuals, and then Alistair can take you for a tour of my house."

"*My* house," Alistair said.

Lady Hellion's smile faltered, and she drew Margaret's arm through hers. "Let's go upstairs."

She sighed as they proceeded back into the entrance hall and up the main staircase. "He still hates me, doesn't he?"

"I have no idea what you are talking about, my lady," Margaret tried to speak, but Lady Hellion kept talking over her.

"Oh, please, call me Frederica. We are almost related now, aren't we? And I am so glad that Alistair has finally found another woman to settle down with. He didn't tell me much about you, but I can already see how he cares for you."

Lady Hellion opened the door into a sun-filled room that faced the formal gardens at the back of the house and walked over to the window to twitch the curtains. Margaret could hear Eileen and Clarkson talking to each other in the dressing room and was glad that she would soon be able to change her gown and restyle her hair.

"I'll leave you to it, then." Lady Hellion smiled at her. "I will await you in the dining room."

"Thank you," Margaret responded as she untied the ribbons of her bonnet.

"Despite Alistair's hostility, I do hope we can become friends," Lady Hellion said hesitantly, her hand on the latch as if she was reluctant to leave.

"I'm sure we will learn to deal excellently with each other," Margaret replied, drawing a relieved smile from her husband's stepmother.

"Thank you."

Margaret remained staring at the door Lady Hellion had just closed behind her. She was nothing like Margaret had imagined. She'd been expecting a cold, disdainful aristocrat, and this enchanting fairy-like creature was nothing like that. It was hard to understand how Alistair could not like her when she'd seemed so genuinely delighted to welcome him back home.

At the moment, the only ungracious and cold person in the house appeared to be her husband...

As if she'd summoned him with her thoughts, Alistair came in and immediately took off his coat.

"CLARKSON! WHERE'S THAT WATER?" Alistair shouted.

"Coming, your grace. Keep your wig on."

Eileen came in, with Clarkson right behind her, bearing a jug of hot water she poured into the porcelain bowl beside the dressing table. Alistair ripped off his cravat, allowing his shirt to fall open at the neck and splashed water over his face.

"I'll see if I can find you a fresh cravat, your grace, seeing as you've ruined that one." Clarkson went back into the dressing room. "And I'll brush out your coat."

"Thank you," Alistair called after him as Eileen helped Margaret unfasten her traveling gown and offered her soap and a towel.

He glanced over at his wife as Eileen took down and brushed out her hair. If it were up to him, he'd take Margaret to bed and never venture down the stairs again. But he had a duty toward his sister that could not be ignored. Just seeing Frederica had unsettled him far more than he'd anticipated. He'd forgotten how charming she could be. He was aware that he'd sounded remarkably ungracious and that Margaret would have noticed.

Eileen disappeared with the crumpled gown and the water, and brought back a new dress for Margaret she had somehow already managed to unpack and iron. After Clarkson delivered his new cravat and brushed coat, he retired to finish the unpacking, leaving Alistair alone with his wife.

"She was not what I expected," Margaret said hesitantly.

Alistair tensed. "What did you expect?"

"She seems... really pleased to see you."

"Of course she is." Alistair retreated to the mirror and spent unnecessary seconds fussing with the folds of his cravat. "She is delighted that she has finally made me return."

She didn't reply, and eventually he had to set the pin in his cravat and turn back to her. She was staring thoughtfully at him.

"What?"

"You are being quite rude to her, which is not like you at all."

"I can be rude if I have to be." He shrugged with a nonchalance he was far from feeling. "I can assure you that she deserves every ill intention I have toward her."

She rose from her seat and settled her skirts around her. "It will certainly be interesting to further my acquaintance with your stepmother."

He offered her an elaborate bow. "Be my guest. I will not be monopolizing her time. I came to see my sister, and that is all."

She paused to study him. "Your behavior toward your step-mother makes her appear a far more sympathetic character than you."

"I am well aware of that." He strode to the door. Part of him foolishly wanted to beg her to believe in him, but he'd told her she was free to make up her own mind, and he had to allow her that choice. "Shall we go down? Perhaps my temper will improve after I have eaten and shown you the house I was brought up in."

Frederica made no effort to actively engage his attention at the dining table, preferring, instead, to enchant his wife. Her lovely laugh rang out constantly as she chatted and sympathized and made friends with Margaret, who wasn't usually the easiest of converts. He offered the odd comment and tried not to appear angry or resentful that the house he loved had been very well taken care of indeed while he was barred from it.

To his relief, Margaret didn't linger for too long at the table, and was more than willing to accompany him on a walk around the house. To his surprise, nothing much had been changed. His father's study, where he had often been called to account for his behavior, looked as if his father had just left the room to walk his dogs.

Alistair swallowed hard, his hand on the mahogany desk.

"I'm surprised there aren't fingermarks embedded in the edge of this desk. This is where my father made me stand when he beat me."

Margaret stroked her hand over the gleaming surface. "Were you often in trouble?"

"Yes. I was nothing like Malcolm, and that, apparently, was a sin. I was too sickly, too pretty, too—" He abruptly stopped speaking.

She came to a stop in front of him and lifted her gaze to his. "Why could he not accept you as you were?"

"Because he didn't accept me at all." He forced himself to meet her eyes. "I was born eight years after Malcolm. He believed my mother had been unfaithful and that I wasn't his son."

He waited for her to recoil, but her gaze remained steady. "Had she?"

"I don't know, but I can tell you this, if she found happiness with another man while being married to my father, I can't begrudge her that." He shrugged. "Whatever happened, my father made sure she repented of her crimes. Eventually, Phoebe was born and my poor, browbeaten mother died in childbirth. As he always treated Phoebe well, I assume he considered her his natural child."

"You don't blame your mother even though her behavior might have made life hard for you?" Margaret asked.

"Even though. He might have suspected I wasn't his child but, according to the law, unless he wanted to create a scandal, divorce my mother, and send us both away, then he was stuck with me."

Her brow creased. "If he disliked you both so intensely, why didn't he do just that?"

"Because, as we had the same mother, that would've made his precious Malcolm a bastard, too, and he wasn't willing to lose his firstborn son, or his daughter."

She cupped his chin, trapping his gaze to hers. "He was a fool. You deserved better, and so did your mother."

Her matter-of-fact statement delivered in her most confident tone made something inside him unclench.

"He was a fool, but he was still my father."

She went up on tiptoes and kissed him gently on the mouth.

"My father struck me once because I dared to criticize his behavior," Margaret said. "He was making my mother so anxious that she became incapable of functioning. I had to take over all the housework, while he gambled and drank away his inheritance with his friends in town. When I confronted him, he said I didn't know my place—that I was too loud and strident and that no man would ever want a wife like that."

"I would," Alistair offered and kissed her back. "In fact, you are exactly what I need." He paused. "He was wrong about you, too."

She made a face. "I *am* opinionated and loud."

"So what?"

"After he hit me, I tried to stay quiet and not complain when we had no money left for food after he'd scraped together enough to pay his workers and pawned all my mother's jewelry." She drew a ragged breath. "I was glad when he died."

"I can understand why, and I felt the same about my father." He paused. "I only wish I'd had the chance to be there with him, so that I could forgive him, but it was not to be. Frederica made sure of that."

"Which is why you can't forgive her," Margaret murmured and wrapped her arms around his waist.

Alistair didn't say anything more as he held her close and

buried his face into the crook of her neck. She might still be reserving judgment about his stepmother, but she was definitely on his side.

Eventually, she drew away from him. "If you wish to finish showing me the house, we should get on. Your family doctor will be here soon."

"He's not my doctor. He's employed by Frederica."

She paused to look up at him. "Does that mean you won't trust his judgment?"

"We'll have to wait and see, won't we?" Alistair took her hand and walked back to the door. "I don't think we have time to see the gardens, but I'll show you my old room."

Just as they reentered the hall, the butler opened the front door to reveal a young man who handed his hat over and smiled agreeably.

"Good afternoon, Mr. Mortimer. Shall I go straight up to see our patient, or would Lady Hellion like to see me first?"

"She said to go straight up, sir, and she would meet you afterward in the drawing room." Mr. Mortimer stepped back and noticed Margaret and Alistair.

"Your grace. This is Dr. McNeil. He is attending poor Miss Phoebe."

The man went still and turned toward Alistair who was advancing toward him looking very haughty, indeed.

"You're the Duke of Thorsway?"

"Yes." Alistair looked down his nose at the unfortunate man. "Who are you?"

Dr. McNeil bowed. "I'm the local physician. I took over from Dr. Meader just after your father's death."

"How convenient for you. I've often wanted to ask my father's doctors why they neglected to tell me he was so ill and assured me that I could return to India." Alistair gestured toward the stairs. "Perhaps you should go up to my sister? I am very interested to hear your opinion of her current condition."

"As you wish, your grace." Dr. McNeil nodded and started for the stairs. "I must admit to some concern for her recovery."

Margaret followed along behind, quite happy to remain unnoticed and listen to the doctor's summary of Phoebe Haralson's condition. She had a lot of experience in tending the sick, and she was interested in what he might have to say.

"She is lethargic, her skin is often red or swollen, and she suffers terribly from stomach problems. Unfortunately, her inability to nourish herself means that she lacks energy and rarely leaves her room."

"How long has this been going on?" Alistair asked.

"It was a very gradual thing, your grace." Dr. McNeil paused on the landing. "I—often visit the ladies of the house, and I noticed she seemed quieter at Christmas and less likely to join in the festivities." He lowered his voice. "At first, forgive me your grace, I did wonder if she was looking for attention. It must be hard for a young lady to live with a beautiful woman like Lady Hellion, and I suspect they did not always get along."

"Indeed." Alistair inclined his head an icy inch. "When exactly did you manage to tear your gaze from Lady Hellion and start paying attention to the illness of my sister?"

The doctor's mouth gaped open. "I—"

"My dear." Margaret reached forward and grabbed her husband's sleeve. "Perhaps it might be better to save your opinions until Dr. McNeil has seen his patient?"

He glanced down at her. "As you wish, my love."

Dr. McNeil offered Margaret a harried glance, and then knocked on the bedroom door, which was opened by one of the maids.

"Miss Phoebe's awake, Dr. McNeil."

"Excellent." He glanced back at them. "Do you wish to come in with me, or wait until I have completed my examination?"

"We'll wait."

"Thank you." Dr. McNeil hurried into the room and closed the door firmly behind him.

Margaret frowned at her husband. "What exactly were you attempting to do, Alistair? Scare the man into running away, leaving your sister with no one to care for her at all?"

"I don't like him." Alistair moved restlessly down the corridor until he reached one of the windows and stared out of it.

"On *sight?*"

"Yes. He's far too young and handsome. He's obviously besotted with my stepmother; so besotted, in fact, that he failed to notice my sister was very ill."

"You might at least give him a chance." Margaret wasn't mollified.

"I have." He flung his hand out toward the door. "He's in there with her right now, isn't he?"

She stared at him until he sat down on the window seat beside her and let out his breath.

"I'll listen to him first and then decide whether he is competent, all right?"

"Thank you." Margaret took his hand and smoothed her thumb over his palm until he brought her fingers to his mouth and kissed them.

After the clocks chimed the quarter hour, the door opened again, and Dr. McNeil poked his head out and beckoned to them.

"She is in good spirits today and eager to see you."

"Thank you." Alistair paused at the door to look down into the doctor's eyes. "Please don't rush off. I wish to speak to you after I've seen my sister."

"I usually take tea with Lady Hellion and apprise her of her daughter's condition."

"Her *step*daughter." Alistair nodded. "Then we will see you there."

They went in, and Margaret stayed slightly behind her husband so as not to disrupt his reunion with his sister.

"Alistair?" the girl on the bed whispered, her eyes wide. "Is it really you?"

"Phoebe." Alistair went toward her and gathered her in his arms. "Yes, it's me."

She pushed against his chest. "You should not have come back! You *know*—"

"I had to come." He smoothed her hair away from her face. "I had to see you."

"But that's what she wanted!" Hectic color rose on Phoebe's already reddened cheeks. "You have to *go*."

Alistair sat on the side of the bed and held her hand. "I will be careful, I promise you. I do not intend to stay very long. If I can persuade you to return to Hellsdown Park with me, we can be shot of her forever."

He turned toward Margaret who had remained in the shadows observing the young woman in the bed, and held out his other hand.

"I'm married now. My wife Margaret can be your chaperone and introduce you to society if that is what you wish to do."

Margaret came forward and smiled at Phoebe. "It is a pleasure to meet you. I do hope you will consider coming to live with us."

Phoebe simply stared at her and then looked back at Adam. "Does *she* know?"

"That I'm married? Yes, of course," Alistair replied. "I introduced her to Margaret earlier."

"She won't let me leave," Phoebe declared.

"But she isn't the head of the family, I am. If I decide to take you home with me, she can do nothing to stop me."

There was a note of finality in Alistair's voice that reminded Margaret very much of her brother concluding a business deal.

Phoebe shook her head. "She wants to go to London with me for my debut and find herself a new husband. She won't give that up."

"Margaret will sponsor your debut, won't you, my dear?" Alistair looked over at her.

"Yes, of course."

The fact that she had no knowledge of high society, had no acquaintance in town, and the flat accent of a middle-class mill-owner's daughter seemed not to occur to him.

"She won't let me go." Phoebe spoke each word with equal force, her frantic gaze fixed on her brother, and then began to cough, her whole body curling in on itself as she fought for breath.

Margaret rushed forward. "Perhaps we should worry about all that after you are well enough to travel."

"I will never be well enough." Phoebe lay back against her pillows and briefly closed her eyes. "She won't let me."

Alistair squeezed her hand and then stood up. "We will come back and see you after dinner, if that is acceptable?"

Phoebe nodded, her energy seemingly gone as she turned her face into the pillow and fell instantly asleep.

Margaret opened the door and let the maid in to watch over her mistress. Alistair didn't speak as they descended the stairs together and headed toward the drawing room. The sound of Frederica's light laughter and the doctor's deeper tones filtered through the door.

Margaret grabbed hold of Alistair's hand, halting his progress.

"Promise me that you will listen to what Dr. McNeil has to say before you condemn him to Hades."

A muscle twitched in his cheek. "I will do my best to remain civil. Will that satisfy you?"

"I suppose it will have to." Margaret resigned herself to the prospect of Dr. McNeil being forcibly ejected from the hall by her husband.

They entered the drawing room together, and the conversation ceased.

Frederica smiled at them. "How was Phoebe? Dr. McNeil said she was having a good day today. Was she able to speak to you?"

"Indeed." Alistair bowed. "It was a pleasure to see her again." He redirected his attention to the doctor, who was looking remarkably apprehensive. "Perhaps you might further explain her condition and the remedies you are employing to make her better?"

Margaret sat down beside Frederica, but her husband took up position on the hearthrug so that he could best stare down at the poor doctor.

"I... have consulted with several colleagues, and we are at a loss to decide what ails your sister." Dr. McNeil frowned. "Her stomach is weak and averse to many foods. When I bleed her, she sinks even further into lethargy."

"Have you taken her to London to see a specialist?" Alistair asked.

Dr. McNeil shot a quick glance at Lady Hellion, who was looking very concerned. "Her ladyship and I feared that making such a journey might weaken Miss Phoebe too much."

"Then have you written to anyone in London to ask for their assistance?" Alistair looked at his stepmother. "You certainly have the funds to employ the best."

Lady Hellion sighed. "Oh, Alistair, how like you to make this about money, when it is your sister's life that we seek to save!" She dashed away a tear. "I know you have never forgiven me for your father's decision to leave the financial matters of this estate in my hands, but please can you stop being so *petty?*"

"I am hardly—" Alistair started speaking.

Margaret hastened to intervene before Lady Hellion managed to send Alistair off on an unnecessary tangent. "We are planning on traveling onward to London when we leave here. We can take Phoebe with us, and I can care for her on the journey."

All three of the occupants in the room turned to stare at her with varying degrees of consternation. Her husband was the first to recover his composure.

"What an admirable thought, my dear!" He turned to Dr. McNeil. "Perhaps you might care to accompany us to ensure my sister's wellbeing?"

"I—" Dr. McNeil opened and shut his mouth and turned to Lady Hellion. "What do you think, my lady?"

She bit her lip. "I think that his grace is willing to put his sister's life in danger just to score a spiteful point off me."

"Hardly," Alistair said. "I was not aware that you had acquired the knowledge and skills of a physician in my absence, my lady. If not, I would prefer to hear what Dr. McNeil has to say. Would my sister seriously be imperiled by such a journey?"

"If she was well taken care of and thoroughly monitored, then probably not," Dr. McNeil answered slowly.

"I am deeply saddened, Alistair." Lady Hellion applied her handkerchief to her eyes. "You are speaking of the girl I have practically raised as my own, and yet you offer me no say in her welfare?"

"I am her guardian," Alistair said. "My father, at least, made that clear. The only reason Phoebe has remained in your care for so long is that I didn't have anyone female to chaperone her." He bowed to Margaret. "Now I do, and, if Phoebe wishes to live with us, then I will not stop her."

"And what am I supposed to do?" Lady Hellion screwed her

handkerchief up in her fist. "When you deprive me of my last duty to your father?"

Alistair shrugged. "With all due respect, my lady, we are discussing my sister. I am more than willing to discuss *your* future in private, and not in front of the family doctor."

"Then as you have all decided to ignore me, I will remain silent," Lady Hellion said stiffly, her gaze on Dr. McNeil who was blushing intensely. "All I will say, your grace, is that if harm comes to that girl because of your ill-advised decisions, then it will be on your conscience and not mine."

Alistair bowed. "Indeed." He glanced over at Dr. McNeil. "Perhaps I might accompany you to your gig?"

"Yes, of course." Dr. McNeil grabbed his bag and bowed to the two ladies. "I will see you tomorrow, your grace, my lady."

Lady Hellion tossed her head and didn't reply, leaving Margaret to murmur something conventional.

Silence fell after the two men left the room, and Margaret made no effort to break it.

"Are you not worried about your husband's current actions?" Eventually, Frederica spoke. "Does it not seem that in his need to hurt *me*, Alistair might inadvertently hurt his sister?"

"Alistair only wishes what is best for Phoebe." Margaret turned her calmest gaze on Frederica. "Taking her to London, and ensuring that she gets the best treatment possible, is hardly the action of a man out for revenge."

"You obviously don't know him as well as you think you do," Lady Hellion replied, her voice rising. "He hates me so much that he would do *anything* to destroy me."

"With all due respect, my lady, you seem somewhat overwrought," Margaret said sweetly. "Perhaps you should lie down?"

Her companion rose slowly to her feet. "Alistair and I grew up together, did you know that? My father was the curate at the local church."

Margaret said nothing and concentrated on looking composed even as her stomach was tightening.

"So don't ever think you know him better than I do." Frederica pressed a hand to her heart. "He was always *mine*. That's why he hated me for marrying his father. That's why he can't forgive and forget."

She nodded at Margaret. "He may spin you any tale he wishes to protest his innocence, but, as they say, you never forget your first love."

She stormed out of the room, leaving Margaret with much to think about. Despite her suspicions, Frederica's words rang true, but what to make of them, and how did they affect the current situation? Alistair's attitude toward Lilly, who had expected to be the next duchess, had held none of the rage he apparently felt for his father's wife. Why was he so passionate about the one and not the other? She suspected she knew the answer but was unwilling to face it.

Margaret rose to her feet and walked out into the corridor with no real sense of where she wanted to go—except that she wasn't quite ready to face the keen gaze of her husband. He would use his wiles to extract her concerns from her, and then what? Would he deny Frederica's accusations? Would he laugh at her? And what if he didn't? What if his stepmother truly had been his first love, and he hadn't even bothered to mention it?

CHAPTER TWELVE

"*D*r. McNeil will travel with us on the first stage to London and stay overnight at the inn to watch Phoebe," Alistair said as he shrugged into his coat, one eye on his wife who was still sitting up in bed staring into space. "Don't worry, I'll make him ride alongside the carriage, so that we don't have to deal with his presence."

"When do you plan to leave?" Margaret asked.

"Tomorrow, as long as Phoebe is well enough to travel." Alistair settled his coat on his shoulders, and transferred his belongings from the dressing table to his pockets. "If that is acceptable to you, of course."

"I certainly have no wish to stay here." Her smile was a little reserved. "And my opinion is hardly relevant in the matter of your sister's health and wellness."

He paused and turned fully back toward the bed. "Is everything all right?"

"Why should it not be?"

"That isn't an answer." He frowned. "Are you annoyed at my highhandedness? It was your idea to take Phoebe with us to London."

"I am aware of that." She started undoing her braid and threw back the covers. "If we are leaving tomorrow, I will have to ask Eileen and Clarkson to start packing as soon as possible."

"Margaret..."

She looked over at him. "What?"

"I am aware that something is troubling you, but I will admit that I am so consumed with getting my sister away from that woman that I do not have time to coax answers from you." He paused, but she didn't speak. "If there is anything you wish to say that cannot wait, please speak up, and I will do my best to accommodate you."

In truth, there was something about his sister's current condition that worried him greatly. He wouldn't be happy until he had consulted an old army surgeon friend of his who lived in London, and could hopefully lay his suspicions to rest.

"I—appreciate your concern." Margaret paused by her dressing table. Her hair covered her face, making it impossible for him to read her expression. "Anything I have to say can wait until we are away from this house."

"Good." He kissed her briefly on the cheek. "I appreciate that. Are you coming down to breakfast?"

"Yes, I will join you after I have spoken to Eileen."

Alistair left the room and went down the stairs toward the breakfast room where he discovered his stepmother eating toast and reading her morning correspondence.

"You're up early." Alistair helped himself from the array of dishes on the sideboard, wondering again why his stepmother needed such a large amount of food. "Did you visit Phoebe? She seems a lot better today."

"I believe that is because she is pleased you are here." Frederica poured them both some coffee. "When do you plan to leave?"

"Tomorrow." Alistair cut into the succulent ham. "If you wish, I will write and let you know how Phoebe is doing."

She sniffed. "You will not."

"Whatever I might think of you, my lady, I am well aware that you have given my sister a home and have cared for her in the past five years." He buttered his toast. "While I am in London, perhaps you might give some thought as to where you wish to live if Phoebe decides to stay with us?"

She put down her cup, her nose wrinkling. "What do you mean?"

"As I will be attending the House of Lords on a more regular basis, I think this house will become a good place for my family to reside when we are able to leave London, but are unable to travel all the way up north."

"This house was left to me for the remainder of my lifetime."

Alistair sighed. "I hate to mention it, but all the property of the marquisette is now part of the dukedom, and its disposition is again at my discretion."

She set down her spoon with a clatter. "You *cannot* throw me out!"

"I believe I can, but, rest assured, I have no intention of doing so, or leaving you penniless. I am offering you the opportunity to move to a smaller residence, even somewhere on this estate—there *is* a dower house—because I require this property for my own use."

"This is just spite." Frederica's eyes filled with tears.

"If that was the case, I would throw you out for deliberately separating me from my father at the end of his life and persuading him to leave you everything that wasn't entailed."

She snorted. "I hardly needed to persuade him, Alistair. He never liked you. You know that."

"I am well aware of that." He paused to consider his next words. "If you agree to vacate this house, I will not attempt to reclaim my fair share of your present income. And, I will not take you to court over the many questionable decisions my father made in his last days of life." He met her furious gaze.

"I've seen his will, my lady. I found it in the study. You wrote half the new clauses in yourself with the help of your new solicitor. As a beneficiary, I doubt that is legal."

"Your father was too ill to write. I merely wrote down what he dictated."

He was surprised how much this fresh evidence of his father's rancor hurt. He was also aware that he needed to reach some kind of conclusion with this woman who had helped destroy what little relationship he had left with his father.

"As I said, such matters will remain between you and your maker if you simply agree to leave this house and find somewhere else to live."

She stared at him for a long while. "You've changed."

He shrugged. "Who has not?"

"You're... much harder."

"While you were dallying with my father, I was away in India fighting ridiculous and pointless wars, thinking you, my one true love, were waiting patiently for my return. Imagine my surprise when I received my father's letter announcing his new marriage—to you."

"You were away for *years*, I—"

"Chose not to wait?"

"He was kind to me! He understood my impatience, he offered me everything I had ever wanted," Frederica cried.

"Everything that you could've had with me, without the inconvenient wait for him to die?"

"You are cruel." She tossed her napkin onto the table.

"No, you were a fool to marry a man who chose you simply because he hated his own son." Alistair picked up his knife. "He never loved either of us, Frederica. He just wanted to stop me marrying the woman I loved, and you let him."

She reached over and grabbed his hand. "I *never* stopped loving you."

Alistair gently removed her hand from his wrist. "That's a

shame, because I definitely stopped loving you when you married my bloody father."

"He said that he doubted you would ever come back, that you would die out there, and that I would be left a curate's daughter with no dowry and no prospects to dwindle into spinsterhood. He *said* that if I married him we might have children, and that if you died, I would be the mother of a future marquess."

"And you fell for his lies."

"I was young and foolish."

"So was I when I left." He smiled at her. "Why did you want me to come here so badly, Frederica? Did you truly think you could use the love I once had for you against me?"

"I merely wanted to *see* you, to discuss Phoebe's debut, and—"

"You could have written to me about that." He held her gaze. "You thought that if I saw you again I would fall in with all your plans for my sister."

"She is ill!"

"I can see that." He sat back. "You will not be involved in her debut; my wife will deal with that. You will not be invited to stay with us in London, although you will receive an invitation to Phoebe's debut ball when she is well enough to have one."

"What if I choose to live in London?" Frederica raised her chin and stood up.

"I can't stop you, but you will not live in my townhouse, and you will bear the expenses from your own account."

Frederica gripped the back of her chair. "What happened to you, Alistair? You used to be such a sweet, kind man."

"Thankfully, I'm not like that anymore." He paused. "Perhaps, in a way, I should thank you for showing me early on in my life that everyone and everything can be bought."

"Like your wife bought you and your title?" Frederica demanded. "You are a fine one to talk!"

"I did what was necessary to secure my holdings," Alistair stated. "And I did it with the full knowledge of my intended. She knew the state of my finances. I never lied to her."

"She's a mill worker who wanted to be a duchess!" Frederica jeered. "Who wouldn't take that chance?"

"Oh, dear, are you jealous?" Alistair rose from his seat. "If you'd just waited a little longer for me to return, you could've had everything."

She glared at him but didn't speak.

He inclined his head an icy inch. "As I said, thank you for showing me I was mistaken, and that love is not necessarily the best foundation for a successful marriage. I am very content with the arrangement I have."

"Of course you are, you cold-hearted bastard," Frederica said. "I must confess to some sympathy for your poor wife! She will suffer greatly in society, and you won't lift a finger to help her now that you have her money."

Alistair smiled. "Please consider your options while I am in London, and let me know what you decide."

He turned to the door, just as the butler entered.

"Good morning, Mr. Mortimer. Have you seen my duchess this morning?"

"I saw her just a moment ago in the hall, your grace. She asked me for directions into the local village." The butler removed Alistair's dishes from the table.

"I thought she was coming down for breakfast." Alistair frowned. "Did she eat anything at all?"

"I'm not sure, your grace. It's possible that her maid took her up something in bed." Mr. Mortimer paused at the door. "Would you like me to inquire?"

"No, I'll find her myself," Alistair said. "I'd quite enjoy a morning stroll."

∾

HALFWAY ALONG THE LONG, picturesque drive to the house, Margaret had to slow down as the hurt and outrage that had fueled her flight finally deserted her. A marriage of convenience to a millworker, and a man who was supremely happy with that arrangement...

But why was she surprised? He'd never promised to love or care about her. He'd appreciated her saving his neck with her fortune and expressed his gratitude in many ways, including bedding her, but he'd never suggested he expected to fall in love with her.

She stopped completely and breathed hard through her nose, aware of the silence around her broken only by the wind moving through the beech trees. When she'd heard him talking to Frederica she should've retreated to her room immediately, or gone in and held them both to account. But she'd remained at the door, unnoticed and undetected, as they were so focused on each other, and heard far more than she'd bargained for.

"Margaret!"

She briefly closed her eyes as she heard Alistair's shout behind her and considered making a run for it. She already had a stitch in her side and was fairly certain he would come after her and catch her, regardless. So, she remained where she was and waited for him to reach her.

He walked around her and halted, his expression intent. He'd forgotten to put on his hat and his blond hair was disheveled by the wind.

"How much did you hear?" he asked.

"Enough."

"Well, you know what they say—eavesdroppers never hear good about themselves."

She cast him a murderous glare, and his smile faded.

"I am not sure what has upset you. I told her to leave this house because I wish to live in it while I am attending the House of Lords. Would you prefer not to live here?"

Ah, there he went, attempting to divert her into another discussion he might graciously allow her to win. Did he not know what had really upset her, or was he blind? Did she even know, herself?

"Margaret? It is not like you to be so silent." He paused and let out his breath, his expression contrite. "Whatever I said that offended you, I will, of course apologize for it."

"It's not what you said. I am well aware of the circumstances of our marriage." Margaret finally managed to form a stiff sentence.

"Then what is it?"

She stared at him. How to tell him that seeing his interactions with Frederica had made her realize how little she knew him, and how superficial their connection. He'd informed her that he hated to argue and yet had seemed to garner great enjoyment from fighting with his stepmother.

"I don't know." She shrugged.

"That's not a very helpful answer."

"Perhaps I don't wish to be helpful?"

He spread his arms wide. "Then how am I supposed to make amends, if you won't tell me what the damn problem is?"

Her anger rose to match his evident frustration. Maybe it was time to stage a diversion on her own. "It would've been helpful to have known you grew up with Frederica and that you intended to marry her."

His expression went blank. "I told you that I would try not to influence your opinion of her and let you make up your own mind."

"Without that pertinent fact? Can you imagine how I felt when she threw that in my face?" Margaret demanded.

He sighed. "You're right. I should've told you. I didn't think she'd have the nerve to mention that she jilted me for my father, but as usual, I underestimated her malice toward me." He reached for her hand. "Will you please forgive me? That was an abominable situation to place you in, and it was all my fault."

She considered his hand and the uncomfortable tangle of emotion still jamming her throat. There was no way to ignore it. She was jealous of her husband's stepmother, and how could she possibly confess that? She'd made a marriage bargain that hadn't given her the right to feel such things, and, as her brother would certainly remind her, she had to keep her side of it.

She took his hand and managed a brisk nod. "As you said, your time here is better spent worrying about your sister than me, so perhaps we could put this behind us?"

He put his fingers under her chin and raised her face to his, his gaze searching. "What else is wrong?"

She used her most pragmatic voice. "Nothing that won't be fixed when we leave this house, I can assure you."

He kept looking at her, which was quite disconcerting. "Did you think I was unkind asking her to leave this house?"

"It is your house, you have the right to do whatever you want with it, and she hardly deserves your consideration, does she?" Margaret agreed.

It was a relief to return to a discussion where she could use her commonsense. That was, after all, the main reason he had married her.

Alistair hesitated. "Am I remiss in not holding her accountable for meddling with my father's will?"

"That is up to you. I assume you are asking her to vacate the premises in return for your silence?"

"Exactly." He nodded and offered her his arm as they continued down the drive.

"As long as you get her agreement in writing and lodge it safely with your solicitors, I cannot see her causing you any further problems."

"That is a given." Alistair nodded. "I don't trust her. Once I have relieved her of Phoebe's care, my obligation is at an end.

All further communications can be carried out through my solicitors."

Margaret wanted to cheer, but settled on a more demure nod. She had a horrible sensation that Frederica would not be quite so easy to shake off, but she didn't want to mention it right now. Her husband was right about one thing. They needed to remove Phoebe from the house and get her to a London doctor. Once that had been accomplished, perhaps Margaret would have the time to worry about her own feelings. Assisting Phoebe was an attractive diversion.

They reached the end of the drive by the small gatehouse, which was no longer occupied, and Alistair looked up at the gates.

"Do you wish to walk into the village? It is just around the corner."

"I was intending to," Margaret said. "Mr. Mortimer gave me directions."

"Would you like me to come with you?" Her husband's beguiling smile was back as he swept her a bow.

"You aren't wearing a hat or your coat," Margaret pointed out.

"The people in the village won't care. They've known me all my life," Alistair said with all the blithe insouciance of his birth and position. "I'd like to take this opportunity to introduce you to some of them. They will be delighted to see that I have finally taken a bride."

"Then I am more than happy to accompany you, your grace."

Margaret placed her hand on his sleeve, glad that, for now, they had managed to put their problems behind them, and she was grateful for the respite. She had no idea how to handle the unknown emotions that being married to Alistair Haralson had aroused and needed time to think things through.

"Wonderful." Alistair lifted the latch of the side gate and held it open for her to pass through. "After you, duchess."

CHAPTER THIRTEEN

*a*listair strolled along the London street, all too aware of the potential to have his pocket picked or be run down by a coach and four. He'd decided to walk because the streets were so crowded that hailing a hackney cab would've had him sitting twiddling his thumbs while pedestrians walked past him. But it always paid to be wary even in the best part of town.

He checked the address, went down the steps into the basement of the Harley Street house, and knocked on the bright blue door. As he waited, he observed the unusual sight of people walking above him at street level, totally unaware he was down there.

"Hellion, old chap! Come in!"

He grinned at the man who opened the door and stepped over the threshold. "Nash, how are you?"

"Well enough, and happy to be alive, what can I do for you?"

Alistair followed his old friend to the back of the basement apartment into a cozy sitting room.

"I heard you've gotten very top-lofty now," Nash said as he poured Alistair a brandy and handed it over before sitting down in one of the comfortable chairs.

"If you consider being a duke top-lofty, then, yes, I have."

"I'm not surprised your cousin Farrell died young. He drunk far too much, and I suspect he had syphilis."

"It wouldn't surprise me, either." Alistair was unwilling to share exactly how his cousin had died and was glad that the event had happened away from the gossips of London.

Alistair tasted the brandy, which was French, and remarkably good. His friend Nash might choose to ignore his title and live like a modest man, but his family roots went back to the conqueror. His father hadn't approved of his son joining the military as a surgeon, and the two were still estranged. Nash had no need to earn his living but continued to work at one of the emerging London hospitals.

"This issue is somewhat confidential. You are the only physician I trust to act for me on this matter."

"Carry on." Nash waved his glass at him. "I'll keep your secrets. I always have."

Alistair took another fortifying sip of brandy. "Do you remember when we were in India and that colonel died quite suddenly?"

"That's quite an open field, my friend. Being totally unsuited for the climate and equally unwilling to adapt, the amount of British deaths was quite high. Can you be more specific?"

"Colonel Clavering."

"Ah, the miserable bastard who was on his third imported English wife and had an Indian mistress?"

"Yes, that one."

Nash sipped his brandy, his gaze settling somewhere in the past, his expression grim. "He was a drunkard and a terrible officer. He beat both his wife and his mistress and was brutal to his men. When he died so unexpectedly, the matter was hushed up. His widow went back to England, and his mistress was paid off."

"I seem to remember gossip suggested that he might have been poisoned," Alistair said gently.

"Indeed. I was the man who had to write the death certificate and speak to the coroner. If they had been able to convict the mistress, they would've done so, but it appears that the wife was involved as well."

"The two women conspired to kill him?"

Nash shrugged. "That's what I believed, and that's what I told the coroner, who quickly decided that no charges would be forthcoming. In truth, I think the army were as glad to be rid of him as his womenfolk." He eyed Alistair. "What this has to do with you is beyond me."

"Do you remember telling me about the symptoms you observed that made you certain he had died of arsenic poisoning?"

"Yes, indeed." Nash sat up straight. "I saw him twice before his death, but by the time I worked out what was going on, it was too late to do anything."

"Why were you so certain that he was poisoned in this way?"

"Because unlike many of my colleagues, I listened and learned a lot from the local healers and went out with them on their rounds. Arsenic was easy to obtain and occasionally taken by accident, because it was commonly left out to kill vermin. I was able to observe the symptoms and see the progression of the illness."

Alistair nodded. "Would you be so kind as to come and visit my sister?"

"Your sister?" Nash blinked at him. "You think—"

"Yes, I do." Alistair rose from his seat. "Would tomorrow be too soon for you to call?"

"Not soon enough." Nash leapt to his feet. "I'm coming with you now."

MARGARET OPENED the door of Phoebe's bedroom to find her husband and a dashingly handsome black-haired man beside him. Alistair beckoned her to join them, and she closed the door and stepped into the corridor.

"This is my friend, Dr. Nash. I have asked him if he will examine Phoebe."

"Ma'am." The doctor nodded to her and then turned to Alistair. "I would appreciate it if your housekeeper remained in the room while I proceed with my examination."

Margaret raised her chin. "I'm not the housekeeper."

Alistair cleared his throat. "Ah, I apologize for my lack of formality. My dear duchess, may I introduce you to my old friend, Dr. Nash?"

"You're his duchess?" Dr. Nash asked.

"Yes." Margaret met his gaze head on.

"Then I apologize, and ask if you might send for your housekeeper or a maid so that I can proceed."

"I'll be happy to assist you, sir," Margaret said. "I have much experience in dealing with the sick, the elderly, and the dying."

He offered her a skeptical glance, but he bowed, and allowed her to precede him into the bedchamber where Phoebe was sleeping. He set his bag down on the foot of the bed and stood quietly observing his patient.

"Would it disturb her too greatly if you pulled the covers down so that I could see all of her?" Dr. Nash asked.

"She was exhausted after our journey, so I doubt much will wake her." Margaret efficiently lowered the sheets. "Her skin is very red and swollen, and she said she had a very sore throat."

He came forward, sat on the side of the bed, and held Phoebe's wrist, listening for something Margaret couldn't hear. "Her pulse is erratic. Has she complained of stomach pain or nausea?"

"She experienced both on our journey, as well as loose bowels," Margaret said.

"How very unpleasant for her." He leaned in, listened to her breathing, and then stood up.

"Would you care to come with me to speak to Hellion—I mean, the duke?" Dr. Nash asked.

"Yes, indeed. I will ask my maid to sit with Phoebe, and I will meet you in his grace's study," Margaret said.

The ducal townhouse was in almost as bad a state of repair as the house up north, and Margaret had already taken a dislike to it. Evidence of the previous occupant, Alistair's cousin Farrell, was apparent everywhere. Margaret had sought her husband's permission to remove every single item, including at least ten dubious remedies against syphilis, from Farrell's bedchamber.

The current staff was lazy, and had not kept the house up to her standards. As soon as Phoebe was on the path to health, Margaret intended to sit down with Joseph Lang and devise a plan to hire new staff.

After settling Eileen in with Phoebe, she proceeded down to the kitchen, which was disconcertingly empty. The cook was absent, and the butler was drunk and snoring in his rooms. She made a pot of tea and carried it up to the drawing room, which was the only one of the receiving rooms fit to admit guests.

"Let me take that from you, your grace."

Dr. Nash hurried over to relieve her of the tray as if she were far too delicate for such a task. Alistair raised his eyebrows.

"Do we not have staff?"

"The butler is drunk, and the cook has disappeared, probably because I had a few words with them about the quality of the food and service presented to us last night." Margaret poured the tea. "I'd offer you milk, but there isn't any, and the previous occupant drank every drop of brandy in the house."

"This will do nicely," Dr. Nash said. "It's far too early for brandy."

Despite his somewhat scruffy appearance, he had excellent manners to go with the upper-class accent of her husband.

"Well, Nash?" Alistair asked. "What do you think?"

"I think you are correct. Someone has been poisoning her."

"*What?*" Margaret said. "Alistair—"

He held up his hand. "I didn't want to believe what I thought I was seeing, and my first priority was to get Phoebe away from that house." He nodded at the doctor. "Nash was a surgeon in the army. I remembered him discussing a particular case of poisoning just before I left for England, and, somehow, the details stuck with me."

"It's a good job they did," Dr. Nash confirmed. "You might have saved your sister's life."

"Will she survive, though?" Alistair asked, his expression grave.

"If you have taken her away from her poisoner, then yes, there is a good chance that she will recover very well."

"How do you know that?" Margaret intervened.

He turned toward her. "Because I've seen such cases before. Sometimes a person would inadvertently eat a small amount of something that contained the poison and be ill for a few days until they gradually recovered."

"But this illness has been going on for months," Alistair argued.

"Probably because whoever did this didn't want to administer a large dose of poison and kill a young, apparently healthy, woman outright." Dr. Nash glanced over at Alistair. "If that had occurred, I'm fairly certain you would've noticed and done everything in your power to discover why your sister had died?"

"Yes."

"Then this method of slowly weakening her was far more effective. A country doctor who would probably have no knowledge of the effects of such poison would attend her. He would prescribe treatments such as bleeding, which would make her even weaker, until he inadvertently killed her."

Margaret shivered, and Alistair reached for her hand.

"Then you think that if we keep her safe here, she will recover?"

"I don't see why not." Dr. Nash looked from Margaret to Alistair. "Do you know who did this?"

"I have my suspicions," Alistair said grimly. "But I am not at liberty to share them with you at this moment."

"Well, if you need a signed statement detailing what I observed, and my conclusions for any court of law, I'd be happy to oblige."

"Thank you." Alistair nodded at his friend as he stood up. "I'd ask you to stay for dinner, but it appears that my wife has frightened away all my staff."

Margaret smiled. "If it comes to that, your grace, and cook doesn't return, I'll wager I can cook you a better dinner myself!"

"I am almost tempted to stay just to watch her grace roll up her sleeves." Dr. Nash bent to kiss her hand. "A pleasure, duchess."

"Dr. Nash."

Margaret remained by the fire until Alistair returned from escorting his friend to the door.

His smile disappeared as he shut the door and came to sit opposite her.

"Do you really think Phoebe was being poisoned?" Margaret asked.

"Yes, don't you?" He shoved a hand through his hair. "Thank God we got there before Frederica could finish her off."

"But Frederica invited us to the house," Margaret reminded him. "Why would she do that if she knew we might remove Phoebe from her care?"

"She probably gambled that we wouldn't come. You have to remember that for the last two years she's been attempting to get me back to Healdstone Hall, and failed miserably. If Phoebe had died, and I hadn't bothered to come when Frederica had *begged* me to, can you imagine what damage she would've done to my reputation?"

"But she wanted to keep Phoebe by her so that she could go to London and find herself a new husband," Margaret persisted. "Why would she kill the golden goose?"

"Because once I became a duke, she realized that her reign was over, and that I held all the power. She probably thought that if Phoebe was dead, she could go to London, play the part of a grieving stepmother, ruin my reputation, *and* acquire a new husband."

"But what about Dr. McNeil?" Margaret set down her tea cup. "Isn't it possible that he decided to poison Phoebe for his own reasons?" Alistair was looking at her as if she was mad, but she carried on talking. "Why assume that it is all about Frederica trying to hurt you"

"Because it always is!"

She blinked at the intensity of his tone as he took a hasty tour of the room, suddenly aware that they were circling back around to a discussion that she still wasn't ready to participate in.

"As you know your stepmother far better than I do, I will not argue with you." Margaret studied her linked hands in her lap. "Perhaps as a precaution, we should make sure that no one from Healdstone Hall is allowed inside this house."

"I can certainly agree with that." He stared out of the dirt-encrusted window. "I hate this house. I had to stay here by myself sometimes when my father wouldn't allow me to come home in the school holidays. There were two Christmases when, if it hadn't have been for the Nash family, I would've been here on my own, gnawing at a bone."

"Dr. Nash seems to be a good man and an excellent and observant doctor," Margaret remarked, more than willing to take the discussion away from the dangerous waters surrounding Frederica. "If we both dislike this house, perhaps we could sell it and find something more modest?"

"I'm not sure if that's possible." He glanced back at her. "Remember how your brother bought some of my debt? One of those items was the mortgage on this house my cousin took out without my grandfather knowing about it."

"Perhaps Adam…"

"No." He spun around, his expression cold. "Don't even suggest that I ask your brother to release me from a debt of honor."

"*Honor?*" Margaret came slowly to her feet. "What is honorable about a man who tried to bankrupt his own family? Why should you have to be responsible for paying back debts that your cousin incurred?"

"You know why. Didn't your brother do the same thing? Didn't he repay all your father's creditors?"

"He repaid his loans to the bank, and to his friends, but not his gaming debts. Adam did not see them as 'honorable.'"

"But I do." He met her gaze. "If I fail to pay them back, *my* credit will suffer, as will our family's standing in the world."

"With whom exactly?" Margaret asked.

He shrugged. "My peers, the world I inhabit, and the world my children will inhabit."

"So you are saying that if you do not pay back all your cousin's and grandfather's debts that our children will somehow be affected?" The fact that he was currently using "I" rather than "we" rankled more than she had anticipated.

"If they wish to take their place in society, then unfortunately, yes."

"And you agree with this?" Margaret asked.

He sighed. "It's not a question of whether I agree with it or not, Margaret, it's just the way the world works."

"Maybe *my* children will grow up with a different set of

values."

He smiled. "Do you really think any heir to a dukedom would prefer to work in a factory like your brother does?"

There was a hint of amusement in his tone that she didn't care for. But, if she were honest, it was a relief to be allowed to get angry about *something*.

"Maybe if my son is a man with values, then yes."

He straightened, his smile disappearing. "I wouldn't want any child of mine working in a mill."

"*I* worked there." She raised her chin. "It did me no harm."

"But you are an exception to every rule, duchess." He paused. "Would you truly wish to go back to such a life, and for your children to have no choice in the matter?"

"If your son is told he *has* to be a duke, is that not another form of allowing him no choice?"

"Touché." This time he grinned at her. "But I still insist that most men would choose to be a duke, my dear."

"We shall see about that." She sniffed. "Perhaps *my* son will surprise you."

He came toward her, his hand outstretched. "As we have no staff, would you be agreeable to meeting my rather formidable great-aunt Lavinia and having dinner with her? I am hoping to enlist her aid to launch both you and my sister into society."

"How formidable?" Margaret asked suspiciously.

His smile was meant to infuriate her. "You'll see."

"This is your wife?" Lavinia, the dowager countess of Thule, looked Margaret up and down as if she had come to apply for the position of parlor maid. She lived in a large townhouse on Portland Square owned by her son, and the entire family was obviously terrified of her. "I heard that you had to marry for money, Thorsway, but the girl doesn't look too common."

Margaret cleared her throat. "I can speak for myself, my lady, and I can hear you quite clearly."

Lady Thule shuddered and continued to direct her comments at Alistair. "That *voice!* What on earth can we do about it?" She shook her head. "She'll have to say as little as possible until we can teach her to speak properly!"

"I like my wife's accent," Alistair said and squeezed Margaret's hand. "It is original and refreshing."

"Well, that might be so in Yorkshire, but in Town, it *will not do!*"

Alistair guided Margaret to the seat opposite the countess. "I have to go and speak to Mark, I'll leave you two to get acquainted."

Margaret shot him a murderous glance as he left the room and squared her shoulders as the countess offered her some tea.

"Thank you." She set the tea beside her. "It is very kind of you to invite us to dinner. Our cook had disappeared with most of the staff."

"Farrell was a fool who could never keep his servants." Lady Thule sipped her tea. "If I were you, I would start afresh."

"That is exactly what I intend to do," Margaret agreed. "Is there a hiring agency you recommend?"

"Ask my son's wife. She deals with the domestic matters in this house."

"Thank you, I will." Margaret picked up her cup, aware that the countess was watching her intently, and barely refrained from using two hands, slurping the contents, and belching.

"You are quite well-mannered."

"We do have manners up north, my lady," Margaret replied sweetly. "We are not entirely savage."

Lady Thule regarded her with faint approval. "It would seem Alistair has married a woman with backbone."

"I'm not afraid to speak my mind or stand up for myself if necessary." Margaret held her companion's gaze. "But I am aware that I have no experience of London society. I will need help to learn how to navigate my way through it so as not to embarrass my husband or sister-in-law."

"I'm glad that you know your limits." Lady Thule sniffed. "You at least look like a lady, and once you have visited a more fashionable dressmaker, I will make sure that you *look* the part of a duchess."

Margaret held her tongue and sipped her tea. If it were up to her, she would have a few choice words to say to the stuck-up countess, but Phoebe needed to be introduced properly into society, and Margaret didn't have a clue how to accomplish that. She devoutly hoped that Alistair would not wish to live permanently in London, or she feared she and Lady Thule might come to blows...

"I will expect you here tomorrow at two, Margaret." The countess was still talking. "I will summon my dressmaker to attend you."

"Does she not have a shop I could visit?" Margaret inquired.

"A *shop*?" Lady Thule looked appalled. "You are the Duchess of Thorsway, my dear, tradespeople come to *you*."

ALISTAIR WAS STILL LAUGHING at his wife's excellent imitation of his haughty great-aunt when they arrived back at their townhouse. There were no lights on, and Clarkson looked grim as he opened the door.

"Bloody butler's buggered off and so has the cook."

"Good, that saves me the job of firing them." Alistair handed Clarkson his hat and cane. "Is my sister all right?"

"Yes, Eileen's been keeping an eye on her. She made her some gruel, and she ate well before falling back to sleep."

"I'll go and check on her." Margaret headed for the stairs, her bonnet swinging in her hand.

Clarkson waited until she'd disappeared before he spoke again. "That Dr. McNeil tried to get in here this evening. Asking about Miss Phoebe, he was."

"Did he," Alistair said grimly. "I assume you told him to leave and never show his face again?"

"I did, sir, but not in quite the same words." Clarkson cleared his throat. "He said he'd accompanied Lady Hellion to London.

"What?" Alistair went still. "Was she with him?"

"No, my lord, but he did deliver a message from her." Clarkson handed over a sealed note.

"Damn and blast," Alistair muttered as he went through into the drawing room where Clarkson had at least lit the lamps and dealt with the fire.

"Mr. Lang arrived, my lord. I told him to take his pick of the bedrooms, but that whichever one he chose he had to clean it out himself. He took it very well, considering. He's gone to bed now and will see you in the morning."

Alistair sighed. "I don't suppose you managed to replenish the brandy supply, did you?"

"Well, you'd be wrong about that, my lord." Clarkson grinned at him. "I just happened to be going past the pub at the end of the road, and I got us some." He nodded toward the right side of the room. "It's on the sideboard. Help yourself."

"It is at moments like this that I remember why I haven't fired you." Alistair took the glass Clarkson had set next to the bottle, filled it with the cheap brandy, and swallowed it down, only shuddering slightly. "Thank you."

"You're welcome, and you owe me a guinea."

Alistair poured himself another glass and raised an eyebrow. "*How* much?"

"For my time and effort, your grace," Clarkson said primly.

"Which included you already drinking half the bottle?" Alistair got out his purse and searched through his coins. "I don't have a guinea. Add it to your wages for the quarter."

"A crown will do."

Alistair tossed the coin over. "Did you get something to eat?"

"Yes, I bought me and Eileen meat pies." Clarkson turned to the door. "Not sure what we're going to do about breakfast tomorrow, but we'll muddle through."

"Thank you for your vigilance, today," Alistair said.

"Don't you worry, I'll keep them out." Clarkson nodded at his employer. "I'm not letting any harm come to Miss Phoebe, I can tell you that."

Alistair opened the note, which informed him that his stepmother had taken up residence with her companion at Grillons Hotel and requested that he visit her as soon as possible.

After he finished his second brandy, Alistair made sure that the lights were out, and the fire contained, before he went up the stairs. He paused in the open door of the dressing room that separated the two main suites and observed his wife, who was contorting her body in a very peculiar way.

"Do you require some assistance?"

She jumped and tried to look over her shoulder at him. "I can't unbutton my gown properly. Something is stuck."

He strolled over to her. "Indeed it is. Where is Eileen?"

"She's staying with Phoebe."

"Then you will have to allow me to be your maid tonight." Alistair dropped a kiss on the exposed nape of her neck. "It has been quite a trying day, has it not?"

He decided not to mention that his stepmother and her doctor were already pounding at their door. He had other more amorous intentions that such information would destroy.

"It's even worse here than up at Hellsdown Park. At least the staff there wanted to stay on." Margaret sighed as he eased the disobedient button free. "Oh, that's better."

"You are most welcome." He kept unbuttoning her, his hands steady, his gaze fixed on the gradual display of her skin. Making love in Frederica's house had seemed impossible somehow. He suddenly realized how badly he'd missed his wife. "Are you very tired?"

"I am quite tired, yes." She leaned back against him as her dress fell to the floor. He wrapped an arm around her waist and kissed her throat.

"Would you consider staying awake just long enough for me to make love to you?"

Her deep chuckle made him hard. "I'm sure I could manage that."

"I promise I'll be quick."

She pulled away from him and took off her corset and shift, leaving her in just her stockings before moving over to the bed. She glanced at him over her shoulder.

"Well, come on, then."

He walked slowly over to the bed and stripped off his clothes, aware that she was watching him and enjoying her reaction. He slid his hand down over his stomach and cupped his balls, his thumb coming to rest on his shaft.

"See anything you like?"

"Oh, yes." She beckoned for him to join her on the bed. "I have... missed you, and this."

He pinned her to the sheets, spreading her thighs wide with his knee. "This? Being naked and ready to take me inside you while I kiss and caress every inch of your skin?"

She nodded as he bent toward her and kissed her soft, willing mouth. "I love the way you have no shame in wanting me back."

"Should I feel shame?" She eyed him uncertainly.

"No, never, not with me." He trailed kisses over her throat to her bosom and set about making her nipples as hard and wanting as his cock. He slid one hand down over her stomach and settled his fingers against her already slippery flesh. "I love the way you are so wet for me, too."

She moaned as he plunged two fingers deep inside her and

thumbed her bud until she was raising her hips against each thrust. He loved this uncomplicated coupling of mutual need where the world of debts, class, and difference no longer mattered, and she was simply his.

Her strong, capable fingers clasped the back of his neck, holding him fast against her breast as he grazed her nipple with his teeth. She gasped his name, her body convulsing against his thrusting fingers, driving him mad with need.

He eased back and slid his stiff cock inside her, pausing only when he was fully embedded to experience the sensation of her clenching flesh gripping his hardness.

He breathed out slowly and raised his head, only to find she'd shut her eyes and was not aware of his regard.

"Duchess," he ordered. "Look at me." She opened her eyes and he smiled down at her. "That's better."

"Why?" She sounded almost as breathless as he did.

"Because I like to watch you when you come."

Her already rosy cheeks took on a darker hue. "I suspect I looked hideous."

"When you lose control, scream my name, and scratch my back?" He eased away and then rocked into her. "When your eyes go dark and wide, and all you care about at that moment is my cock filling you and the pleasure awaiting you?"

He kissed her slowly and lavishly. "If you hate it so much, then perhaps I should make you wait awhile, delay the inevitable, so to speak."

She glared at him and he smiled. "Maybe I'll hold back until you are begging me to finish it, to let you come? *Begging* me, duchess."

"You wouldn't—" She clutched at his shoulder.

"Oh, I would." He settled himself deep inside her, and drew her hands over her head. "In fact, now I feel compelled to do so. Watch and learn, my duchess, and let's hope both of us survive the experience."

CHAPTER FOURTEEN

"*Well*, that at least is settled, Mr. Lang. Tell the agency that we will hire all three footmen, the boot boy, and the four maids we have seen so far." Margaret smiled at her husband's new secretary. "I must confess that I expected the process to take much longer than this, but the quality of the applicants is very high."

"Yes, your grace. We certainly have more choice than we did up north." Mr. Lang nodded as he wrote something in his notebook. "Now we just need a butler, a cook, a housekeeper, and an entire stable yard."

Margaret checked the list he had given her. "We are interviewing cooks and housekeepers later this afternoon. Let's hope we are equally as lucky."

"You ask excellent questions, your grace." Mr. Lang looked approvingly at her. "And, if you don't mind me saying, you have a formidable air about you."

Margaret stood up and stretched. "I suppose there isn't any point in asking what might be for luncheon?"

"Unless there is anything left over from that magnificent

breakfast you cooked this morning, then we'll probably have to get something in." Mr. Lang sighed. "The quicker we find a cook, the better."

After waking early and going down to the kitchen to make sure the range was still alight, Margaret had ended up cooking eggs, frying ham, and making toast for her husband and the rest of their staff. They'd all sat down together at the kitchen table, marveled at her competence, and enjoyed her food. For the first time in a long while, Margaret had felt really useful. Being able to feed her family had always been important to her.

"I have to go and visit Lady Thule at two," Margaret said. "But I intend to be back by four. If I am delayed, please go ahead with the interviews. I trust your judgment."

"Thank you, your grace." Mr. Lang bowed. "If you are not present, I will draw up a shortlist for you to peruse at your leisure."

Margaret headed for the door. "Do you know where his grace went off to in such a hurry this morning?"

Mr. Lang paused to hold open the door for her. "I believe he said he was going to Grillons Hotel, your grace. I have no idea why."

Neither did Margaret, but she had already decided she was not going to be the kind of wife who expected her husband to be dancing attentively at her side at all times. Alistair had many acquaintances in town and a dukedom to maintain, which meant many meetings with financial institutions and their owners. He had also married her for her money.

She had just stepped into the entrance hall when there was a knock on the door, and Clarkson went to open it.

"What do you want?" he growled in a most inappropriate and unwelcoming way.

"Good afternoon, I was wondering if I might leave my card?" The man on the doorstep bowed. "I was a good friend of

Farrell's. I wanted to express my condolences for his death and meet the new duke."

"He's not here," Clarkson said.

"Then will you take my card?"

Clarkson gave a long-suffering sigh. "Give it here, then." Without giving the man any further chance to reply, he took the card, and closed the door. "Silly bugger."

Margaret went over to him. "That is hardly the way to behave toward our guests, Clarkson."

"He wasn't one of ours. He's a friend of the bloke what's dead. From what I can tell, none of those men are worth knowing, your grace."

"Surely that's up to me to decide?" Margaret asked.

"Nope, because you've only got to deal with the ladies." Clarkson gave her a stern look. "No gentleman would come here expecting to speak to you when your husband's not present. That wouldn't be proper at all."

Margaret repressed her thoughts as to the idea of Clarkson telling her what was proper, took the visiting card, and read the engraved script.

"The Honorable Garston Pritchard."

Clarkson snorted. "He didn't look very honorable to me."

"I think that's a form of address for the son of a titled gentleman." Since her marriage, Margaret had been avidly studying the old copy of Debretts she had found in the Hellsdown Park library.

"I know *that*." Clarkson gave her a look.

He opened the door again and stared out. "He's buggered off nicely, and there's a fancy carriage with a crest on the side stopped outside, which I reckon is for you, your grace."

Margaret glanced over at the clock and turned to the stairs. "It appears that Lady Thule is expecting me to arrive earlier than I planned. Will you inform Mr. Lang that I will be unable to join him for lunch?"

Clarkson chuckled. "Don't worry, your grace. I'll take him down the pub with me. He'd probably much prefer it anyway."

Margaret hurried upstairs to put on her coat and bonnet, checked that Phoebe was awake and that Eileen was aware of her plans, and went back down to the hall.

"You shouldn't be going off like that on your own," Clarkson observed as he opened the front door for her. "His nibs wouldn't like it."

"I'm sure Lady Thule isn't planning on kidnapping me," Margaret said tartly. "And I suspect I can make it unaided from the house to the carriage."

"Good, because it's starting to rain." He looked her up and down. "I don't have an umbrella, and I don't want to get my feet wet, so off you go."

Margaret slammed the door hard after she went through it and picked up her skirts to descend the steps down to the pavement.

"May I assist you, ma'am?"

She startled as a hand came up under her elbow.

"Thank you." She disengaged herself from the man's firm grip as one of the footmen accompanying the coach sprang down to open the door for her.

"Am I perhaps, addressing the new Duchess of Thorsway?"

"Yes." Margaret looked searchingly up at the man's face.

He bowed. "I apologize for my bad manners, but may I introduce myself? I'm Pritchard. I was a good friend of the late Lord Farrell—in fact I was with him the night he died."

He paused expectantly, but Margaret didn't speak, so he continued. "I was hoping to have a quiet word with you about what happened that night."

"With me?" Margaret wrinkled her nose. "Why not with my husband?"

"Because what I have to say might enrage him." He hesitated.

"I thought that as his wife, you should be made aware of the kind of man you have inadvertently married."

Margaret stared at him for a long moment, taking in the lines of dissipation already showing around his hard, unsmiling mouth.

"What if I simply tell my husband you have approached me, and that you claim to have information against him?"

Mr. Pritchard shrugged. "Then I will submit my 'information' to the correct authorities, and let them deal with him in the courts. I assumed that as a young bride, you would care what happened to your husband, and would wish to protect his reputation, but perhaps I was mistaken."

Behind her, the Thule footman gave a discreet cough and shifted his feet, reminding her that it was pouring rain.

Margaret made her decision. "Perhaps you could give me your address, and I will write to you for further details."

"A pleasure, your grace." He offered her another card. "I look forward to hearing from you."

She got into the carriage, aware that she was now rather wet, and considered what had just happened. Mr. Pritchard seemed to be implying that Farrell's death had something to do with Alistair. She already knew her husband had been present that night along with Viscount Grafton, but had heard nothing at Hellsdown Park to implicate him in any dastardly plot to inherit his cousin's title.

She looked out of the window at the dreary streets. Everyone at Hellsdown had disliked Farrell intensely. Was it possible that they were so glad to be rid of him that no one had thought to inquire as to the particulars of his actual death? Despite their indolent exteriors she couldn't ignore the fact that both Alistair and Francis Grafton had been in the army and were perfectly capable of killing.

Should she tell Alistair? Or would it be better to extract as much information from Mr. Pritchard before handing the matter over to her husband? She was an excellent judge of character and unlikely to be bamboozled by a man like Mr. Pritchard. In truth, the thought of being useful to Alistair was quite exhilarating.

The carriage stopped, and the footman opened the door for her. Margaret picked up her reticule and prepared to descend, her mind made up. She would deal with Mr. Pritchard in her own way, and hope that Alistair would never have to hear a word about it.

～

"GOOD MORNING, MY LADY." Alistair bowed to his stepmother who sat on the sofa in her suite at Grillons. She was still in her dressing robe, if a gauzy confection of ruffles and lace could be considered such a mundane garment. "I apologize for my early arrival. Would you prefer it if I leave and return when you are dressed?"

"Oh, Alistair, sit down and don't be such a prude." She laughed and patted the seat beside her. "I swear that you have become incredibly stuffy since you became a duke."

"I prefer to stand, my lady," Alistair returned stiffly, aware that he might just be proving her point. "I am wondering why you felt it necessary to follow me to London?"

She opened her eyes wide. "Dear Lord, do you really believe that my every action is dictated by you? If so, I regret to inform you that you are sadly mistaken." She pushed a displaced curl into place. "With Phoebe safely in your hands, I decided I *deserved* a trip to London."

"With Phoebe's doctor in attendance?"

She chuckled. "He is no longer her doctor, he is my friend, and I am a widow, which means I am quite above reproach."

"He certainly seems very taken with you."

"Do I detect a hint of jealousy?" Frederica asked archly. "Perhaps I should warn your wife that you still have feelings for me, after all."

"I believe you've already tried that. Luckily, Margaret isn't a fool," Alistair said repressively. "You asked to see me. What do you want?"

"I merely wanted to advise you of my presence in London." She bit her lip. "I knew that if you discovered I was here without me notifying you of my intent, you would be angry with me and perhaps force me out of my house even more quickly."

"I am not 'forcing' you to leave," Alistair said. "I have explained my reasoning quite clearly. If you choose to stay, then you will have to deal with the consequences."

"You are cruel." Her eyes filled with tears, and she looked away from him, one hand grasping the lace flounces of her robe over her bosom.

Alistair didn't reply. What was there to say? He was no longer willing to allow her to ride roughshod over him, especially now, when he suspected her involvement in a scheme to poison his sister. At least if she was in London, he supposed he knew where she was.

"I intend to look at property here," Frederica said, changing the subject with a suddenness Alistair had become used to in the past. She hated to be challenged and had always possessed the ability to quickly move onto something else and pretend the previous conversation had never happened. "Would you be willing to allow the Thorsway solicitors to act on my behalf, if I find something I like?"

Alistair shrugged. "As the affairs of the marquisate are now part of my estate, I can see no harm in that."

"Thank you," Frederica said. "Dr. McNeil has offered to accompany me on my search."

"How kind of him." Alistair inclined his head.

She looked up at him. "When may we come and visit

Phoebe?"

"She is not well enough to receive visitors at this time," Alistair said.

"I am hardly a visitor," Frederica objected. "I am her stepmother."

"After consulting with her new physician, be assured that I will inform you when she is able and *willing* to receive you." Alistair bowed. "If that is all you have to say, then I will be on my way."

"There is one more little thing," Frederica said hesitantly.

"If you need money," Alistair said, "I regret to inform you that I have none to spare."

"Really? Not even after you married a mill heiress? I find that quite hard to believe, but no matter."

Alistair smiled, but said nothing until she started speaking again.

"I had a letter from Bottomly. Do you know him?"

"I believe he was a friend of Farrell's." Alistair tried hard not to let his wariness at this unexpected development show.

"He wrote me a most *peculiar* letter, offering condolences for Farrell's death, and asking whether you had attended *your* father on his death bed." She peered up at him through her lashes. "Do you have any idea why he might ask me that?"

"Seeing as I wasn't at my father's deathbed, surely the question is moot?" Alistair kept his tone light and disinterested. "If you bothered to reply, I do hope you corrected his mistaken assumptions."

"Indeed I did." She paused. "He hasn't replied, so one must assume he was satisfied by my answers."

"If I see him when I'm out and about, I will certainly ask him why he wants to know," Alistair said and bowed again. "Good day, my lady."

"Goodbye, Alistair." She smiled up at him. "Perhaps you

might bring your wife to have tea with me here, seeing as I am apparently barred from my old home."

"As the house belongs to the dukedom, and Farrell occupied it, I doubt you've even set foot in it." Alistair turned to the door. "But I'll certainly pass on the invitation, never fear."

He finally managed to leave and went down the stairs to the entrance of the hotel. As usual, his stepmother had given him a lot to think about, none of it good. Her revelation about Bottomly was worrying and, worse, she was astute enough to realize it might cause him a problem and pursue it.

He decided to go to his club and see if he could ascertain where Bottomly was likely to be found. Margaret was safely at his great aunt's, Clarkson was guarding the house, and Nash was taking care of Phoebe, which meant he could focus on tracking down his prey.

He'd known Bottomly at school. He had always struck Alistair as a follower rather than a leader, the sort of man who admired fools like his cousin Farrell and enjoyed associating with them. He'd never thought Bottomly would be the kind of man to write to Frederica in an attempt to gain information without someone else pulling the strings.

Had Frederica been the one to contact Bottomly? He paused on the corner of the street. Had she heard rumors of what had happened the night Farrell had died and reached out to a gullible man in an attempt to get information to damage Alistair still further? He reminded himself not to get too carried away. Maybe she had a point that he always thought she was out to get him. Francis had been with him that night and so had Dr. Nettles. He had witnesses as to what had happened and, therefore, nothing to worry about.

If he'd been a betting man, he would've wagered that Pritchard would be the one causing problems. He'd always disliked Alistair and had been Farrell's closest friend for years.

Even as Alistair hailed a hackney cab, the tenseness in his

stomach refused to relax. He trusted his gut. It had saved his life on more than one occasion. Something wasn't right, and, until he cleared it up, he would not rest easily. What with dealing with Frederica, making sure that Margaret and Phoebe were protected, and saving the dukedom, he predicted his days were going to be remarkably busy.

Francis was due to join him in London to help further smooth the complicated reconstruction of the ducal finances and repair the all-important personal relationships that Farrell had so carelessly destroyed. Despite his reputation, Francis was begrudgingly recognized as a tough negotiator and was well known in the financial community, whereas Alistair had kept far away from anything involving finance after his stepmother's coup. He therefore had a lot to learn, and he was very grateful both for Francis's help and Margaret's keen-eyed financial acumen.

He leaned back against the worn seat and briefly closed his eyes. London was exhausting at the best of times, and he'd barely settled in. He pictured Margaret sleeping in their bed and found himself smiling. She might have married him under unusual circumstances, but it was rapidly becoming clear to him that she was the perfect wife. She held him accountable, she didn't allow him to divert her attention away from the matter in hand—a skill he thought he'd perfected—and she met him as an equal in bed.

Of course, the vast differences in their upbringings were bound to cause the occasional misunderstanding, but he relished her opinions, liked being challenged, and enjoyed arguing her into bed. She also didn't demand that he love her above all else, something Frederica had insisted on. Frederica's emotional demands had exhausted him and made him realize that love never came without a price and was therefore to be avoided.

His smile widened. In all the turmoil surrounding him, it

was good to know his wife was firmly on his side, and, as his friend, would always be honest with him, even as he sought to conceal certain things from her... She wouldn't like that at all, but, as soon as he had solved the problems, he would confess everything, and accept her wrath with due humility.

"Whites!" the hackney cab driver bellowed as the carriage came to a halt.

"Thank you." Alistair gave him some coins and went up to the door of his club. It was raining hard now, and the streets were almost empty. He would spend some time greeting old friends, getting the latest gossip, and find a way to bring Bottomly into the conversation as unobtrusively as possible.

Once he had discovered the man's whereabouts, he would pay him a visit, and hopefully find out exactly what was going on.

~

"I DON'T LIKE IT," Margaret repeated as the dressmaker looked inquiringly back at the dowager. "I'm too old for frothy lace and pastel colors, and I will not wear them."

"With all due respect, my lady, I tend to agree with the duchess." Madame Violet, the dressmaker, straightened up. "With her strong coloring and height, she will look magnificent in darker colors and jewel tones."

Lady Thule sighed. "Make her look matronly and stern if you must. Such plainness in dress brings to mind a governess, not a duchess."

"We will compensate for the lack of additional trimmings with expensive and unique fabrics, my lady." The dressmaker winked at Margaret. "I can assure you that her grace will look just as she ought."

"Hmmph." Lady Thule glared at Margaret. "If I allow you your way on this, you must accept my decision as to your court gown, which I will pay for. It is *imperative* that it follows the correct protocols."

"I will certainly cede to your superior knowledge on that matter, my lady," Margaret agreed. "One would not wish to offend."

"I will also teach you how to curtsey properly to your monarch and how to back out of the receiving room without tripping over your feet, standing on your train or, even worse, falling to the floor."

"It sounds quite intimidating," Margaret confessed as she put on her gown and came to sit beside her hostess.

"It is, and it is meant to be." Lady Thule fixed her with an terrifying stare. "And I intend for you to represent our family properly."

"I'll certainly do my best."

Margaret had never seen a member of the royal family, let alone met one in person. The idea of being dressed up like a doll in wide panniers, ostrich feathers, and a train, and paraded in front of the queen and her family was, quite frankly, ridiculous. She knew Adam might tease her but would secretly be delighted that she had risen so high, and that Lottie would pout and laughingly wish that it had been her.

Lady Thule pointed her closed fan at Margaret. "You will not fail. It is not allowed."

"Will Phoebe need to be introduced as well?" Margaret asked, anxious to leave the subject of her shortcomings behind.

"Not immediately. A lot of young girls wait until they are married, these days."

"Then, at least I will not have to worry about her." Margaret turned to the dressmaker, who had finished packing up her things, and jumped to her feet. "Thank you for coming. Do you need any help down to the carriage?"

"No, thank you, your grace." Madame Violet smiled at her. "I will visit you at Thorsway House as soon as I have something ready to show you."

She left, and Margaret returned to her seat to find the dowager scowling at her.

"You do not offer to help the staff!"

"Why not?" Margaret rang for some refreshments. "She was carrying rather a lot.

"Because it is not done! Being familiar with those of the serving class leads to a lack of respect and a blurring of the lines."

"So?" Margaret frowned in return. "Surely, respect is earned?"

"Good Lord! Has Alistair married a radical?" Lady Thule pressed a hand to her bosom. "I'll wager you'll be telling me next that every man should have the vote!"

"Oh, I'd go further than that." Margaret smiled sweetly. "I don't see why women shouldn't vote, too."

Luckily, the maid arrived with the tea because Margaret feared her hostess might explode into a thousand pieces. She had to admit to a certain amount of enjoyment in battling with the dowager. She also knew that society would judge her far more harshly, and that she had better decide how she was going to deal with it. Should she remain quiet, hide her "common" accent, and attempt to pass unnoticed through the ranks of the peerage, or should she try her hardest to be herself and ignore those who had already decided she was beneath them?

Apparently, because she and Alistair were still officially in mourning for the duke and his son, she could avoid balls and parties until the following season, but private dinners and the occasional musical evening were deemed acceptable. Lady Thule was determined to introduce her into society, and Margaret was more than willing to accept the help. She didn't want to let Alistair down, and although he might laugh and say it was all nonsense, she knew in her heart that it was still his world, and that he expected to be part of it.

As Lady Thule started lecturing her on the correct way to deal with morning callers, Margaret settled down to listen. She'd married not only a man, but also a duke, and she would just have to live with it.

CHAPTER FIFTEEN

hree days later, Alistair walked into the breakfast room and found his wife already at the table. The pleasing smell of sausages and bacon rose to greet him from the silver-covered dishes on the side table.

"I assume we now have a cook?"

"Yes, her name is Mrs. White." Margaret smiled up at him. "She seems very pleasant."

Alistair filled his plate and took the seat opposite her. He'd marveled at his wife's quiet confidence in the kitchen and had enjoyed sitting at the kitchen table eating with his loyal staff. "I will reserve judgment until I have tasted her offerings. I suspect she will not be as proficient as you. It's good to know that if Ruby Delisle gets her way and the aristocracy are brought down, we'd still be able to survive."

Margaret raised an eyebrow and returned to her correspondence.

"What are all those?" Alistair pointed at the growing pile of cards by her elbow.

"Invitations. I was going to ask you what you want to do about them. Lady Thule says it is acceptable for us to attend private dinners and musical soirees held in people's homes, but not to go to balls, public parties, or the theater." She glanced down at the stack of cards. "The thing is, I don't know any of these people."

"Then hand them over, and I'll go through them," he offered obligingly.

"Finish your breakfast first. I doubt any of them are emergencies, and I haven't finished going through everything yet."

He added more food to his plate and she poured him another cup of coffee, and proceeded to open the next letter, and then the next.

"You have something from Grillons." She passed it over, her nose wrinkling. "Doused in perfume."

He took the folded billet. "Ah, that would be from my mistress, it's quite admirable that she has taught herself to read and write."

Margaret's head came up, and she stared at him.

"Your mistress?"

"Do you really think I would tell you if it was?" he asked. "And why would I need one when I have you?"

She glanced down at her plate. "I have no illusions about our marriage, sir. You are quite free to seek out... others."

He sat back in his chair, the note lying unopened beside his now tapping fingers.

"Do you really value yourself so little?" His question came out more sharply than he had intended, perhaps because her words had hurt him more than he had anticipated. "You must know I was merely jesting."

She finally looked up at him. "Yes, I've noticed that you do that quite often when you are trying to avoid having a real discussion about something." She nodded at the note. "Who is it really from?"

He considered her for a long, fuming moment. "Lady Hellion."

"She's in London?" Margaret asked, and then her eyes narrowed. "You went to Grillons four days ago. Has she been there for all this time and you haven't bothered to *mention* it to me?"

He shrugged. "I'm mentioning it now, aren't I?"

"Only because I have forced the discussion on you." She shook her head. "In truth, I'd rather it had been your mistress."

"Why's that?" he asked with a lightness he was far from feeling.

"Because Lady Hellion is—" She abruptly stopped speaking.

"Is what?" Alistair knew he should stop, but he'd never learned to be careful.

"Too important to you." Margaret rose from the table and shoved in her chair with unnecessary force. "If you will excuse me, I have a dressmaking appointment in half an hour, and then I will be going out. Please let me know which invitations you wish me to accept and which to decline."

"Margaret."

She paused at the door to look back at him.

"Maybe this is why I use humor, to avoid upsetting you unnecessarily?" Alistair inquired. "Now we are at odds for no reason at all."

"No reason? When you deliberately concealed the arrival of the woman who you believe poisoned your sister? How am I supposed to keep Phoebe safe with Lady Hellion around?"

"*That's* why you are angry with me?" He raised an eyebrow.

"I—" She raised her chin. "Your decision not to inform me of her arrival was unfair and shows how little you trust me."

"You were the one who assumed I had a mistress!" he countered. "Where's your trust in *me*?"

"I did *not*—" She drew herself up and glared at him for several seconds before letting out a frustrated breath. "It is obviously pointless trying to argue with you."

"Which is what I originally suggested." Alistair smiled sweetly. "I don't like arguing."

"You are infuriating!"

She turned on her heel and walked away, leaving him alone at the table. A minute later he heard a door slam shut upstairs and winced. Didn't she understand that he'd been trying to protect her? Even as he justified his behavior, a small voice in his head insisted that his wife had a point.

Why hadn't he told her that Frederica was in town? He glanced up at the ceiling, but everything had gone quiet again. Why did she care if he spoke to his stepmother?

"You know why," Alistair muttered out loud to himself. "That's why you didn't mention it in the first place."

He considered following Margaret upstairs and begging for forgiveness while persuading her into bed and realized that would simply prove her point. But if his wife didn't care if he took a mistress, why did she care if he spent time with his stepmother?

He feared he knew the answer to that question, too. Margaret might insist that their marriage was merely a financial bargain, but he was fairly certain she cared for him...

"Devil take it!" Alistair flung down his napkin and got to his feet. And there it was—another subject that he carefully avoided because he didn't want to admit that he'd started to care for her, too. So much for there being honesty between them.

MARGARET WAS BRUSHING the mud off the hem of her coat with some force and muttering under her breath when the door opened, and the last person she wanted to see appeared. Her husband sauntered in, one hand in his pocket, and halted beside the four-poster bed, the epitome of fashionable elegance.

"I probably owe you an apology," he ventured.

"Probably?" Margaret refused to look at him.

"I was… hurt when you assumed I would take a mistress."

She stopped what she was doing and slowly raised her head. "*Hurt?*"

He shrugged. "Yes. I would not have married you if I intended to break my vows."

"Then perhaps it is I who should be apologizing to you," Margaret replied, aware that as gratifying as this was, he was still not prepared to talk about his obsession with his stepmother.

He offered her an enticing smile. "Perhaps we should apologize to each other? It never occurred to me that you would expect me to take a mistress."

She shrugged. "You are a peer of the realm, and, from what I have observed, such behavior is commonplace amongst your set."

"Not for me."

"Then, as I said, I was wrong." She offered him a direct look.

"And I was wrong to tease you about such a matter."

She waited for him to expound on his words to include why he had deceived her about his stepmother, but he had apparently finished speaking.

"Well, then, as it appears that we have agreed to keep our marriage vows, the matter is settled, and we can both proceed with our days. As I mentioned, I am expecting Madame Violet any minute now." She looked expectantly at him.

He shoved a hand through his hair. "I know that because we were virtual strangers when we married, that there are bound to be difficulties between us, but I hope that we can continue to be honest with each other."

"Indeed." Her fingers curled into her palm. He was a fine one to talk about honesty when he still hadn't told her what his stepmother was doing in London. "I will certainly bear that in mind in our future interactions."

She turned back to her coat, horribly aware that he was still standing there. She hoped he would have the sense to leave before she threw the brush at his stupid blond head. After being part of a plain-speaking family who settled their disagreements in a straightforward manner, dealing with her chameleon-like husband was sometimes exhausting.

"I will see you later, then, duchess."

He finally left, and Margaret's shoulders sagged. His refusal to discuss his stepmother made her feel better about concealing her communications with Mr. Pritchard. She had agreed to meet him at two in the afternoon beside the Serpentine, where he had promised to reveal all to her. If Alistair believed he could deal with Frederica without her assistance, she could certainly deal with Mr. Pritchard.

Margaret sighed. There was no point in denying it. After six months of marriage, she had come to care very deeply for her husband. She sensed that admitting it would not endear her to him, and that he might even turn it into a joke, which would hurt her very deeply. It was a lowering thought, which was why she truly wished to solve the issue with Mr. Pritchard. If she couldn't tell Alistair that she cared for him, perhaps she could show it in another more practical way?

"DUCHESS." Mr. Pritchard bowed low and offered her his arm.

"Mr. Pritchard." Margaret signaled for Eileen to fall in behind them as they took a path down toward the water. "Are there likely to be many people out walking here today?"

He glanced down at her. "Are you worried about being seen with me?"

"Hardly. I doubt more than half a dozen people in London know who I am," Margaret said serenely. "I was concerned on your behalf."

"Don't worry about me, your grace. I'm fairly certain that my reputation will stand it."

Margaret focused her attention on the pleasing vista opening up in front of her. There were several majestic swans and ducks floating on the pond, which was surrounded by large trees and pleasant paths.

"You said that you had information about my husband." Margaret had no wish to spend more time than necessary alone with the obnoxious Mr. Pritchard. "Obviously, I am concerned about his reputation and wish to hear more."

Her companion sighed heavily. "I fear you will be shocked, duchess, *shocked* at the depravity and dishonesty of the man you have married."

"How so?" Before he could answer her, Margaret instantly regretted her direct question, and tried to imagine how her sister Lottie would've answered it. "I mean, I cannot imagine that my beloved husband has done anything wrong; he is a true gentleman."

"Alas, you are mistaken, your grace." Mr. Pritchard paused dramatically. "On the night in question, your husband and his accomplice, Francis Grafton, deliberately attempted to lure me and my companion away from the study so that they had Farrell alone and in their power!"

Margaret gasped and pressed her gloved hand to her lips. "I cannot believe such a thing!"

"Believe it, your grace. Unfortunately for them, I returned too quickly and saw what happened through the half-open door. Your husband attacked Farrell with the poker, bashed his head in, and then ran crying to the doctor that his dear cousin had fallen and banged his head on the fireplace."

"Why would he do such a thing?" Margaret let her voice quiver.

"Because he wanted to be a duke, your grace, why else?"

"Did you instantly report this matter to the coroner and the local magistrate, sir?"

Mr. Pritchard spread his hands wide. "How could I, when they were all in the dukedom's pocket? Who would've believed *me*, an innocent bystander?"

Margaret halted beside the lake and looked up at Mr. Pritchard, who was enjoying his role far too much for her liking.

"Which is why you have come to me, because the authorities *will* believe me, and justice will be served." She gazed worshipfully up at him. "Thank you, sir. Thank you for offering me this opportunity to right a terrible wrong."

"Ah, I wouldn't recommend you doing that, your grace," her companion said hurriedly.

"Why ever not?"

"Because, firstly, no court will allow evidence from a man's wife, and secondly, legally your husband would still be the heir, and, as he has been confirmed by his peers, it is too late to take the title away from him."

Despite everything, Margaret could not help but admire his quick thinking.

"But I wouldn't care if I was no longer a duchess if that meant justice was served. I do believe you can still charge a duke of a crime?"

"Yes, he can be tried by a court of his peers in the House of Lords, but I still doubt they would convict him." Pritchard sighed. "And in the meantime, I live in fear that the current duke will destroy me."

"Why?" Margaret asked.

"Because he can," Mr. Pritchard said bitterly. "He has already spread rumors that I am in debt, and he's filled my father's ears with poisonous untruths, which have led to him cutting my allowance." He fixed his gaze on Margaret. "In fact, I don't know how I will be able to survive if my finances are not bolstered."

Margaret allowed a long pause to develop and for Mr. Pritchard to start to sweat before she answered him.

"I have lots of money. I could help you with that."

"Why on earth would you help me, your grace?" He stared at her. "I am the man who could bring your husband down?"

"Perhaps we could come to some mutually agreeable arrangement about that?" Margaret asked.

"Are you offering me a bribe, duchess?" He took a hasty step away from her. "Do I look like the kind of dishonorable man who would take money from a *woman*?"

She desperately wanted to say yes, and had to admit that she was quite enjoying herself at this point.

"Of course not!" She placed a hand over her heart. "It was so brave of you to come forward with this information at such risk to yourself. I believe you should be *rewarded*."

"Well, when you put it like that..." He nodded. "I can quite see the advantages to both sides."

Margaret smiled warmly at him. "Then will you consider how much money you would require to clear your name and your debts and let me know the total?"

"If I must." He sighed again. "You are very kind." He indicated the path ahead. "Would you like to walk on with me? It is such a fine afternoon and we are quite alone."

"That would be delightful." Margaret placed her hand on his arm.

After they had toured that particular area, he led her back up the slope toward the main carriageway, where she hoped the new Thorsway coachman would be awaiting her. It was far busier than when they had arrived. Margaret noticed several riders on horseback and fashionable conveyances driving slowly along the promenade.

When they reached her carriage, she inclined her head to Mr. Pritchard. "I will expect to hear from you, then, sir."

"Indeed, duchess." He bent to kiss her fingertips, and she

barely repressed a shudder. "You have been most understanding."

As she turned to get into the carriage, another vehicle slowed to go around them, and Margaret caught sight of the unmistakable face of Lady Hellion. The door was shut behind her, and she took her seat.

"Damn and blast it!" Margaret said in a very unladylike way. "Why on earth did she have to see me now?"

CHAPTER SIXTEEN

"*A*re you ready, Margaret?" Alistair went through the dressing room into the bedchamber, his cloak over his arm and his hat in his hand. "Aunt Lavinia hates unpunctuality."

"I am well aware of that."

He stopped in the doorway as she stood up, shook out her skirts and turned shyly toward him.

"What do you think?"

"You look beautiful."

She fixed him with a patient look. "We have had this discussion before, sir, and we agreed that beauty is beyond me and that I should strive for elegant."

Her gown was a dark green, with black embroidery and lace, and bared her shoulders and made her waist look tiny.

He walked forward and slowly circled her. "It suits you very well." He leaned in and kissed her throat. "Very well, indeed."

She shivered slightly and went to pick up her fan, shawl, and reticule that lay on the bed.

He watched her carefully, aware that she was quieter than usual.

"Are you worried about tonight?"

"Yes." She turned back to him. "Lady Thule believes I should try not to speak too much because I sound like a millhand. Do you agree with her?"

"What a stupid question!" Alistair said. "Of course not."

She gave a small, satisfied smile. "I told her you would say that."

"Well, thank God." He frowned at her. "I expect you to be my very own opinionated duchess who will not be cowed by anyone."

"I will do my best."

He took her shawl and placed it around her shoulders. "I wish I could bedeck you in jewels, but I fear our current financial situation will not allow for such luxuries."

She touched the delicate emerald necklace around her throat. "This is perfectly appropriate for this particular dress and occasion. In truth, Lady Thule warned me not to display my wealth like a vulgarian."

"She would." A laugh shook through him and then he thought better of it. "Is she upsetting you?"

"Not at all." She raised an eyebrow. "It is refreshing to meet someone who speaks the truth to one's face."

"Indeed." He held her gaze, noted the hint of defiance in it, and decided to proceed with caution. "Shall we go?"

Although his cousin and wife were the official hostesses of the gathering, Lady Thule had placed herself at the center of the proceedings and was the first to greet them when they arrived.

"Hmmph." She looked Margaret up and down. "You look quite acceptable."

"Thank you." Margaret curtsied.

"I have invited a carefully selected group of my friends to view you here in the privacy of my home, and I expect you to behave accordingly."

Alistair frowned. "My duchess is not a prize pig being judged at the county fair. Your guests will keep their opinions to themselves, or, if they truly wish to comment, I suggest you send them to speak to me."

"For goodness sake, Alistair." Aunt Lavinia tapped him on the arm with her fan. "You know nothing about the complexities of our current society, and I do. Now go and introduce your wife to the guests who are assembled in the drawing room, and leave the rest to me."

Alistair offered his great-aunt a glare that was returned in full measure, placed Margaret's gloved hand on his sleeve, and moved away. He immediately became aware that his duchess was shaking and drew her back into the shadows of the entrance hall.

"Don't let her upset you. If you wish to leave—"

She pressed her hand to his chest and raised her face. "You… you likened me to a prize-winning pig at a county fair."

He slowly grinned back at her. "I did, didn't I? I do apologize."

She was laughing so hard that he had to kiss her. The kiss turned wild until they were both breathless, and he was pressed fully against her. He eased away and she patted her hair.

"We should go in," she said unsteadily.

"Yes." He stayed where he was until she raised her eyebrows.

"What's wrong?"

He glanced down at his trousers. "Give me a moment, unless you wish to shock all the guests?"

"Oh." She blushed and bit her lip. "I see."

He took her hand again. "I'll just hide behind your skirts, which seems appropriate anyway."

They entered the drawing room and were immediately the center of attention. Alistair made sure he had a firm grip on Margaret's hand and turned to the first couple on his left.

"Duchess, may I present you to Lord and Lady Cooperdale?

The family has long been friends of the Thules and the Haralsons."

He proceeded around the room until his aunt joined them and supplied some of the missing names. From what he could see, she had gone to an immense amount of trouble to introduce his wife to people who would help her fit into society with as little fuss as possible. Despite their differences, he was grateful to her.

When dinner was announced, he reluctantly released Margaret's hand, and she was borne away to the opposite end of the long table by her dining partner. He couldn't hear what she was saying through all the chatter around him and also had to pay attention to his own companions.

The ladies left the room, leaving the gentlemen to their port, and talk turned to politics and horse racing. Lord Cooperdale nudged Alistair's elbow.

"Thank you for selling Farrell's racing stable. I acquired some excellent horses."

"You're welcome." Alistair liked Cooperdale, who was only about five years older than him. "I have no interest in racing and couldn't afford to keep them eating their heads off for no purpose."

"Farrell will be turning in his grave," Cooperdale said. "Are things really that dire with the dukedom?"

"Not now. It's more a question of priorities," Alistair explained. "For example, I'd rather have a sound roof over my head than a win at Newmarket."

His companion looked horrified. "I'm not sure if I could choose between those two things at all! I assume that your recent marriage has... helped things?"

"Indeed, if it hadn't been for my wife's dowry, I'd be facing a debtor's prison."

"That bad, eh?"

"Yes, I have much to be thankful for." Alistair nodded.

"Her grace was very pleasant. In truth, my wife was quite surprised by that, seeing as she had heard..." Cooperdale paused. "I wouldn't normally pass on gossip, but I think you need to hear this."

"What?" Alistair set his glass down on the table.

"That her grace was uncouth and badly spoken."

"I wonder who said that?"

"I'm not sure." Cooperdale finished his port. "I just thought you should know that it is being said."

"I appreciate that. Would you object if I asked your wife for more details?"

"Not at all. She thinks your duchess is very nice, so don't worry that she'd spread such a rumor."

Alistair helped himself to more port as the decanter was passed around again. He didn't have to think very hard to imagine who might be maligning his duchess, and he would make sure to address the matter as soon as possible.

"And did you attend school, your grace?"

Margaret turned toward the woman who had inserted her question into the cordial discussion about education she had been having with two of the older ladies by the fire.

"I was taught at home, ma'am."

"You had a governess?" Lady Tillington arched a condescending eyebrow.

"No, my mother taught us." Margaret smiled, but didn't receive one in reply. "She was an excellent teacher."

"She didn't have to work in the mill?" Lady Tillington asked with a slight titter.

There was a sharp intake of breath behind Margaret, and she became aware of the avid stillness around her as everyone waited for her reply.

"My father owned the mill. My mother stayed at home to raise her children."

"Oh! I suppose that does make a difference." Lady Tillington nodded. "I must have mistaken what I heard about you."

Margaret raised her chin. "What was that?"

"That you worked in the mill, yourself."

"Isabelle..." One of the older women leaned forward. "This is hardly an appropriate conversation. You are bordering on being impolite."

"When we were shorthanded, I worked, what of it?" Margaret asked. "Would you not have done the same?"

"Did you, indeed?" Lady Tillington's smile was victorious. "How *brave* of you to admit something so damning."

"Isabelle." Mrs. Godson, the woman beside Margaret frowned. "This is quite uncalled for. What the duchess did before her marriage has nothing to do with you. Personally, I have nothing but respect for any woman who has supported her family in whatever way necessary." She turned to Margaret, deliberately shielding her from Lady Tillington. "You were telling me about the schools you set up in your brother's mills; do, pray, continue."

Margaret started talking, aware that Lady Tillington had retreated to a corner with two of the other women and was now whispering and casting furtive glances back at the group still gathered around the fire.

"Please pay no attention to her, your grace. She does not represent the feelings of everyone here," Mrs. Godson murmured. "In truth, I look forward to many future stimulating conversations with you about how we can reform education in this country. Now that you have married a duke, you have more influence than you might imagine, my dear."

∽

LATER, on the way back in the carriage, Alistair took her hand in his.

"How did it go with the ladies?"

"Most of them were very pleasant." Margaret debated how much she wanted to tell him. She had a fair idea who might have been spreading gossip about her, seeing as there was only one other female member of the *ton* who had met her. She was quite capable of fighting her own battles and was more than willing to deal with Lady Hellion herself.

"It was very kind of your aunt to organize the dinner for us. I received several assurances that I would be called on in the next few days."

"That's excellent."

It occurred to her that he was looking quite distracted, too.

"Did you enjoy yourself?"

"Yes, it was nice to be among my peers and not feel like a beggar." He smiled and brought her hand to his lips. "Thank you for marrying me. Everyone thought you were delightful."

The carriage drew to a stop, and he got up and opened the door to help her down before the footman reached it. For the first time in over a week, she enjoyed coming into the house, which was finally well-staffed and clean.

"There is a note for you, your grace." The butler handed her a folded letter.

"Thank you." She paused to look at the direction. "I'll read this now."

Alistair had already shed his hat and cloak and was heading for the stairs.

"Are you coming, duchess?"

"In a moment." She smiled at him. "I have to attend to this matter and then make sure that Phoebe is well."

He went off up the stair, and she returned to the back parlor where she had established her desk and sewing basket. She lit a candle and opened the note.

Your Grace, a thousand pounds should prove sufficient for my needs, yours respectfully, Garston Pritchard.

She ripped up the note and cast it onto the embers of the fire before sitting down at her desk and writing a reply, and one other letter to her brother. After sealing and addressing the letters, she carried them back out to the hall where the butler was shutting up the house.

"Can you have both of these delivered tomorrow?"

"Yes, of course, your grace."

"Thank you." Margaret went up the stairs, knocked softly on Phoebe's door, and went in. Her sister-in-law was sitting up against the pillows reading a book. They had spent a lot of time together over the past weeks, and were well on the way to becoming good friends.

"Good evening, Phoebe." Margaret smiled. "It is good to see you looking so much better."

"I feel much better," Phoebe admitted. "Dr. Nash says I'm a medical marvel. He says he wants to speak to you and Alistair tomorrow about an experiment he wishes to perform." She set the book down. "How was the dinner party?"

Margaret grimaced. "Everyone was very nice—except for one lady who said she'd heard gossip that I worked in a mill."

"Who would know you well enough to spread that kind of rumor?" Phoebe asked.

"Guess," Margaret invited her.

"Not Frederica?" Phoebe curled her lip. "What am I saying? Of course she would do that. Did you tell Alistair?"

For the first time Margaret hesitated. "No, I—"

"I'm not surprised. He still thinks the world of her, doesn't he? I cannot understand it at all." Phoebe reached for Margaret's hand. "He was so in love with Frederica that Father deciding to marry her instead of him changed him immeasurably."

As Margaret didn't wish to know what Alistair was like when he was in love with another woman, she said nothing.

"I never liked her," Phoebe confided. "She doesn't like other women. We are all competition for her. She manipulated my father, she rarely let me see Alistair when he returned home, and she refused to allow me to attend your wedding."

"Well, we have you with us now," Margaret said and squeezed her hand. "And we will take care of you until you are better, and then launch you into society where you will meet your future husband, fall in love, and live happily ever after."

"Just like you and Alistair." Phoebe smiled and then yawned. "Please excuse me, I still get very tired."

"Then I will leave you in peace." Margaret rose from the bed and turned toward the door. "Goodnight, Phoebe, sleep well."

Margaret went out into the corridor, her steps slowing as she recalled Phoebe's words. Alistair didn't love her, he loved Frederica. It was blindingly obvious, and yet it still hurt. She stopped walking. But when had she decided that he *should* love her? That hadn't been part of the bargain she'd proposed at all. She'd offered him her money, and he had accepted it—that was it.

It was stupid of her to expect more. Just because her feelings toward him had deepened, didn't mean that his had to do the same. He treated her with great respect, she was fairly certain that he genuinely liked her, and he was an excellent lover. It was more than she had ever expected, and far more than many women ever achieved within a marriage.

Margaret straightened her shoulders and started walking again. Her brother Adam would be appalled at her weakness and critical of her decision to accept the wrong bargain and then want to change it. She was no beauty like Lottie or Frederica, she had done very well for herself, and she had to crush her foolish, *silly* yearnings underfoot and accept her lot.

Apart from a single candle left by the door, her bedchamber was in darkness. She took the candle, walked through into the dressing room, and managed to remove her clothing without needing any assistance. She could hear Alistair's slight snoring as she went back through to the large four-poster bed and climbed in.

He turned to her, wrapping her in his arms, and gave a very contented sigh. She lay still, staring into the darkness, breathing him in. If everything went to plan, they would soon be rid of the obnoxious Mr. Pritchard, and Alistair would never know that he had been threatened at all.

CHAPTER SEVENTEEN

*D*espite his best efforts, it appeared as if Bottomly had been warned that Alistair was looking for him and had gone to ground. Alistair wouldn't stop searching for him, but he had begun to doubt he would succeed. He glanced over at his wife, who was reading through her morning correspondence. She'd been quiet since the dinner party. Beset by his own problems, he was guiltily aware that he hadn't really made much effort to find out why.

Alistair finished his breakfast just as Nash arrived. Knowing his friend's appetite, he asked the butler to bring him into the breakfast room. Nash appeared with an unknown man carrying a large leather bag alongside him.

"Good morning, your grace, duchess." Nash pointed at the other man. "This is Mr. James Marsh. He works as a chemist at the Royal Arsenal in Woolwich. I asked him to come and help me today."

"Why?" Alistair offered both men a seat. "Are you planning on blowing something up?"

"On the contrary." Nash grinned as he helped himself to coffee and offered it to his companion. "Mr. Marsh has developed a very interesting testing procedure that I think might help produce evidence for your particular needs."

Alistair raised an eyebrow and turned to the chemist. "Please, do explain. I am all ears."

Mr. Marsh cleared his throat and sat up straight. "I have developed a test to detect arsenic poisoning, your grace."

"Indeed." Alistair studied the man's earnest face. "Does it work?"

"Yes, although I have yet to use it as evidence in an actual court case, your grace, but I am certain it would pass muster."

"How is such a test administered?" Margaret asked.

"I simply need a specimen of tissue or body fluid from the victim."

"That's where I come in," Nash intervened. "Mr. Marsh can set up his experiment in a safe part of the house. He doesn't need to see or identify our patient."

Alistair transferred his attention to Nash. "Do you think it is worth doing?"

"It can't hurt." Nash shrugged. "But of course, I would need your and your duchess's permission before I can proceed."

"What about the patient?"

"We have already discussed it." Nash smiled. "The patient is very happy to be part of the proceedings."

Margaret looked over at Alistair. "I see no harm in this, do you?"

"None at all." He nodded at Mr. Marsh. "Please proceed."

"I'd best set up somewhere near your kitchen, your grace," Mr. Marsh said. "A scullery with a large wooden table would be best."

"We have just the thing," Margaret said. "We will take you there as soon as you have finished your breakfast."

Mr. Marsh looked longingly at the sideboard full of dishes. "But I haven't—"

Nash nudged his friend in the ribs. "What her grace is trying to say, old man, is that you and I should start eating."

While Margaret went up with Nash to speak to Phoebe, Alistair followed Mr. Marsh down to the scullery and watched in fascination as the man carefully unwrapped a simple glass apparatus.

"What are you going to put in there?" Alistair asked curiously, pointing at a rounded bottle.

"Zinc, sulphuric acid, and the potential victim's body fluid or tissue."

"Then what happens?"

"If arsenic is present, then arsine gas will be produced along with hydrogen. Igniting this mixture will oxidize the arsine into arsenic and water vapor." Mr. Marsh produced some more items from his bag and assembled a line of three connected glass contraptions that were all slightly different. "If we hold a cold ceramic bowl in the jet of a flame of the final solution, it will become stained with a silvery black deposit of arsenic, proving the person has been poisoned."

"Ah, I see." Alistair wasn't sure he understood any of it, but he trusted that Mr. Marsh knew what he was doing.

"I can explain in more depth if you wish, your grace?" Mr. Marsh looked up inquiringly from arranging his glass vials.

"No, I think I grasp the principle," Alistair said hastily. "I look forward to seeing how it works."

LATER THAT DAY, after Mr. Marsh had completed his experiment and left to write up an official report of his findings, Margaret, Alistair, and Dr. Nash met in the drawing room.

"So now we know that Phoebe was definitely being poisoned, what are we going to do about it?" Dr. Nash was the first to speak, his expression grim.

"Does Phoebe know?" Margaret asked.

"I haven't told her," Dr. Nash said. "I thought that was up to you."

"Then we should tell her immediately," Margaret said. "If she wishes us to prosecute Lady Hellion, then—"

Alistair cut across her. "We still have no proof that it was her, my dear."

Margaret blinked at him. "What are you saying? It *must*—"

For the second time, he interrupted her. "Perhaps we should wait to have this discussion in private? No offense, Nash."

"None taken." Dr. Nash got to his feet. "I'll take myself off. I'm due at the hospital. Let me know what you decide and how you wish to proceed."

"Thank you." Alistair shook his hand. "If it hadn't have been for you, we might never have discovered what was going on."

"If you hadn't have suspected foul play in the first place, I wouldn't have been able to help, would I?" Dr. Nash turned to Margaret. "Duchess, a pleasure."

He left, leaving an uneasy silence behind him. Margaret folded her hands in her lap and kept her mouth shut as Alistair paced the room. He finally took the chair opposite her.

"We don't know if it was Lady Hellion."

Margaret kept her gaze downward.

"It could've been Dr. McNeil," Alistair continued.

There was so much that she wanted to say to him, but she was afraid that once she started speaking, she might never be able to stop.

"I just don't want us to rush to conclusions."

"As you wish." Margaret managed to force the words out of her stiff lips.

"You are determined to make this difficult, aren't you?" He sat back, one arm resting on the back of his chair.

"I merely agreed that it was up to you to decide how you wished to proceed. Phoebe is your sister, not mine."

"I want to proceed with caution, what's wrong with that?" His fingers tapped on the armrest in a restless tattoo.

"Nothing at all."

"The repercussions of accusing a peer's wife of murder would be severe and affect the security and reputation of our family name."

"As I know little about such matters, I defer to your judgment."

He continued to frown at her. "I think I prefer it when you shout at me."

"But you don't like arguing." She opened her eyes wide. "I am merely acquiescing to your wishes."

"I'm going to speak to Phoebe." He rose to his feet. "There is absolutely no point in talking to you when you are being so annoying."

She smiled up at him. "Please let me know when you have reached a decision on this matter."

He turned on his heel and marched out, slamming the door behind him. Margaret allowed herself a small self-congratulatory smile. Let him stew; let him feel the frustration she experienced when he refused to engage with her.

Her smile died. Yet again, he was more concerned with protecting Frederica Hellion from the consequences of her behavior than doing the right thing. In Margaret's view it was impossible that Dr. McNeil had acted without his employer's knowledge. Surely, any person seeing their charge grow sicker in the care of one doctor would have brought his patient to London?

But did Alistair have a point about the scandal such an accusation would bring? She didn't care about her own position in society, but she did care about Phoebe's, and her husband insisted she should also care about their future children. Suddenly, she wished she were back in the millhouse with just Adam and Lottie to take care of and no other worries than whether she could make his wages stretch for the week.

There was a knock on the door, and the butler came in.

"Your grace, a carriage has just arrived from Millcastle."

Margaret had barely entered the front hall before Captain Grayson came through the door. He bowed low and doffed his hat.

"Good afternoon, your grace. I have brought you a surprise." He stepped aside to reveal her sister.

Margaret took an unsteady breath and almost burst into tears. "Oh, Lottie." she ran toward her sister and embraced her. "I am so *very* glad to see you."

"AFTER ADAM RECEIVED your letter about the money, he insisted that I bring it with me rather than him sending it with a messenger." Lottie was curled up on the sofa next to Margaret in her bedchamber. They'd eaten their dinner upstairs together while Alistair took Captain Grayson out to their club. "I was quite happy to oblige him, as I've only been to London once before."

"I did ask him for rather a lot," Margaret confessed, "And, due to the specific nature of my request, I'm glad he didn't risk sending it. Goodness knows what might have happened if it had fallen into the wrong hands."

Lottie finished her tea and sat back to study her sister. "You look very well, Margaret. Marriage obviously suits you."

"I am... quite content."

"Content? You are a duchess, you are married to a very handsome and charming man, and you get to take part in London society. What more *is* there to life?"

"Nothing more." Margaret smiled. "I am very lucky."

"Has something happened?" Lottie sat up straight again, her smile fading. "Is Alistair unkind to you?"

"Not at all, it's just that—" She paused and then remembered that Lottie was the only person in the world apart from Adam who really understood her. "I think I care about him too much, and that wasn't part of our bargain."

Lottie frowned. "Surely he would be pleased about that? He is a man, after all."

"I haven't told him," Margaret confessed.

"Why not?"

"Because it wasn't part of our agreement. We are supposed to be good friends who trust each other."

Lottie gestured at the bed. "So you haven't consummated your marriage?"

"Of *course* we have, in fact—" Margaret became aware that she was blushing. "I have nothing to complain about in that particular area."

"Then you are already more than friends." Lottie regarded her seriously. "It's not like you to be scared of sharing your feelings, Margaret. Why are you hesitating now?"

Margaret took a deep breath and told Lottie all about Frederica Hellion, which took quite some time as her sister asked lots of questions.

"Well, I can see why his behavior might alarm you," Lottie eventually said. "But you have to remember that he can't marry her anyway."

"I know that." Margaret glared at her eminently practical sister. "So how can I tell Alistair that I am jealous of his regard for her?"

"Stop being jealous of nothing?" Lottie suggested.

"I suppose you are right, but it is hard for me to hold my tongue when he constantly finds excuses for her behavior." She hesitated. "And, because he knows that something is amiss, he deliberately avoids initiating those important conversations with me."

"Do you love him?"

Margaret stared at her sister. "Yes, but as I said—"

"Then that's all that matters, isn't it?"

"Not if he doesn't love me back. He's never suggested that such a thing is even possible," Margaret objected. "The only woman he has ever loved is Frederica."

Lottie wrinkled her nose. "That was over ten years ago, and she is now his stepmother. Soon she will be gone from your life, Alistair will be free of her, and you can devote yourself to proving to him that you are his one and only love."

"You make it sound so easy," Margaret grumbled.

Lottie nudged her elbow. "It's always easier when it's someone else's problem. Now, what did you want all that money for? Doesn't Alistair pay you an allowance?"

"I need the money to pay off a blackmailer," Margaret said.

Lottie's mouth opened to form a perfect O. "Good gracious, sister, your life has certainly become far more exciting than mine will ever be!"

"I'm glad that you are here, Francis."

Alistair passed his friend the bottle of brandy the waiter had left on the table between them. They were seated in a quiet corner of White's far away from the gambling and betting men where they stood less chance of being overheard.

"I said I'd come down, and Caroline was quite happy to release me for a week or so."

"Is she well?"

"Very well, and getting rounder by the minute." Francis took a sip of his brandy. "It is most peculiar. I never expected to be a father."

"I suspect you will be very good at it and far more under-standing than either of our fathers ever were."

"I'll certainly try to be," Francis agreed. "How is your duchess settling in? Caroline told me specifically to ask."

"She's holding her own." Alistair found himself smiling. "My great-aunt Lavinia has taken her under her wing, and that has definitely helped."

"Good Lord, that dragon?" Francis shuddered. "I suspect the Margaret Blackthorn I knew is perfectly capable of standing up for herself. Have you seen your sister?"

"I brought her with me to London," Alistair said. "I was not... happy at how she was being treated at my stepmother's house."

Francis raised an eyebrow. "You're still at odds with the beautiful Frederica?"

"It's hard not to be when she consistently invites my atten-tion." Alistair took a restorative sip of brandy. "She recently had a most peculiar letter from Bottomly."

"The fool that was with Farrell when he died?" Francis frowned. "What the devil did he want with her?"

"He seemed to be implying that he knew something was off about my cousin's death, and wondered if I might be implicated in my father's death, too. I believe Frederica was at least able to reassure him that, thanks to her, I wasn't even in the country when my father died."

"The last time I saw Bottomly that night he was passed out in a flowerbed," Francis commented. "It is impossible that he saw anything that went on in the duke's study."

"But Pritchard was there, wasn't he?" Alistair reminded his friend. "When I left to rouse Dr. Nettles, I went past him at the door."

"So, if there is anything suspicious going on, then it is prob-ably Pritchard who is behind it. Is he in town?"

"I believe so, but I haven't been able to see him or Bottomly." Alistair smiled. "It's almost as if they are avoiding me."

"With good cause," Francis said. "If I see either one of them, I will make sure they know that their underhand tactics are pointless."

"Thank you." Alistair toasted his friend. "I don't think they have the nerve to openly challenge me assuming the title, but gossip and rumor can be effective to destroy a family's reputation. Frederica blackened my name after my father died, and I still haven't lived it down." He drank more brandy. "I did wonder if Frederica had sought out Bottomly to make trouble for me."

Francis rolled his eyes. "You're obsessed with the woman. Why should she do that when her social prestige is higher because her stepson is now a duke?"

"You sound like my wife."

"Your duchess has always struck me as a remarkably sensible woman. Perhaps you should listen to her," Francis said. "At some point Bottomly or Pritchard will reappear in society, and we will be ready for them."

"I appreciate the 'we,'" Alistair said drily.

"I was a witness to what went on that night, and Dr. Nettles can confirm what I saw," Francis reminded him. "You have nothing to worry about."

"Let's hope that you are right," Alistair agreed, even though he had a nagging sensation that things were far from settled. "The poor old dukedom can definitely do without any more scandal being attached to its name."

The waiter returned to let them know that their table was ready in the dining room. Alistair followed Francis through the throng of gentlemen, stopping to acknowledge acquaintances, and accept congratulations on his marriage and his new title. It was strange how many men were willing to tolerate his existence now that he was a duke and not a somewhat questionable marquess.

Margaret had made no objection to him taking Francis out

of the house on the night on his arrival. Her joy and relief at seeing Lottie had been all too evident. Had he failed her so badly already? He'd vowed to be everything she wanted and was already aware that he was letting her down.

He took his seat and remembered to thank the waiter. He had a terrible sense that a reckoning was coming, and he still wasn't sure whether either he or Margaret would survive it.

CHAPTER EIGHTEEN

"*L*ady Hellion." Alistair bowed as his stepmother came rushing toward him.

"Alistair, darling, thank you so much for coming."

Did she ever get dressed? As usual, her hair flowed around her shoulders in luscious waves and her dressing gown was untied. He could easily see the shape of her breasts against the thin fabric of her nightshift.

"You said there was an emergency concerning my wife."

He still couldn't believe he'd actually responded to her anguished note, but while he'd been at the bank with Francis, Margaret had gone out with Lottie that morning and had not yet returned. If something had happened to her, it was highly unlikely, but possible, that Frederica had been informed if he was not available.

"I thought you should know as soon as possible." Frederica was speaking again. "Yesterday when I was out walking in the park, I met Lord Bottomly and his friend, Mr. Pritchard." She looked expectantly up at him, but Alistair was done with playing her games.

"And?"

"They asked me about you again. Mr. Pritchard said that he was a close friend of your cousin Farrell's, and that he couldn't believe that a young man in such good health would die from hitting his head."

"Farrell was a drunkard; he was hardly in good health," Alistair said dismissively. "Is there a point to this story, or did you merely wish to attract my attention again?"

Frederica fingered the lace of her gown. "The thing is, a few days ago, I saw your wife with Mr. Pritchard."

"That's extremely unlikely."

"He was helping her into your carriage. I noticed the Thorsway arms on the door." Frederica paused, her gaze avid. "Did she not tell you about this?"

"She might have done. I can't say I would have taken much notice if she had." Alistair managed a shrug even as his mind was racing.

"Mr. Pritchard said he was meeting her again today by the Serpentine at two."

"Well, her grace has developed a great fondness for ducks, so perhaps they will be feeding them together?" Alistair inclined his head. "Is there anything else you wish to speak to me about? I have a meeting in an hour."

"Alistair, this isn't a matter for levity." Frederica touched his arm and paused dramatically. "What if your duchess is conspiring with these men against you?"

"To do what exactly?" Alistair inquired. "Throw me a surprise birthday party?"

"What if Mr. Pritchard thinks he can accuse you of Farrell's murder?"

"There's nothing stopping him accusing me to my face. He hardly needs my duchess's approval to do that." Alistair retrieved his hat. "If he's toadying up to my wife rather than facing me like a man, then he's probably in for something of a shock. She doesn't suffer fools gladly."

"You care about her, don't you?"

"She's my wife."

"But it's more than that, isn't it? And she is such a *practical* creature and so lacking in finesse and, dare I say it, class. The poor dear probably isn't capable of reciprocating your feelings, as she only married your for your title." Frederica sighed. "What a shame it is that you always fall in love with the wrong people, Alistair."

"The only person I've loved who betrayed me is you, my dear." Alistair turned to the door. "And, in truth, I'm beginning to think that my father did me a huge favor."

He had barely shut the door before something smashed against it. His smile died as he went down into the hotel entrance hall. If she was right and Margaret had somehow gotten herself involved with Pritchard, he was going to wring her bloody neck.

~

"I AM COMING WITH YOU," Lottie announced as she came into Margaret's dressing room. She wore a cherry-red bonnet, a brown coat with matching red buttons, and a very determined expression.

"No, you are not. Eileen will accompany me." Margaret frowned at her sister and wished not for the first time that she hadn't told Lottie what she was intending to do.

"I swore to Adam that I would make sure the money was correctly delivered."

"Which you have done, thank you." Margaret shot her a repressive look.

"Not quite, if Mr. Pritchard is the person you intend to deliver it to," Lottie countered somewhat piously.

"Lottie, if he sees you, he will disappear," Margaret said as she buttoned up her blue coat and put on her matching bonnet.

"If you insist on coming, you will have to stay completely out of his way."

"If I must." Lottie's sigh was large enough to turn a windmill. "But if he does anything terrible, I will come and save the day."

"That will not be necessary, as I am quite capable of saving myself!" Margaret reminded her, earning her sister's chuckle. "It is all very simple. I make Mr. Pritchard sign a letter renouncing all claims to further payments and some other matters that Adam's solicitor made sure to include in this letter. I hand over the money, and that is the last we will see of him."

"I do hope you are right." Lottie didn't sound very convinced as she followed Margaret out of the door.

"I am always right," Margaret said. "If you insist on accompanying me, you will stay in the carriage until Mr. Pritchard and I have reached the banks of the Serpentine."

"As you wish," Lottie acquiesced.

There was no sign of the new butler in the hallway, but the carriage was already outside awaiting them. Margaret glanced anxiously over at Alistair's study. She hadn't seen him all day and devoutly hoped he would remain busy with Francis Grafton sorting out their finances well into the evening.

She still felt a little guilty at deceiving him, but if her plans came to fruition, and he was no longer bothered by the obnoxious Mr. Pritchard, then she would be more than satisfied.

When she arrived in the park, she made sure Lottie stayed hidden and alighted from the carriage with Eileen at her side. She walked down to the place where she had agreed to meet Mr. Pritchard and sat down on the bench to await him. She had deliberately arrived a little early just to make sure she had time to review her plans and prepare herself for any eventualities.

She took a deep, steadying breath and focused her attention on the pair of swans currently gliding along side by side on the smooth surface of the water. She'd been told that swans mated for life and raised their chicks together and was suddenly and stupidly envious of the beautiful pair.

A light touch on her shoulder made her gasp and swing around to see, not Mr. Pritchard, but her husband, behind her.

"Good afternoon, duchess. Whatever are you doing sitting here all by yourself?" He paused, his blue gaze furious enough to convince her that any attempt at subterfuge would be pointless. "Would you care to explain?"

ALISTAIR HELD the door of his study open, and Margaret walked past him, her head held high. He shut it behind her and leaned against it, aware that even after the carriage ride, when she had refused to say a word in front of Eileen and Lottie, that he was still angry.

She stopped, took off her bonnet, and placed it and her reticule on the top of his desk.

"Well?" he demanded.

She raised her eyebrows. "As I assume someone has been telling tales, so why don't you start?"

"Because I am not the one consorting with my husband's enemies?"

"Has it not occurred to you that if you had not interfered, you would've had one *less* enemy?" Margaret asked.

He felt his temper rise. "It is not your job to save me from anything or anyone. What exactly were you trying to achieve by meeting with that man?"

"I was trying to protect you." Margaret wasn't backing down, and in some part of his soul, he was pleased about that. "I had a *plan*—"

He cut across her. "Please humor me and start at the beginning when you first conceived of this hare-brain notion that I needed 'protecting', and that you were going to lie to me."

"I haven't lied!" Margaret protested.

"You've not been completely honest with me, either, have you?" The incredulous look she gave him made him come away from the door. "What?"

"You are hardly the epitome of honesty, yourself, your grace."

He glared at her. "Stop trying to change the subject. What were you doing with Pritchard?"

She leaned back against the front of his desk, her arms folded over her chest. "He thought to blackmail me."

"About what?"

"He said that he was there the night your cousin Farrell died, and that he witnessed you hitting your cousin with a poker and then covering up a murder."

"Did he, now." Alistair released a slow breath. "And what did he want for his silence in this matter?"

"Money, of course." She shrugged. "Which is why he came to me."

"And you were going to *give it to him?*" His fingers curled into the palms of his hands.

"Well, not exactly. I asked Adam—"

He interrupted her again. "You asked your brother for money?"

"Yes." She studied him uncomprehendingly. "Only because I knew he could help me with this particular matter."

Alistair took a short turn around the room, and ended up back where he had started, facing her calm expression as his anger turned to ice.

"Your brother should have told you to go to the devil."

"Why?" A small frown appeared on her forehead. "He has great faith in me and understood my plan and what I needed from him."

"Because…" Alistair shook his head, aware that the thought of her turning to another man, even her own brother, made him even more furious. "You should *never* have approached him in the first place! If you needed money, if you needed to deal with a blackmailer, you should've come to me! Your husband!"

He was only aware that he was shouting when she winced.

"I thought—"

He pointed his finger at her. "You damn well did not think. What if he'd taken the money and a month later had come waltzing back? What would you have done then? Asked your darling Adam for more? Bled your own brother dry because you're too much of a coward to have an honest conversation with me?"

"No, of course not." She blinked and looked away from him. "I'm not stupid. What would you have done if I'd told you what he was claiming?"

"I would've sought him out, held him publicly accountable for his ridiculous suggestions, and made him apologize."

"And what if he hadn't apologized?" Margaret asked.

"As a man of honor, I would've called him out," Alistair said.

"And that is preferable to me tricking him?" She advanced toward him, hands on her hips "You dying in a stupid, pointless duel?"

"I wouldn't have died."

She rolled her eyes at him. "You don't know that. Mr. Pritchard isn't exactly an honest, honorable gentleman."

"Nevertheless—"

It was her turn to interrupt him. "If you had let my plan proceed, he would never have shown his face in society again."

"Don't be ridiculous." She bit down on her lip at his contemptuous tone. "You handled this very badly, very badly, indeed. If Lady Hellion hadn't told me about your meeting with Pritchard today—"

Her head came up. "Lady Hellion told you?"

"Yes." He held her gaze. "What of it?"

She didn't look away, so he had the awful pleasure of seeing her eyes fill with tears.

"Ah, of course it would be her." She swallowed hard. "How fitting." She opened up her reticule, and carefully placed a parcel and a letter on the desk before picking up her bonnet. "Good day, your grace."

"You can't just walk away in the middle of our discussion," Alistair protested.

"I can if I don't think there is anything left to say." She gestured at the parcel and walked toward the door. "Perhaps when you have time, you will read the letter and examine the money I intended to give to Mr. Pritchard."

"I can do that right now while you watch," he counter-offered, aware that she would no longer look at him and more disturbed by that than he had anticipated.

She paused at the door, her hand on the latch. "I'm feeling rather tired. I need to go and lie down."

"It's not like you to run away from a fight, Margaret."

She finally looked at him, and he wished she hadn't. "No, that's normally you, isn't it? Or you laugh at me and expect me to forgive and forget, make light of my concerns, tease me or bed me, anything to distract me from getting close to you or upsetting you."

"That's neither true nor fair."

She smiled. "It doesn't matter anyway, does it? We made a marriage bargain. I promise you that in the future I will stick to it."

"That has nothing to do with our current disagreement," Alistair said. "If the fact that Lady Hellion told me about your meeting disturbs you, I am sorry for it, but I'm glad she told me."

"Of course you are." She nodded. "I'm sure she will be delighted when you go and give her your thanks."

"Why does it always have to come back to this?" Alistair

demanded. "Your ridiculous fear that I am somehow still in thrall to my stepmother?"

"Because you *are!*" She took a hasty step toward him. "I've seen you with her!"

"Then you know how much I loathe and despise her."

"I've seen how easily she gets under your skin, how she arouses such passion in you—you who laugh and make light of everything else in the world—including me." She forced a smile. "You loved her once; you still love her."

"I bloody well do not. She taught me a good lesson," Alistair snapped. "I don't love anyone, and I never will."

Her sharp intake of breath as she turned to the door, one hand pressed to her bosom, made it look as if he had wounded her physically. He cursed himself for a fool as she fumbled for the door handle and fled.

But what could he say?

She'd summed up the entirety of his miserable and selfish existence quite eloquently. It also occurred to him that at no point had she ever doubted Pritchard was lying about him. He slammed the flat of his hand against the door and cursed like the lowest born soldier in his ranks.

After a deep, steadying breath he opened the door and walked out into the hall, his gaze going upward. He had to go after her—had to reassure her that— That what? He'd misspoken? She'd seen the truth in his eyes. Nothing he could say, even though he desperately wished he could take the words back because he had started to care very deeply for her, would make any difference to his plain-speaking wife.

The butler opened the front door and Francis appeared. He halted at the sight of Alistair standing by the stairs and scrutinized him carefully.

"Is everything all right?"

"Yes, of course." Alistair advanced toward his friend. "Am I supposed to be meeting with you this afternoon?"

"No, but I found Bottomly drinking at Whites, and from the state of him I don't think he'll be leaving any time soon." He gestured at the door. "I have a hackney cab waiting. Do you want to come with me?"

Alistair realized he was still dressed in his outdoor coat. He hastily picked up his hat and followed Francis out onto the street. If he couldn't yet think of a way to deal with Margaret, perhaps venting his frustration on Bottomly would provide some relief.

MARGARET WENT up the stairs and locked both doors into her bedchamber, which would hopefully keep Lottie and Eileen out until she was ready to see them. She took off her coat and carefully laid it over the back of a chair before sitting down to remove her half boots. She noticed that Eileen had been in and left her some hot water, so she obediently washed her hands and face and then returned to sit in her chair.

Would Alistair appear, full of contrition after reading her letter to Mr. Pritchard and beg her forgiveness? She held herself stiff and still, listening to the business of the house murmuring around her. She wasn't sure she was capable of looking at him, let alone forgiving him for anything yet, but still...

The front door banged twice and she risked a glance out of the window. Her husband and Francis Grafton were leaving in a hackney cab together. Her faint hope died, and she clenched her jaw hard against the sudden pain in her heart.

For some reason there seemed to be little else she was capable of doing except sitting in her chair. She couldn't even cry; she didn't have the right to. It reminded her of when her father had died, her mother's hysterical weeping, Adam's terrifyingly blank face, and Lottie's bewilderment. She'd been the one to look after everyone then, but who would look after her?

I don't love anyone, and I never will.

Her husband's voice rang in her head. It was stupid to compare her current situation with her father's suicide. She would survive the notion that her husband didn't love her far better than the fact that her father had deliberately killed himself. Alistair was still alive, still her husband, and she owed him her loyalty. That was the bargain she had made, and that was all there was to it.

Margaret took an unsteady breath. Now, if she could only convince her heart that the matter was settled and that nothing had really changed at all. She'd been stupid to hope for more. Alistair hadn't lied to her. She was the one who had changed, and that was her problem and hers alone.

A tear threaded its way down her cheek and fell onto the pale green cotton of her gown. It was soon followed by another one until Margaret had no other option than to find her hand-kerchief and let the tears fall. Her first fiancé had treated her with obvious contempt. Alistair would never do that. He was a gentleman, and she wasn't the sort of woman to inspire love and devotion from any man. She was too plain, too practical, and too managing. Both her father and Matthew had told her that. Perhaps Alistair was just too polite to say it to her face.

She blew her nose and sat up straight. One good thing was that her husband wouldn't mention their disagreement unless she pushed him into an argument. As she had no intention of ever doing that again, the discord between them would swiftly pass, and they would move forward together in friendship and harmony.

Margaret repeated the words to herself, but still had no inclination to leave her seat. At four o'clock, she was due to visit an educational institution with Mrs. Godson. She would attend that meeting and direct her thoughts and energies into the considerable influence she held as a duchess. Perhaps hard work and surviving the bad times was amusing to women like Lady

Tillington, but Margaret had always found that such matters prevented her from thinking too hard about the stupid things she could not control.

She blew her nose again and remained sitting in the chair, carefully gathering her common sense, practicality, and hard-won confidence around her. When she emerged from her chamber, no one would ever know that she had any weaknesses at all.

Except her husband, but as she intended to avoid him as much as possible, and he would be very grateful if she never referred to love again, there was nothing to worry her at all, was there?

CHAPTER NINETEEN

"*B*ottomly." Alistair looked down at the sprawled form on the couch at Whites. "Just the man I wanted to talk to."

Bottomly opened and closed his mouth like a fish gasping for air as Francis grabbed him by the shoulders and forced him to his feet.

"Come and sit with us."

"I'd rather not," Bottomly hiccupped gently. "Pritch wouldn't like it."

"As he is not here, and neither his grace or I will ever mention that we saw you, let alone spoke to you, I think you are quite safe."

Alistair took hold of the other side of Bottomly's sagging form, and he and Francis manhandled him out of the main areas and into a quiet, deserted office toward the rear of the property.

"What do you want?" Bottomly asked nervously.

Alistair sat opposite him while Francis watched the door. "Why did you write to my stepmother, Lady Hellion?"

"She *told* you?" Bottomly boggled at him. "But Pritch said you were mortal enemies."

"Oh, we are, but it is far more complicated than that," Alistair said smoothly. "Why were you so interested in whether I was at my father's deathbed?"

"Because—" Bottomly looked surreptitiously over at the door Francis was leaning against. "Pritch asked me to ask her."

Alistair held onto his temper. "Why did Pritchard want that information?"

"I'm not sure." Bottomly frowned. "Something to do with gathering information against you, but for what I'm not quite clear."

"Are you trying to tell me you didn't know that Pritchard was planning on accusing me of murdering my cousin Farrell?"

"Good Lord, no! Was he?" Bottomly's horrified expression was so ludicrous that Alistair almost wanted to laugh.

"Because if you *did* know, I will be mentioning your name to my lawyer when I sue Pritchard in court."

"You don't understand." Bottomly poked himself in the head with his index finger. "Pritch doesn't tell me everything because he knows I'll get confused and let the cat out of the bag."

Alistair's lips twitched at Bottomly's earnest tone.

"Were you aware that Pritchard has also contacted my wife?"

Bottomly considered that as he chewed his fingernails. "He did say something along those lines. He thought the best way to get back at you was through your womenfolk because they would be easier to deal with, and more likely to give him money."

"Do you have his address?" Alistair asked.

Bottomly sat back and crossed his arms over his chest. "I'm not telling you that. He's my best friend."

"Then will you give him a message from me?" Alistair raised an eyebrow. "Ask him to call at my house in the next two days. Tell him that if I don't hear from him, I will be pressing charges against him for attempted blackmail."

"Oh, I say, your grace, that's rather harsh," Bottomly

protested. "The man's only trying to make a living now that his pater has cut him off."

"Well, he's not making a living off me." Alistair stood and flicked his gaze over to Francis, who stepped away from the door. "I suggest you sober up and go and find him. The longer you take to deliver my message, the less time Pritchard has to decide what to do about it."

Bottomly rose shakily to his feet and hung onto the back of his chair. "I'll find him, don't you worry about that."

"Good. See that you do." Alistair nodded and followed Francis out of the room.

"What a complete and utter buffoon," Francis commented as they descended the stairs to the street level.

"Indeed," Alistair agreed and despite everything that was wrong he couldn't help chuckling. "That went a lot more easily than I anticipated."

"Blessed are the drunk and lacking in brains," Francis said. "What a fool. Do you think Pritchard will dare show his face to you?"

"I don't know. I'd rather he left town, but I suspect he'll still be after that money he thinks he can collect from my wife or my stepmother."

"Why would Lady Hellion give him money?" Francis hailed a hackney cab.

"Because she would appreciate having something to hold over my head again now that I have extracted Phoebe from her clutches."

"But wasn't she the one who told you about the note?" Francis asked when they were settled. Alistair had spent most of the carriage ride to Whites filling Francis in on the current state of his affairs.

"She did tell me, but only to judge my reaction to the news with her own eyes. It wouldn't surprise me if she was in league with Pritchard."

"Which probably explains why she told you she saw your duchess with Pritchard as well."

"How so?" Alistair asked.

"She's jealous." Francis shrugged. "It's obvious that you care for your wife. From what I've seen of Lady Hellion, she would hate to think that she was no longer the most important person in your life, and she would be very willing to help destroy that relationship."

"She told me because she was worried about Margaret," Alistair insisted.

Francis made a disgusted sound. "Come on, Alistair, don't be a complete fool. She wishes nothing but ill on your wife. I'm surprised you even listened to her."

"Well, it's a good job I did, because I stopped my duchess getting involved in a blackmailing scheme," Alistair countered.

"I doubt your wife is that much of a fool." Alistair glared at his friend, who refused to look away. "I'm fairly certain she took Pritchard's measure and was planning to deceive him in some way."

As that sounded far too likely, Alistair abruptly ended the conversation by staring out the window. But Francis's words kept revolving in his head. Had he misjudged his wife yet again? Had her scheme to defeat her blackmailer had merit after all? He hadn't bothered to read her letter or investigate the parcel she had left with him. Perhaps it was time he did, but was he ready to have another conversation with Margaret?

The hackney cab stopped and Francis paid off the driver. Alistair looked up at the windows above the front door where his bedchamber was. Was Margaret there? Maybe the question he should be asking himself was whether *she* would deign to speak to him.

∾

Margaret braced herself as she went into the drawing room where Lottie, Francis, and her husband were already assembled for dinner. She'd delayed her arrival for as long as possible, but she couldn't put it off any longer. If she wanted to set the tone for how she wished things to go in her marriage, then there was no better time than now.

"Oh, there you are, Margaret." Lottie called out to her. "I was just telling Captain Grafton about our visit to the Bethnal Green school today."

"It was most interesting." Margaret offered a bright smile that encompassed all three occupants of the room. "I intend to go back as soon as possible and decide exactly where to direct my efforts."

"I'm sure they'll be delighted," Francis commented. "Caroline is insisting that we involve ourselves in the movement to ensure that all children receive some basic form of education in our factories."

"That is an excellent project and one I am also interested in," Margaret agreed. "I will write to Caroline when I return to Hellsdown Park."

Francis bowed. "She will be delighted to hear from you. I've already been given my orders as to what I should vote for if it comes up in the House." He glanced over at Alistair. "I am fairly sure you will receive an equally attentive ear from the duke."

The butler appeared at the door and cleared his throat.

"Dinner is served."

"Thank you." Margaret placed her hand on Francis's sleeve. "Shall we go in?"

She suspected her voice was too light and her smile unnatural, but it was the best she could do until she reclaimed her old role of defensive, practical prickliness.

As they walked through, Francis leaned in close. "I'm not sure what is going on between you and Alistair, and I'm also aware that it is none of my business, but don't give up on him just yet."

"I will do my best," she offered him a heartfelt smile.

"Thank you. He might pretend not to care about anything, but that is far from the truth, and I believe he cares about you very deeply."

Margaret's eyes filled with tears and she had to turn away. Unfortunately, that meant her gaze locked with her husband's. He took a hasty step toward her before she abruptly fussed with her chair and sat down.

It was a relief to let Lottie chat away about all the wonders of London that she had seen and all those she was still anticipating. Margaret simply had to add a word in here and there to keep the conversation moving. Alistair did the same with such charming ease that Margaret had to try even harder.

When she and Lottie rose from the table, she addressed her first direct remark to her husband.

"Lottie and I are going to a musical evening at Lady Thule's, so do not worry about having to meet us in the drawing room after your port."

He looked up at her, his face unsmiling, his blond hair gleaming in the candlelight. "I am more than willing to accompany you."

"There is no need." Margaret offered him a firm nod. "Her carriage is picking us up in less than an hour, and I know you do not enjoy such amateurish musical events."

His gaze turned cool. "As you wish."

She swept out of the room, Lottie at her side, and let out a breath she hadn't realized she'd been holding.

"I assume you and Alistair are still fighting?" Lottie asked as they went up the stairs.

"Not at all," Margaret said. "We have both said our piece, and that's the end of it."

Lottie snorted. "Yes, I can see that from the cordial way you spoke to each other all evening. I had to talk a *lot!*"

Margaret squeezed her sister's arm. "And I appreciated your efforts." She stopped outside her door. "Will you be ready to leave in half an hour?"

"Yes, I only have to change my dress and redo my hair." Lottie smiled at her. "And then go to a musical evening at the house of a viscount." She broadened her accent. "Who'd have ever thought that, Margaret, lass?"

"Where you will outshine all the other ladies and be fighting off suitors," Margaret reminded her.

Lottie shrugged. "The men here don't interest me that much. I prefer those back in Millcastle who make their own money and work with their hands."

"I thought I would marry one of those men," Margaret said slowly. "Instead, I married a duke."

Lottie's expression softened. "He's still a good man, Margaret, and he cares about you."

Margaret didn't have an answer for that, so she went into her room, rang for Eileen, and let herself be immersed in the process of picking a suitable gown for her evening entertainment.

Lady Thule paused by Margaret's chair and leaned in to speak to her above the babble of conversation. It had been a surprisingly pleasant evening. Margaret had relaxed and simply enjoyed the music without worrying about her husband. Lottie had disappeared off to the supper room with a crowd of admirers after telling Margaret to stay put and not fret about her.

"I'm surprised that Alistair didn't come," Lady Thule remarked.

"He is entertaining his friend Captain Grayson and sends his apologies," Margaret said. "It is a shame he has missed such a wonderful collection of talented performers."

Lady Thule looked smug. "I only allow the best to perform here, my dear." She paused. "I hear very good reports of your conduct from my friend, Mrs. Godson. She speaks very highly of you."

Margaret smiled. "Mrs. Godson has been very kind to me."

"Perhaps involving yourself in good and pious works will mask your other more obvious deficiencies."

"Let's hope so, shall we?" Margaret wasn't in the mood for sparring with Lady Thule. "I would hate to embarrass you."

Lady Thule straightened and stared down at her. "I doubt you will do that. Have a pleasant evening, my dear."

Aware that she had possibly been paid a compliment, Margaret half-smiled as the dowager moved away from her. There was plenty of work for her to do here in London and back in Millcastle. If she occupied herself with that, she wouldn't have time to worry about her relationship with her husband.

"Margaret, my dear."

She turned to see that Frederica Hellion had taken the vacant seat beside her. She wore a pink gown with silver lace and her hair was a mass of ringlets. She looked more like a debutante than a dowager.

"What do you want?"

Frederica settled her silken skirts around herself. "I... just wanted to explain."

"What exactly?"

"Why I told Alistair that you were seeing Mr. Pritchard."

"Oh, I think I understand your motives perfectly, ma'am. Did it not occur to you to come and tell *me* why my meeting with Mr. Pritchard was inappropriate?"

"You don't understand." Frederica sat forward. "I promised

Alistair that I wouldn't say anything to you. He was *most* insistent."

The thought of her husband conversing with Frederica about anything still set Margaret's teeth on edge.

"I'm not sure I understand *you*. How did you even know about this whole scheme?"

"Because Alistair told me. When he realized that Mr. Bottomly and Mr. Pritchard were asking questions about his cousin's death, he asked me to write to Bottomly and see if I could coax any information out of him." She patted her curls. "Bottomly has always been one of my court. When he replied and suggested that Mr. Pritchard was *indeed* up to no good, I told Alistair. That's actually why I came up to London—to warn him."

Margaret just stared at her, her mind racing as she struggled to think how to respond.

"I can see that you are still confused." Frederica reached out and patted Margaret's clenched fist. "Bottomly told me about your meeting with Mr. Pritchard in the park, and I made certain to be there just to make sure that he was telling the truth." She opened her eyes wide. "I was surprised to see that you had been so easily duped and thought it my duty to tell Alistair what I had seen before any harm was done to you."

"Am I supposed to thank you?" Margaret raised her eyebrows.

"I don't see why not. Despite everything, we are still family." Frederica's smile was beguiling. "I told Alistair that you wouldn't like me being involved in all this, but you know how he is."

"I do, and I find it difficult to believe that he involved you at all."

Frederica sighed. "I'm sorry that it hurts you that he still loves me. I've told him to stop, *told* him that he should be paying attention to you, and yet he persists. What am I supposed to do?"

"There is no need for you to worry in that respect, my lady. A man cannot marry his stepmother, can he?" Margaret held her gaze. "If you had only waited for Alistair to come home, then you could have held my position, but you didn't, and he's mine now, and I'd appreciate it if you remembered that."

"You know nothing about why I married his father." Frederica pressed a hand to her bosom and her eyes filled with tears. "I had no choice! Alistair had abandoned me and gone back to India, and I was with child! What would you have done in such circumstances, your grace?"

Margaret felt as if someone had pulled the mat out from under her and she was now hurtling down a long, dark mineshaft. She wasn't sure what hurt the most, the thought that Alistair had bedded Frederica, or the idea of him having a child he didn't know about.

"Didn't he mention that? Oh dear, I did try and tell you that you would never know him as well as I do." Frederica rose to her feet, her expression triumphant. "Good evening, your grace." She pushed past Lottie and walked over to the door, head held high, her smile in place as Margaret's world crumbled around her.

"Are you all right?" Lottie took Margaret's hands in hers.

Margaret could only shake her head.

Lottie urged her to her feet. "Let's go and get our cloaks. I'll say our goodbyes to Lady Thule, don't you worry about a thing."

Margaret was sitting in the carriage and almost back at the house before she finally managed to speak. "I... don't want to see Alistair."

"Then you can sleep in my bed with me."

"Thank you."

Lottie nodded, her expression unusually grim. "Was that the infamous Lady Hellion who was talking to you?"

"Yes." Margaret shuddered. "She said—"

Lottie patted her shoulder. "Tell me when we're safe inside, and then we'll decide what to do about it."

ALISTAIR WOKE up to find Margaret missing from his bed. He got up and walked into the dressing room where Clarkson was whistling away and folding his shirts.

"Did her grace already arise?"

"How would I know?" Clarkson gave him an aggrieved look. "I don't spend my time worrying about what goes on in your bed, your grace, now, do I?"

"Has Eileen been here?"

"Haven't seen her." Clarkson laid a coat over the back of the chair. "Is this one all right? The brown matches your surly expression."

"It's fine." Alistair washed hurriedly, dressed, and put on his coat, sitting down to pull on his boots. He'd drunk rather too much brandy after Francis had left him in his study last night. Not only did he have a headache, but he had slept in.

He needed to make things right with his wife. Even a day of her stepping back from him had been painful. He didn't want a lifetime of politeness and deference to his wishes; he liked her just the way she was.

His heart lightened as he heard female voices in the breakfast room. Perhaps she had simply woken before him, after all. He paused at the doorway, his gaze shifting from Lottie to his sister Phoebe, who was looking very pleased with herself.

"Good Lord." Alistair smiled at her. "Look who's here!"

"Dr. Nash told me to attempt to join you for breakfast. I'm not sure how long I can stand the excitement, but it is good to be part of things once more."

"Indeed." Alistair helped himself to some food and sat down

next to her. He encouraged her to talk to him even while his glance kept sliding over to the door.

Eventually, when Phoebe was talking to the butler, he managed to look across the table at Lottie.

"Have you seen Margaret this morning?"

She eyed him steadily. "Yes, I have."

"Ah, has she gone out?"

"She went for a walk. She asked me to say that she would like to speak with you in your study at ten if that is convenient."

"There's no need for such formality. She could just barge in like she normally does." Alistair hid the stab of hurt beneath his attempt at humor. "But, please tell her I will await her there."

BY TEN O'CLOCK, he was as nervous as a new foal and twice as wary. He sat at his desk and pretended to sort through the monthly accounts, but his heart wasn't in it. When the door opened precisely at ten, he forced himself not to jump to his feet and throw himself on her mercy.

"Duchess, what can I do for you this fine morning?"

"Good morning, your grace."

She came and sat on the chair in front of his desk, her hands folded in her lap, her hair drawn back into a plaited coronet on top of her head. She looked composed but desperately tired, and his heart clenched at the sight of her.

"I had a letter from my sister-in-law, Emily, asking me to return to Millcastle with all haste. She is expecting another child and is currently bedridden with nausea."

Alistair blinked at her. "Why do you have to go and not Lottie?"

"Lottie isn't married yet. I think Emily will be more comfortable with my help."

"When are you hoping to leave?" Alistair thought about his

own plans. Pritchard might be turning up to see him today, and he'd arranged a meeting with his solicitor about Phoebe being poisoned and who to engage as a barrister if such a thing became necessary. He couldn't walk away from any of it yet.

"Today." She looked him right in the eye. "I think it would be for the best."

"Best for whom?"

"Both of us?" She studied her clasped hands. "We are married, we both want the dukedom to succeed, and perhaps we can be more successful apart than together."

"What does that have to do with Emily Blackthorn needing your help?" Alistair asked, but she didn't reply.

He considered her, the silence lengthening as his mind ran in endless, pointless circles. He couldn't leave right now—not that she'd even suggested it.

"I don't understand your haste," he said slowly. "Can you not wait a few more days?"

"I've already arranged to leave today."

"What do you wish me to do?" Alistair asked. "How can I stop you from leaving? And how can you leave, anyway? Phoebe needs your chaperonage."

"Lottie has offered to stay with Phoebe until she is well enough to travel up to Hellsdown."

Alistair was aware of anger stirring somewhere in his chest. "You promised me honesty when we married. Tell me what is wrong and how I can fix it."

"Nothing is wrong." She smiled at him. "I have to help Emily, and I just need some time to..." For the first time her voice faltered. "To myself."

God, that hurt. He let out a long breath. "Am I so objectionable?"

She didn't answer, and he fiddled with the pens on his desk. Obviously, he was. It was an opinion that many of the people who were supposed to care about him had already expressed. Perhaps he really was that unlovable.

He made one last effort to put off the inevitable. "Is there anything I can say to persuade you to stay and tell me why you are intent on running away? This is not like you."

"I know." She managed a small smile that almost broke his heart. "I don't want to fight with you over this."

"Why not?"

"Because I don't think I can win." She looked up at him. "May I go back to Millcastle, *please*?"

"You don't need my permission." He shrugged. "I'm not going to lock you in your room and keep you here if you don't want to stay."

"Thank you." She rose from her seat. "Will you... come back to Hellsdown at some point?"

"If you want me, you know how to find me, otherwise I will leave you in peace." He stood as well, aware that she was about to leave him, and that, as usual, he had somehow been found wanting. "Let me know when you are safely home."

"I will." She stayed where she was as if she were memorizing every inch of him and then turned to the door. "Goodbye, then."

"You don't have to go, you know." He reached her in three quick strides. "I... don't want you to go."

Tears started in her eyes, and she shook her head. He hated seeing her so defeated.

She left his study, and he stood there like a fool, feeling as if someone had ripped out his heart. How had their disagreement over her plan to deal with Pritchard by herself escalated so badly that she was for all intents and purposes *leaving* him?

SHE WAS GONE WITHIN AN HOUR, her bags loaded into the carriage, Eileen alongside her. Alistair played his part, handed her into the carriage after kissing her averted cheek, tried to pretend that all was well even as the future he had started to believe in came crashing down around him. All he had to do was beg her to stay and yet the words stuck in his throat. What would he do if she refused again? He'd become a coward in matters of the heart, and he damn well knew it.

He turned back to the house and went in, his jaw clenched so hard from smiling that his teeth hurt, and he had the beginnings of a headache. He paused to speak to the butler.

"If a Mr. Pritchard calls, please show him straight into my study."

"Yes, your grace."

He went up the stairs and into his dressing room where half the cupboards now stood empty. Clarkson was busy cleaning out the shelves and repositioning Alistair's clothing. He glanced over at his employer, but didn't speak.

Alistair leaned back against a chest of drawers, arms folded over his chest, and glared at him. "Go on, then, tell me what a fool I am."

"Don't need to tell you what you already know, gov."

"I thought you'd be pleased. You never liked her anyway."

Clarkson raised his eyebrows. "My, you are in a snit, your nibs, aren't you? If I were a betting man, I'd say you'll be chasing after her in a day or so, begging her to come back to you."

"I've already begged." Alistair blew out a breath.

"Well, then you'd best forget about her." Clarkson slammed a drawer shut. "Plenty more fish in the sea, especially for a duke."

"What if I only wanted that particular fish?"

"Bit late to work that out, isn't it, seeing as she's up and left you?"

Alistair straightened up. "Thank you for your continuing support."

"You're welcome, your grace." Clarkson stared at Alistair.

"Now, if you wouldn't mind getting out of my way, I'd get things done a lot faster."

As he had no wish to stare at the emptiness around him, Alistair took himself off. Francis had taken Lottie out to the park on some slim pretext, after telling Alistair to sort matters out with Margaret. He decided to go and see Phoebe who had returned to her bed.

When he knocked and was admitted, he found her seated in a chair by the fire, a blanket over her knees and a book in her hand. She put the book face down on her knee and waited for him to come and sit opposite her.

"Is it true that Margaret has gone?" Phoebe asked.

"Yes, she had an urgent letter from her sister-in-law asking for her assistance."

"Oh, well then, I assume she will come back at some point?"

"I think she intends to travel onward to Hellsdown Park to supervise the work that is going on there."

Phoebe frowned. "She didn't mention it to me yesterday."

"I believe the letter only arrived this morning. She asked me to send you her love, and that she looked forward to seeing you as soon as you were well enough to travel up north."

"I like her very much, Alistair," Phoebe said. "She has been far kinder to me in the last weeks than Frederica ever was. And, she loves you far more than that woman ever did." She hesitated. "Although I was quite young when you left to join the army, I was well aware that she continued to flirt with every available gentleman, including our father at every opportunity."

"That doesn't surprise me," Alistair said dryly. "I was a romantic fool where our stepmother was concerned."

"Margaret thinks you still care for Frederica."

"I know she does." He tried to find a smile. "But I really don't."

Phoebe looked as if she wanted to contradict him, but held

her tongue, and it was Alistair who impatiently filled the silence.

"Why doesn't anyone believe me?"

"Alistair, you think she might have been poisoning me, and yet you are still giving her the benefit of the doubt!" Phoebe blurted out.

"I am merely trying to make sure that we have all the evidence and the facts before I confront her."

"Dr. Nash said that he and Mr. Marsh are willing to testify against her. What else do you need to know?"

"Whether it was her or Dr. McNeil? Have you considered that?"

"Yes, I have." Phoebe grabbed his hand and stared into his eyes. "Even if he did administer the poison, we all know who was behind it. *I* know."

"I do not wish you to be caught up in this mess. Your reputation will suffer."

"I don't care about that! I just want that woman to pay for what she has done to our family and not allow her to keep inflicting further pain!" Phoebe's color was now hectic, and she started to cough.

Alistair found her some barley water and waited until she was composed again. What *was* wrong with him? When had he decided that it was easier to laugh everything off and never take a stand? Margaret had pointed out the same thing and he hadn't attended to her either, which was why he was in his current sorry state.

He took Phoebe's hand. "I promise I will sort everything out. Will you try and believe that?"

"If I must."

He left her room and continued on down to his study. There was still no sign of Lottie or Francis. He worked on his morning correspondence with Joseph and instructed him to cancel Margaret's social events. He ate a solitary lunch at his desk and wondered how he was going to fill the rest of the day with no duchess to entertain.

He opened his drawer to find a new sheet of writing paper and stared down at the letter and parcel that Margaret had left on his desk a few days before. He took both items out and studied them before using his knife to cut open the seal on the letter.

He read through the legalese that presumably Adam Blackthorn had concocted with his solicitor, appreciating the tightly worded sentences that left no room for error if Pritchard decided to break the terms of the agreement. There was even a clause against future demands, which was stringent enough to have made even Pritchard pay attention.

Alistair opened the package and studied the pile of bank notes, his gaze stopping on the third one down. He retrieved his magnifying glass and focused in on the details of the engraving, a smile emerging as he realized exactly what Margaret and Adam had intended to deliver to Pritchard.

"Forged notes," Alistair murmured.

No wonder Margaret had specifically asked for her brother's help. He must have received them at some point, and kept them for future use. Alistair returned to the letter, noting how specific it was about the cash payment. He guessed that as soon as Pritchard had taken the bribe, Adam Blackthorn would have alerted all the banks in the country as to the forgeries, and Pritchard would've had an impossible time using them.

"Clever." Alistair sat back and found himself smiling. No wonder Margaret had been annoyed with him for ruining her scheme. It was remarkably well thought out. If Pritchard had been caught consistently using forged notes of high value, his reputation would have suffered and no one would want to engage in a financial transaction with him. A fitting revenge on a blackmailer, indeed.

Joseph came in with the letters he had prepared and placed

them on the desk. "Captain Grafton and Miss Blackthorn have just returned, your grace."

"Good, would you ask Miss Blackthorn if she could spare me a moment of her time?" Alistair asked.

When Lottie came in to his study, he could immediately tell that he was in for a battle. Lottie might be beautiful, but she was as stubborn and forthright as her older sister.

"What do you want, your grace?" Lottie asked suspiciously.

Alistair gestured at the chair in front of his desk. "I suspect there are many things you wish to speak to me about, but can we suspend hostilities until we have dealt with the matter of Mr. Pritchard?"

Lottie, who hadn't taken the seat he offered, frowned. "*You* are the person who stopped us from completing our scheme, why would you want my help now?"

"Because I can't fool Pritchard. I was hoping that you might see him instead?" Lottie just stared at him so he continued speaking. "I'm sure Margaret would approve of your involvement."

"You want me to give the forged money and letter to Mr. Pritchard?"

"Exactly. He is supposed to turn up here today. I suggest that you waylay him in the hall, offer him the money, and get him to sign the letter on behalf of your sister. Then you can write to her and your brother so that the rest of the scheme can unfold as planned."

"You guessed what Adam intends to do? Report the forgeries?"

Alistair shrugged. "It seemed obvious once I thought it through."

Lottie came forward and took the letter and package. "It's a shame you didn't think it through earlier!"

"I'm not going to argue with you about that." Alistair went to open the door for her. "I'll make myself scarce, and tell the butler to direct Mr. Pritchard toward you."

She paused in the doorway to look up at him. "When I have obliged you in this matter, you will oblige *me* by explaining exactly why Lady Hellion upset my sister!"

"When?" Alistair frowned.

"At Lady Thule's."

He blinked at her. "I have no idea what you are talking about, but I'm fairly certain you are going to tell me."

"Oh, you can count on that, your grace," Lottie said grimly. "Let me just get rid of our blackmailer first."

EILEEN TURNED the covers of the bed down and smoothed the sheets.

"At least the linen is well-aired, your grace, seeing as we didn't have time to bring our own."

"It's very pleasant here, indeed."

Margaret had been bowed into the largest bedchamber by the landlord and lady and promised the best dinner the inn could provide. She was currently sitting by the fire in her stockinged feet enjoying a cup of tea. Traveling as a duchess was so far removed from her previous experiences that she might as well enjoy it.

They'd made good time on the roads and were at least fifteen miles away from the house in London. Margaret contemplated the flames and for the hundredth time since she'd left, pictured her husband's face when she'd told him she was leaving. He'd masked his dismay quickly, but she knew that at some level she'd hurt him and that he was struggling with how to respond to her.

She'd half hoped he would tell her that he loved her, but why would he when everyone he loved in his life had repudiated him in some form or other? His older brother, his father, Frederica...

Did she really believe he had left Frederica pregnant, thus forcing her to marry his father? The more Margaret considered Frederica's words, the more unlikely they became. And why hadn't she been brave and told Alistair what had been said? Why had her much-vaunted plain-speaking and honesty deserted her? Because she'd been afraid, that's why, afraid of what she might have seen on his face—that she wasn't good enough.

If Alistair knew about the child, then what was there left to say? And if he didn't know? Surely it wasn't her business to inform him. Margaret sipped her tea. Perhaps that was what Frederica had counted on all along—that Margaret's unwilling-ness to test the strength of Alistair's affection for her would tear them apart.

But she hadn't even given Alistair the opportunity to state his feelings, had she? She'd given him an ultimatum, had run away, and allowed him to hide from her behind his charm. If they were to have any kind of marriage together, she had to be honest with him. If he didn't love her, she would accept that, and be grateful for everything else he gave her that she already missed.

A bargain was a bargain.

Margaret set the cup down. "I've been a fool."

"I beg your pardon, your grace?" Eileen looked up from her folding.

"I need you to go and tell our coachman that we will not be proceeding farther on our journey north tomorrow. We're going back to London."

CHAPTER TWENTY

*P*ritchard finally turned up around five in the evening, and Alistair let Lottie deal with him. He had watched from an upstairs window as the grinning fool exited the house with the forged notes in his pocket, leaving his witnessed signature on the copy of the letter Lottie had asked him to sign.

Alistair hadn't yet had time to speak properly with Lottie as Francis had whisked him away to Whites for the evening, and then taken him to a series of financial meetings the next day that had kept him remarkably busy and focused. He suspected his friend was driving him deliberately hard until he could bear dealing with the fact that he'd allowed his duchess to leave him without saying a word about how he really felt.

He'd already decided that, as soon as Nash said Phoebe was fit to travel, he was going to return home to Hellsdown Park, find his duchess, and make everything right with her—if she'd let him. Not seeing her, not touching her, not laughing and working alongside her, had left such a hole in his life and in his heart that he couldn't imagine not being with her again.

He spent the afternoon with his solicitor, going through the evidence against Dr. McNeil and his stepmother, settling on which legal avenue to pursue against them. He'd already decided to take Francis along with him when he finally confronted Frederica and the doctor. He'd definitely need a witness.

He returned to the house as it was getting dark, and paused on the step to admire the welcoming lights before the butler let him in. Margaret had provided the staff and the necessary authority to make the place function again, but without her it was not the same.

"Dinner is just about to be served, your grace, if you wish to go through?" the butler murmured as he relieved Alistair of his hat and coat.

"Thank you, I will." He still needed to speak to Lottie. Phoebe had mentioned that she might come downstairs to dine, and he couldn't miss that.

"Good evening, everyone." He paused in the doorway, his startled gaze drawn to the foot of the table where his duchess was sipping her soup. She looked up and smiled at him, her gaze steady, and his whole world righted itself. She was here; she'd come back to him.

"I apologize for my absence for most of the day." He took his seat at the head of the table between Lottie and Joseph Lang. "Did anything of interest occur?"

Phoebe tittered and covered her mouth with her hand.

"Nothing in particular," Francis commented as he lifted his wine glass to toast his friend. "Although, I do need to leave for Millcastle tomorrow, because Caroline will surely murder me if I miss our child being born. If you wish me to accompany you anywhere, can you make it happen soon?"

Alistair's gaze slid to his duchess, who was finishing her soup. "Thank you for everything that you have done, Francis, but I don't think I will need your services, after all. I suspect her grace would be more than willing to accompany me to visit Lady Hellion this evening."

"Shall we, duchess?"

Alistair placed Margaret's hand on his sleeve and headed for the front door. She hadn't had the opportunity to speak to him privately yet, and she still wasn't sure what she would say to him, anyway. His unguarded expression when he'd seen her sitting in her usual seat at the table had been worth everything.

He helped her into the carriage and got in behind her. The moment the door shut, he picked her up, dumped her on his lap and kissed her hard.

"Don't you ever bloody walk away from me again," he murmured, his voice rough. "Fight me, shun me, *hate* me, but don't ever leave. I can't bear it."

She struggled to free her arm, but only so that she could wrap it around his neck and keep him where she needed him.

"God, I'm so sorry, Margaret, I'm a fool, I—"

She pressed her gloved fingers to his lips. "Shall we agree that we are both fools?"

"I'd certainly prefer not to be the only one," he replied, his expression wry.

"Can we also postpone this very important discussion until we have seen Lady Hellion?"

"Why?" His blue gaze was intent.

"Because there are certain… things that we need to clear up with her."

"What the devil has she been saying to you?" Alistair demanded.

The carriage drew to a stop, and Margaret slid off his lap. "Why don't we ask her that together?"

As Alistair knew the way to Frederica's suite, and he was a duke, no one challenged them as they went up the stairs and knocked on the relevant door. Dr. McNeil, who wasn't wearing his coat or a cravat, immediately recoiled after opening the door.

"Good Lord, I thought you were one of the maids."

Alistair moved swiftly past him. "Good evening. I'm glad you are here. I wanted to speak to you and Lady Hellion about Phoebe's current condition."

Frederica appeared in the door of the bedroom, her expression aggrieved.

"What on earth do you want at this hour of the night?"

Alistair reached back and took Margaret's hand. "As I just told your doctor, I wished to speak to you about Phoebe, but I'd also like to know why you upset my duchess the other night."

Frederica's smile was aimed at Margaret. "Did you tell him? I'll wager you didn't because you don't really want to know the answer, do you?"

Alistair turned to Margaret. "What did she say?"

Margaret gathered her courage. "Lady Hellion claimed that when you went back to India she was with child, and that she married your father because she had no other choice."

Alistair glared at her. "And you damn well *believed* her?"

"She was very convincing."

"Of course she was! Haven't you worked out that she is a master dissembler? She said that to upset you, and to make you doubt *me*."

He turned back to Frederica. "What utter balderdash. Firstly, I didn't bed you. I was far too young and idealistic. Secondly, even if I had, if you'd written to me, I would've done everything in my power to come back and marry you."

"Lady Hellion did tell me in my medical capacity that she had once been pregnant, your grace," Dr. McNeil volunteered. "She also told me that the child was yours."

"Of course she did," Alistair said. "Did the child live?"

"No, I understand that her ladyship had a miscarriage early on in the pregnancy just after her marriage to your father."

"That is true. I was *devastated*." Frederica, who had sunk down onto the couch, dabbed at her eyes.

"Seeing as you'd achieved your object and become the Marchioness of Hellion I doubt that," Alistair said, which even made Margaret wince. "I'll wager you told my father it was his child, didn't you?"

"I did what I had to do to survive after you refused to listen to my pleas and stay in England!" Frederica said. "I begged you not to go back, but you *abandoned* me!"

"I was in the army, Frederica," Alistair said helplessly. "You can't just… leave."

"I am tired of everyone blaming me for merely doing my best to survive!" Frederica continued. "It's hardly my fault if men always let me down."

Faced with such monumental self-absorption, Margaret could only shake her head. The fact that she had almost allowed Frederica to ruin her marriage was rather embarrassing.

Alistair met Margaret's gaze. "Now that we have cleared that matter up, can we move onto the issue of Phoebe's health?" He turned back to the doctor and his stepmother. "I have reason to believe that while Phoebe was in your care, she was being poisoned."

"What on earth are you talking about?" Frederica gasped and pressed her hand to her breast. "Now you're going to accuse me of being a poisoner? When will my torment end?"

"Would you like to comment on the issue, Dr. McNeil?" Margaret kept her attention on the doctor, who had gone pale. "We have expert witnesses who will testify that Phoebe was indeed the victim of an attempt to poison her with arsenic."

Frederica turned to her doctor. "Don't listen to them, my dear sir. There are no such tests or witnesses."

Dr. McNeil cleared his throat. "Actually, there are, my lady."

He looked briefly down at the ground and then up again. "If I confess, will that absolve Lady Hellion?"

"Why would you wish to absolve her?" Margaret couldn't keep quiet. "If you did what you did with her permission and encouragement?"

Frederica had gone very still.

"Perhaps I did it so that she would turn to me and love me?" Dr. McNeil swallowed hard and looked over at his employer, who was studiously avoiding his gaze. "I swear that she never told me directly to do anything."

"Again, I doubt that is true, and I hope that if this comes to trial, then you will confess the full truth." Alistair gestured at the door. "There is a man waiting outside to escort you to Bow Street Magistrates' Court where you will be able to make a full statement about the charges I have laid against you."

Alistair walked back to the door and opened it. After a murmured conversation, a man wearing the uniform of a Bow Street Runner escorted Dr. McNeil out.

Even as the door shut, Frederica was on her feet heading for Alistair. "You must believe that I didn't know! I have looked after Phoebe most faithfully and was eagerly anticipating her Season in London. Why would I wish her dead?"

Margaret held her breath as Alistair looked down at his stepmother.

"If you don't wish to be caught up in another scandal, I suggest you leave London, go home, pack your things, and leave for an extended tour of the continent."

"Or what?" Frederica was crying now, her hands fisted at her side. "What worse thing can you possibly do to me than accuse me of murder and evict me from my home?"

Alistair slowly took out a piece of paper from his inside coat pocket and unfolded it. "This is a statement from Phoebe. Would you care to read it?"

Frederica grabbed the paper and read it through. "More

lies!" She ripped it into shreds. "There! That's what I think of your sister's jealous plot against me."

Alistair stepped back and reclaimed Margaret's hand. "Good evening, my lady."

"You can't just leave me!" Frederica shouted.

She was still screeching as Alistair guided Margaret out of the room, down the stairs, and into their waiting carriage. He let out a shuddering breath as they pulled away.

"What did the letter say?" Margaret had to ask him.

"Phoebe insisted on writing a statement that said that not only had she seen Frederica doctoring her food and drink, but that she also suspected her of poisoning my father."

Margaret slapped his sleeve. "And you *let her go*?"

He glared at her and rubbed his arm. "Of course not. After the authorities have dealt with Dr. McNeil, they'll be coming back for Frederica Hellion."

He frowned. "Not that it will be easy to prosecute a peeress. From what my barrister told me, such a thing is rarely attempted. I hope that just the threat of being brought to trial will persuade Frederica to leave the country. If she does choose to stay, or tries to return too quickly, we will hopefully have built a strong enough case to attempt to prosecute her to the full extent of the law."

"What if Dr. McNeil accepts the blame and refuses to incriminate his employer?" Margaret asked.

He grimaced. "Then we are in the basket."

"That's not good enough."

"I know." He inclined his head, his expression quizzical. "Now, as to you believing that I had not only bedded her, but fathered her child…"

Margaret grabbed hold of his waistcoat. "Don't you *dare—*"

He bent his head and kissed her, and the rest of her sentence was lost in the wonder of his mouth.

"I'm sorry," she whispered against his lips. "I should not have run away from you."

"And I should not have allowed that woman to control my father and my sister for so long. I was a fool and a coward." He held her gaze. "If there is any way to bring her to justice, I swear I will pursue it with all my might."

She kissed him, and, for a long while, there was nothing else that mattered except being in his arms and being alternately scolded and loved.

"As soon as Phoebe is well, we will all go back to Hellsdown Park," Alistair said as they arrived home. "Nash says that it will take her months to regain her full strength, and that the fresh air up north will do her the world of good."

"I am more than willing to leave London," Margaret confessed. "Although I suspect we will have to come back down next year for Phoebe's debut and my appearance at the queen's drawing room."

"That's a year away; let's not bother ourselves over that." Alistair kissed her cheek. "Did Lottie tell you that she delivered the money to Pritchard?"

"Yes, she did. From the sound of it, she was far more convincing than I would ever have been."

"I should have had faith in you and let the scheme progress in the first place."

"And I should have told you what I was doing." Margaret sighed. "So much for honesty."

"Here's some honesty for you." He cupped her face in his hands and gazed into her eyes. "I love you, Margaret Jane Blackthorn Haralson."

For a moment she wanted to tell him that it wasn't necessary to say the words, that she wasn't yet worthy of them, that—

"Duchess, I'm waiting."

Behind his lightly uttered command, she heard his uncertainty echoing hers and bravely met his gaze.

"I know."

He frowned. "What do you know?"

"That you love me, and that I love you, too."

"I knew it!" His smile reemerged and became triumphant. "Now to get you into bed so that I can prove it to you for the rest of our lives."

Dear Reader,

I hope you enjoyed book 3 in the Millcastle series, which features Margaret Blackthorn, Adam's forthright sister, and Alistair Haralson a distant relative of Captain Grafton. When an industrially acquired fortune meets a bankrupt dukedom, what could possibly go wrong?

If you enjoyed this book, please consider leaving a review at your favorite retailer.

If you want to read more of my books, please check out my website and consider joining my newsletter for the fastest updates and early contests to win new books.

katepearce.com/newsletter

Thank you for reading!

Kate Pearce

CONTINUE THE SERIES WITH *JACK OF ALL TRADES*...

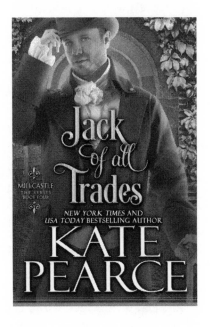

Prologue

Millcastle 1839

Alice Collins stepped out of the mail coach and looked apprehensively around her. The George and Dragon coaching inn was an old black and white building set low in the ground with a small and remarkably crowded cobbled yard to one side.

"Mind out, miss."

She instinctively stepped back as one of the ostlers moved past her and dumped the baggage from the top of the mail coach to the ground beside the door. She spied her bag, quickly reclaimed it, and headed inside the inn.

"Are you wanting a room, dear?" A blond woman Alice assumed was the proprietress came over, her smile welcoming.

"No, thank you. I merely wished to ask for directions to Grafton Hall."

"You'll need to rent a gig for that journey. It's too far to walk."

"I... don't have sufficient funds to do that." Alice gripped the handle of her bag more tightly. "But thank you, anyway." She glanced at the door. "Can you at least advise me as to which direction I should take?"

The woman sighed. "Go out of the stable yard, turn right, and follow the lane back up the hill until you come to the common. Keep the high hedge on your left and go on about a mile until you see a stone gatehouse. That's the entrance to Grafton Hall."

"Thank you." Alice nodded.

"Do you have business with his lordship, then?" The landlady's tone turned slightly sharper.

"You could say that."

"You do know he is happily married with a child?"

"I'm very glad to hear it." Alice curtsied. "I won't keep you from your customers any longer, ma'am.

She escaped through the door and studied the scene in front of her. The mail coach was being readied at some speed for its onward journey. New horses had been hitched and the coachman was intent on gathering his flock of passengers by threatening to leave any latecomers behind. Alice wondered how long the mail coach would survive after the new-fangled railway came to town.

She'd already spotted the massive construction works in the valley leading up to Millcastle, a brash new scar through the hills that looked as if it would never heal. From her view of the town below, she saw half the old market square was in the process of being torn up to create the necessary grand station. The air tasted acrid, and her clothes were already dirty from the spoil billowing out of the numerous factory chimneys. The mill owners would probably welcome the railway to improve their businesses.

A harsh place, Millcastle, and not one she would've chosen to visit unless desperate. She turned right and began to trudge up the hill. At least it took her away from the town limits and back into the countryside. A glance up at the cloudy sky told her that she would be lucky to avoid the rain, and that if she didn't pick up her pace, she would arrive in the dark and possibly miss the entrance to the estate.

Her boots were already patched, and she hoped they'd last the journey. What would happen if she was sent on her way again? How would she survive? Alice quashed down her fears and concentrated on the uneven path ahead of her. One thing she had learned in the last painful year was not to look too far ahead or court trouble.

～

"Francis?"

Viscount Grafton-Wesley, who preferred to be known simply as Captain Grafton, looked up as his wife Caroline came into his study.

"What's wrong, my dear?"

"Barker just informed me that a woman arrived at the front door and asked to see you."

He set down his pen. "What kind of woman?"

"Young, beautiful, and soaked to the skin."

"And you believe I invited her here?"

"You're not that foolish." She regarded him steadily. "But this wouldn't be the first occasion when one of your previous paramours has unexpectedly dropped by for a visit, would it?"

"That is true." He stood up. "Do you want me to tell Barker to throw her out?"

"In the rain?" Caroline looked appalled. "Perhaps you might consider speaking to her first."

He sighed. "As you wish." He offered her his arm. "Where is the girl?"

"In the small front parlor."

"You will accompany me."

"Naturally." She sniffed. "I had no intention of allowing you to go in there alone."

"How is our son?"

"Sleeping soundly for once, which is why I was downstairs and able to intercept Barker before he came to get you."

"In case I threw our uninvited guest out in the rain or ran off with her?"

"Exactly."

He bowed and held the door open for her. The woman standing by the fire swung around to stare at them. She was indeed both young and beautiful, with fair hair and very brown eyes. She was also soaked to the skin and dressed in garments that, in his opinion, should've been torn up and sold to the rag man years ago.

"Viscount Grafton-Wesley?"

"Yes. What do you want?"

She took a deep breath, straightened her back, and looked him right in the eye. "I believe we might be related."

Aware of his wife stiffening beside him, he held up his finger. "How old are you?"

Her brow creased in apparent confusion. "I'm twenty-six, but I'm not sure what that has to do with anything."

"Not my child, then. I wasn't even in this godforsaken country when you were conceived—unless your mother came out to India?"

"She... did not, sir, and I am definitely not claiming to be your child."

"Thank God for small mercies." Francis nodded. "Continue."

"After her recent death, I found out that the man who... kept my mother was a gentleman called Thomas Grafton."

"Ah, now it begins to make sense." Francis turned to his wife. "My father was a randy old bugger."

"This woman is claiming to be your half-sister?" Caroline asked and turned to the woman. "Do you have any proof?"

She took out a letter and offered it to Francis, her hand shaking the paper so hard it fluttered like a fan. "My mother wrote this on her deathbed."

Francis quickly perused the letter and handed it to Caroline. "I'll get my solicitor to look into the matter. Is this your previous address on the letterhead?"

"Yes, sir. When she died, the bailiffs came and told me I had to leave because the rent hadn't been paid for months." The woman swallowed hard. "They said my mother had considerable debts and that they would sell the contents of the house to recoup her losses."

"And left you out in the street?" Francis inquired. He wasn't shocked. He'd had to deal with plenty of tenants in the past and evicted more than a few. "I assume you have no other relatives?"

"Not that I am aware of. My mother's family refused to acknowledge her."

"Sanctimonious old pricks," Francis muttered. "Then you will stay here until the matter is resolved to my satisfaction."

"You... aren't going to throw me out?"

"Not immediately." Francis turned to his wife. "Can you find her some clean clothes and somewhere to sleep until we resolve this nonsense?"

"Of course." Caroline smiled at the younger woman. "What is your name?"

"Alice Collins." She looked from Francis back to Caroline and her voice broke. "I can't believe you are allowing me to stay."

"Neither of us are of a mind to send anyone in distress away,

Miss Collins. We know desperation when we see it." Caroline placed a gentle hand on Alice's shoulder. "Now, come with me and I'll help you settle in for the night. Everything will look far better in the morning."

"Somehow, I doubt that," Miss Collins said. "But I have had little reason for optimism in the past few months."

"I'll be in my study." Francis kept the letter and followed them back out into the hall. *"Collins..."* For some reason the name sounded vaguely familiar.

He lit another branch of candles after returning to the study and set it beside the bookcase containing his father's estate records. Despite his dislike for his old man, he had to admire his meticulous record-keeping. If there was some record of Alice's mother in the papers, it would be within the pages of these leather-bound volumes.

He returned to his desk and spent a few minutes writing to his solicitor about the matter in hand and was just sealing the letter with his signet ring and red wax when Caroline returned.

"How is she?"

"She is well spoken, obviously hasn't been eating properly, and her clothes have seen better days."

"That wasn't what I asked you."

"I know." She sighed. "She reminds me of myself when I first met you—full of pride and not much else."

"You had much more than that to offer, my love."

"No, I didn't. I was terrified all the time." She met his gaze, her expression thoughtful. "I suspect Alice is in a similar situation."

"Penniless and desperate?"

"Exactly—except there is no Captain Francis Grafton around to entice her into a devilish alliance."

"I certainly hope not." Francis addressed the letter and set it to one side.

"Francis... if she proves not to be related to you at all, would you still consider allowing me to help her?"

"*Allowing* you?" He raised an eyebrow. "When have you ever done anything I have asked you to? If you wish to keep her and find her a useful occupation, I will hardly object."

"Thank you." She came over and kissed him full on the mouth.

"You're welcome. Shall we go to bed?"

She wrapped her arms around his neck and smiled. "Yes, please."

Alice got out of the bath and wrapped herself in the large drying cloth the maid, who had identified herself as Martha, had left warming by the fire. There was also a long linen nightgown, a dressing gown to put over it, and a pair of knitted socks. Alice was beginning to feel as if she was dreaming. She hadn't dared to think beyond handing over the letter to the current viscount. On first seeing his harsh face, she'd assumed she'd be shown the door immediately, but he had proven to be not only extremely direct, but gruffly kind.

She climbed into the large, comfortable bed, discovered someone had warmed the sheets, and almost cried. Despite the hall's closeness to Millcastle, there was no noise and no glow from the factory furnaces to disturb her rest. She settled against the feather-filled pillows and closed her eyes. Tomorrow she would be more in command of herself. Before she could even manage another thought, she fell asleep.

Alice smoothed down the skirt of her new day dress and followed Caroline into the viscount's study. She'd been at the hall for over two weeks and had just begun to feel safe again. She loved spending time with Caroline and Ivy, who was Caroline's sister, and also the viscount and Caroline's son, Joseph. She already knew she would miss them if she had to leave.

Viscount Grafton sat behind his desk, a cigar in one hand and a letter in the other. "Ah! There you are. I believe we finally have an answer as to your parentage."

Alice sat down before her knees gave way. Despite Caroline's assurances that whatever the outcome she was welcome to stay, she still had her doubts.

"Mr. Palmer helped me discover the necessary documentation held in my father's accounting books and supplemented the information with correspondence between your mother and my father. He definitely paid the rent on your mother's house. When I claimed the title, my solicitor stopped the payments. He had no idea who your mother was until I enlightened him."

"Then it is true?" Caroline asked.

"Indeed, it is. Welcome to the family, Alice. I can only apologize for my father's appalling behavior." He glanced over at his wife, who nodded for him to continue. "I intend to offer you an allowance, of course, and if you wish to continue to live here, we would be delighted."

"But... I'm not legitimate." Alice finally managed to speak.

"So what?" Francis raised an eyebrow. "I don't care about that."

"Most families would."

"Well, we're not most families," Francis said firmly. "Now, if you will both excuse me? I have business in town that can't wait." He stood up. "If you wish to read through the correspondence, it's here on my desk."

"Thank you," Alice said. She waited until he'd gone out of the room before turning to his much more approachable wife. "I know you cannot possibly share the viscount's attitude to my status."

"Why can't I?" Caroline looked amused. "I have two sisters. Adding you to the family will be a blessing."

"But—"

"Alice, dear. Why don't you read through the correspondence from the solicitor and come and find me if you have any further questions? I'll be in the nursery."

End of Sample
To continue reading, be sure to pick up Jack of All Trades at your favorite retailer.

ALSO BY KATE PEARCE

FOR A FULL LIST PLEASE GO TO KATEPEARCE.COM/BOOKS

The Diable Delamere Series
Historical Romance
Completed Series

Regency dukes, disinherited aristocrats and a plot to assassinate the Prince Regent create plenty of problems for all the heroes and heroines as they struggle to trust each other in an ever-changing game of love, deceit and treachery.

.

The Millcastle Series
Historical Romance

On the cusp of the industrial revolution in the northern town of Millcastle the old and the new clash both in matters of business and of the heart. Can love flourish among the rush to make a profit?

.

The Harcourt Twins Duology
Historical Erotic Romance
Completed Series

Identical twins Gideon and Gervase Harcourt share more than a birthday and an insatiable interest in sex. They also believe in sharing their sexual expertise with the women they lust after in whatever combination is required. But when two very different women enter their lives will they be able to reconcile their complicated needs with their desire to fall in love?

.

The House of Pleasure Series
Historical Erotic Romance
Completed Series

Enter a Regency house of pleasure where nothing is forbidden and every sexual desire you have ever imagined can come true...

.

The Sinners Club Series
Historical Erotic Romance
Completed Series

When intrigue collides with heated passion behind the closed doors of the Sinners Club there is nowhere left to hide.

.

The Morgan Ranch Series
Contemporary Western Romance
Completed Series

A Northern Californian ranching family torn apart by tragedy reluctantly return home to discover not everything was as they thought it was, and that love, and forgiveness can sometimes go hand in hand.

.

The Millers of Morgan Valley Series
Contemporary Western Romance
Completed Series

When the mother you haven't seen for twenty years asks to visit your family ranch and set the record straight, how will her ex and six adult children react? The loves and sometimes messy lives of a ranching family.

.

The Three Cowboys Series
Contemporary Western Romance

The Three Cowboys series centers on three retired Marines living on a ranch in Northern California coming to terms in their own different ways with their experience in combat. From grumpy Noah and an unexpected baby to unruffled Luke who hides things almost too well, and the prickly puzzle of Max, each man will find the perfect woman to bring them to their knees—but not without navigating a lot of bumps in the rocky road to true love along the way.

.

The Turner Brothers Series
Contemporary Erotic Western Romance
Completed Series

As the oldest sibling in a spectacularly dysfunctional family, Grayson Turner has made it his life's mission not only to distance himself from his famous father, but to connect with the half-siblings his father's multiple marriages scattered across the country. Getting to know his siblings and creating trust between them hasn't been easy, but Grayson is determined to succeed because he, Jay and Dakota all deserve a happy ending with the women they love.

.

The Obsidian Series

Sci-Fi Romance

Join a renegade band of telepaths roaming the galaxy to protect and rescue their race from the evil empire intent on destroying them.

.

The Planet Valhalla Series

Sci-Fi Erotic Romance

Completed Series

One human female crash lands on a planet full of men descended from the Vikings, one of whom is the King who claims her as his mate— what could possibly go wrong? A sexy romp through the stars with excessive sex, a touch of humor and some very satisfied women...

.

The Triad Series

Sci-Fi Erotic Romance

Completed Series

Welcome to an imaginary world where civilizations, clash against the new and unknown, where telepaths are revered and reviled, and where your destiny can be preordained by a living oracle. Add in a group of super-soldier telepaths rescued from Earth and forming sexual triads for life becomes even more complex and life changing.

.

The Kate Pearce Holiday Paranormal Romance Series

Paranormal Historical Romance

A collection of lighthearted historical paranormal holiday novellas centered in a mystical faerie-ridden village in Cornwall. If you enjoy love at first sight, mistaken identity, ghostly and mystical advice, and fated lovers then you're in for a treat!

.

The Kurland St. Mary Mysteries Series

Historical Mystery

Writing as Catherine Lloyd

Completed Series

Join wounded cavalry hero Major Sir Robert Kurland and Lucy Harrington the rector's eldest daughter as they solve crimes in their quiet little village and gradually learn to appreciate each other.

.

The Miss Morton Mystery Series

Historical Mystery

Writing as Catherine Lloyd

Miss Morton, the daughter of a disgraced peer, is forced to seek employment and navigate her way through a society that no longer wishes to acknowledge her existence. But with her no-nonsense employer at her side, Caroline discovers her rebellious nature and that family and friends can be found in the most unlikely of situations—even while investigating the occasional murder.

ABOUT KATE PEARCE

New York Times and *USA Today* bestselling author Kate Pearce was born in England in the middle of a large family of girls and quickly found that her imagination was far more interesting than real life. After acquiring a degree in history and barely escaping from the British Civil Service alive, she moved to California and then to Hawaii with her kids and her husband and set about reinventing herself as a romance writer.

She is known for both her unconventional heroes and her joy at subverting romance clichés. In her spare time she self publishes science fiction erotic romance, historical romance, and whatever else she can imagine. You can find Kate at katepearce.com.

a amazon.com/author/katepearce
g goodreads.com/katepearce
BB bookbub.com/authors/kate-pearce
f facebook.com/KatePearceAuthor
twitter.com/kate4queen

Manufactured by Amazon.ca
Bolton, ON

40862447R00166